Warrior Class
Sky Cutter

Other Books by S. L. Kassidy

Please Baby

Scarred Series
Scarred for Life - Book 1
New Cuts, Old Wounds – Book 2
Bandages – Book 3
First Degree Burns - Book 4
Learning to Walk Again – Book 5

Warrior Class
Sky Cutter

S.L. Kassidy

Desert Palm Press

Warrior Class - Sky Cutter

by S.L. Kassidy

ISBN-(book): 9781942976813
ISBN-(epub): 9781942976820
ISBN (pdf): 9781942976837

Desert Palm Press
1961 Main Street, Suite 220
Watsonville, California 95076
www.desertpalmpress.com

Editor: Glenda Poulter
Cover Design: Jamani Hawkins-El (http://www.maddrandom.com)

Printed in the United States of America
First Edition July 2018

Dedication

This book is dedicated to my family, who support my writing long before I thought it was worth anything, and to my friends, who helped me believe in myself and allowed themselves to be conscripted into betareading stories, whether they wanted to or not. Thank you all.

.

In the world of Prism, during antiquity, a small tribe in the Far East exploded onto the world stage, becoming a mighty empire.

Chapter One

THE AIR SMELLED AND tasted different. There was a sweet quality to it that lingered on the tongue. It made Ashni Akshay's blood rush, but then again, lately everything made her blood rush. On the ship across the sea, she could hear her blood over the roar of the water and the odor of destiny had drowned out even the salty smell of the ocean. Now, it was worse. It engulfed her and could drown her if she wasn't careful.

She was hyperaware of the differences around her since leaving for the West. The air seemed calm compared to the sea, and especially compared to home, even her great city of Khenshu. In Khenshu, the air felt as if it could breathe itself and smother those who opposed it. But, this air caressed her, begged her for attention, and she would give it her all. She could feel the buzz around her, threatening to make her hair stand on end. Every nerve in her body popped. Her very essence wanted to interact with the West.

Ashni dug her boot-clad feet into the rich earth and inhaled deeply. Here she was on ground her father had never seen, planning to consume it all, and create something so much greater. He might have dreamed, but she would do. She turned her eyes to the sky. The sky was hers, vast and infinite. She could bend the sky to her will, so she would bend all things to her will.

"Stay with me, Father. It will all be ours."

The cry of an eagle caught her attention and Ashni immediately sought it out. A brief breeze caused her teal cloak to flutter behind her. She nodded. That was enough of an answer for her. This would all be hers by the grace of her father, the son of the Great Eagle, the king of the gods, Khurshid.

She turned her attention to the land in front of her. From the hilltop, she could see the small, confined meadow, choked by trees on three sides. It was not the ideal place for a battle, but she and her forces

1

would make do. They had fought in worse places and come out victorious. The memories put a smile on her face.

Their ships pulled up to shore, bringing her and her army to this unknown territory, they were prepared for battle, but they had been disappointed. Villages on the coast surrendered to their numbers, and the first group that opposed them had been broken minutes after the fighting commenced. Her warriors were starving for true combat.

"Are you sure you want to have this battle here?" Adira asked, coming to stand beside Ashni. A small frown marred Adira's dark features as her sharp eye stared below them. "The sun will be in their eyes and the space is too open, but closed off by forest. We're already outnumbered according to the scouts. Our archers and spearmen are out of range and wouldn't be able to use their weapons until the enemy is already mixing with our soldiers."

"I want them to think they have the upper hand here. Are you worried?" A teasing smirk tugged at Ashni's face as she side-eyed Adira.

Adira snorted, throwing her head to the side a little. She looked down at Ashni with her good eye, dark mahogany trying to cut into Ashni. The other eye barely opened with an angry scar cutting through it, going from Adira's forehead to halfway down her cheek. Adira waved the whole matter off with a flick of her wrist.

"I worry more about being home late. I stopped being worried when Amir Khalid saw fit to let me ride with him."

Ashni's smirk became a proud grin as she tilted her head to the clear sky. "Then what's the problem? Not ready to see him yet?"

Adira folded her arms across her chest, covering the lion emblem on her breastplate. "Can you be serious for a moment? You know I hate having battles where the enemy actually wants the battle, especially barbarians."

Ashni sniffed, rolling her eyes. "But, this is where I want the battle. They only think they want it here."

Adira didn't argue. She stared off in the distance and pressed her palms together. With her hands at her mouth, she took several deep breaths. Ashni waited, taking in miles of green grass, flanked by lush trees. If Adira truly didn't approve of having the battle here and had valid reasons, they'd have to come up with something else quick. It wouldn't be the first time. *It won't be the last time either, despite Adira's nervousness.*

"You put the princess and her shadows in those woods over there?" Adira pointed to thick brush to the side of the battlefield.

Ashni rolled her eyes again. *Is she serious?* Of course, she knew the answer to that. Adira was being a worrywart. *By Khurshid's great wings, it's a good thing I don't have to pay her for worrying.*

"You were there. You watched her leave. You're the most cautious person I've ever met," Ashni said.

Adira nodded. "One of us has to be. If it were up to you and the princess…" Her words trailed off as her upper lip curled into a sneer.

Ashni shook her head. She snatched Adira's helmet from under her arm. She put the golden helm on Adira's head, its proud white feathers standing at attention on top. Ashni knocked on Adira's temple, barely missing the ivory eagle wings on the side of the helmet. Adira looked her in the eye and Ashni beamed.

"We're here, Adira. We're here!" Ashni pounded both fists against Adira's chest. She felt the sky pulse with her as her nerves danced with anticipation. The very air moved with her, ready for action.

"I know, which is why we need to be careful. We can't rush in and throw it all away," Adira said.

"I'd never."

"There are tens of thousands of men beyond those trees, ready to stop us. Ready to keep us from our destiny."

"I know, but they won't. Now, bring me what I want, Adira. Show me what you're made of, General." Ashni placed her hands on Adira's wide shoulders, clutching the edges of Adira's flowing, sky blue cape.

"I think it's time you show us what you're made of," Adira said.

Ashni chortled, her golden eyes sparkling with excitement. "You're right. Let's go rally the troops. We need to stay on schedule or Princess will rush out too soon and ruin the whole thing."

Adira scoffed. "You mean you'll rush out after her and ruin the whole thing."

Ashni waved the matter off, even though that was partially true. She had done it before. Still, the troops needed to be rallied and she needed to get moving before she lost one of her more valuable soldiers. She marched off to her horse.

Midnight Thunder was ready for war and had been since she managed to shove him on a ship. Her favorite horse had paced the entire voyage and continued when they made it to land. He stared down the first people they encountered and they cowered before him, undoubtedly never seeing a beast like him. His eyes burned crimson with destructive desire. She'd give him this battle. As soon as she was on his massive, muscular back, they were both ready for destiny.

"Prepare the bull," Ashni ordered before riding off toward the front lines. Even if Khurshid and her father were with them, she would pay the gods their proper respect.

Adira frowned. "Prepare the bull? There are slaves for that, you know," she called after the queen.

Ashni's response was to throw her middle finger in the air, a gesture she picked up from the Westerners meaning 'fuck you.' She didn't care if Adira, or anyone else, felt they had to do a job that wasn't theirs. There was a battle to win, after all.

Ashni smiled to herself as Midnight Thunder trotted to the front lines. Her troops were starved. They didn't need her to rally them, but they expected it and she wouldn't let them down. Not when they were so close, not when she could virtually taste success. Everyone was clad in their best armor and their helmets glinted in the dazzling sun. They were bathed in the heavens' blessing. It was a good day.

"Troops, today we make history. We are about to do something that even my father, the great god and the Son of the Fire Eagle, couldn't do. We are the first of the Roshan to touch these shores, the first Roshan to breathe the West's air, but we will not be the last. My father desired to have the entire world under the Roshan and we are the ones who will make his dreams come true. Are you with me?" Ashni roared.

Weapons, shields, and helmets were thrust in the air. The cheers reached the Sun itself. She knew her soldiers were as hungry as she was. Still, the sound sent a tingle up her spine. Ashni beamed and turned just as slaves brought a large, black bull to her. She slid off Midnight Thunder and circled the bull three times, murmuring a prayer as she went. Rubbing her palms together, she clapped and threw her hands up. Thunder clapped and echoed through the air. She took a knife from a slave and slit the bull's throat in one swift motion, the blood splashing into the dirt. The bull didn't make a sound and slaves caught it before it hit the ground. The gods were definitely with them.

"If victory be ours, then the great God Khurshid will share this bounty with us," Ashni said.

Her troops hollered and raised their weapons again. A grin slowly spread across Ashni's face as she looked at Adira. Her best general smiled back. The army's energy hummed through the air, ready for anything. The world was theirs.

"Into position, General," Ashni called, just to be annoying. It didn't need to be said and Adira would be offended if she dared to mention it.

Adira sucked her teeth. "I know. If anything, you need to get into position." She rode off.

Ashni mounted her horse once more and put her helmet on, making sure the golden eagle head faced forward. White feathers with golden tips rose off the helmet. She rode down the lines to make sure everyone was in place. She stopped in front of the best pieces of weaponry she had for this mission—the catapults. They were new and begged for use. She took in the sight briefly before moving to the side of the weapons.

"Ready!" Ashni put up a hand. She looked out across the field where their enemies thought they were safe, thought her archers couldn't reach. They were in for a surprise. "Fire!"

The sound of thick ropes letting lose their strain snapped through the air. Spears flew like the promise of a hundred prayers toward her foes, whistling through the sky, *her* sky. Her insides trilled as she watched the missiles land within the ranks of her enemies, taking from them their precious high ground and cover. The heavy bolts splintered surrounding trees, tearing off large bits, causing chaos and opening up a line of sight to the opposing army. Birds screeched and shot up from the woods, briefly blocking out the sun as they fled.

As expected, the enemy moved toward them like charging bulls. Little did they know they were running toward the waiting jaws of lions. Ashni put her hand up again, signaling for archers to prepare to fire. She waited for the exact range and then dropped her hand.

"Fire!"

The twang of bowstrings fluttered over their enemies' battle cries. Blazing arrows shot over her head and rained down on her foes. Ashni watched the enemy throw up their circular shields and continue to creep closer through the shower of arrows.

A crooked smile curled onto Ashni's face. "Now, to bring the thunder with this storm."

Clicking her tongue, Ashni drove Midnight Thunder to the cavalry ranks. The smell of smoke, blood, and mud already flooded the area, but it was too soon to move. Once the enemy was near enough and had lost a sufficient amount of men to her bolts, arrows, and javelins, it would be time to engage. Her blood seethed, and her muscles quivered. She was certain every hair on her body stood on end. She took one glance at the sky.

"Father, protect Princess since I'm too far to save her from herself and we both know Naren can barely keep up with her," Ashni prayed, and then she turned to her troops. She drew her right sword, *The Golden Feather*, from her back. The single-edged, curved blade glinted in the light, earning its name.

"Charge!" she screamed at the top of her lungs, pointed her sword forward, and urged Midnight Thunder on.

The sound of her troops behind her, their horses' hooves beating against the ground ran up and down Ashni's spine, delighting her more than a fine wine could. They sounded like thunder, *her* thunder. Her dream and the dreams of thousands burned in her soul. The dream of her father. *It's mine.*

Ashni couldn't contain herself. She felt like she'd come out of her skin. Standing on the back of her horse and pushing off of her saddle, she dived into the fray with a mighty roar, needing to be part of the battle as soon as possible. She landed with the grace all of her troops expected of her. Her impact was like a tiny explosion, pushing up dust and rocks, blowing back grass, and covering her in smoke.

Any enemy near her jumped back, not sure what happened. Her opponents lucked out, moving just out of the reach of *The Golden Feather*. Ashni wasted no time unsheathing her other sword, *The Ivory Claw*, from her back and holding both blades, ready for war.

"It's the devils' leader!"

"It's Death's Daughter!"

Ashni chuckled darkly. "Is that what you're calling me? Let me tell you gents something." Thunder clapped overhead. "I'm the daughter of the Golden One and the Chosen. I cut the skies. Fear me!" Lightning blazed out of the sky and she thrust her swords up.

The lightning hit the tips of her blades and she could hear the gasps as the blue-white energy enveloped her. With a howling battle cry, Ashni flung her arms out and the ground around her exploded, tossing her enemies out of the way.

"I am the Chosen One and Daughter of the Heavens themselves," Ashni declared before charging into the crowd. Her swords sang through the air as she cut down her opponents, chopping through soldiers—armor, shields, and all. They barely had time to make a sound.

Foes came at her from all directions and she worked her blades against them, through them. Twisting, twirling, and grunting as she put down anyone who stood before her. Blood splattered her face, the odor making her more determined. Each scream fueled her, pumping through her, driving her to devour other souls. When they fell, she turned to more. Roaring as she caught sight of people to annihilate, she felt her whole body vibrate.

More men charged her and Ashni cut them down with ease. Both swords slid through bodies, gore dripping down the hilts, but never interfering with her grip thanks to wraps on her hands and on the swords. As she fought through waves of men, she was aware of her own cavalry tearing through the lines. She could hear their cries and grunts as they engaged. The cling of swords clashing ripped through her ears. Dirt flew in her face, yet she moved forward. She could only move forward.

Eventually, she was lost in a sea of her enemies, surrounded by straight blades, and slicing her way through foot soldiers, her dark armor almost totally swallowed by their beige breastplates. For a moment, she allowed herself a glance toward the deep foliage encapsulating the battlefield.

"Princess, wait for the right moment," Ashni muttered.

If Layla noticed how deep she was in the enemy lines, she would join the battle prematurely and ruin the whole plan. While Layla was an amazing warrior, there were times when she didn't use the best judgment and could wreck lots of hard work. Thankfully, there was no movement in the woods.

Turning her attention back to her opponents, Ashni snarled, cutting through men once more. The ground beneath her was slick, but she kept her footing. More foes pushed against her and she forced them back. Her muscles burned, which she ignored.

She took a quick glance around, checking on her soldiers. They were being engulfed, the enemy closing in, ready to consume them. Soon, it would be too late, soon their dreams would die with them, but her army pressed on, trusting in her, trusting in their ability. *Was this too much? Are there too many?* Her heart pounded in her chest as wave after wave of Westerners clashed with her warriors, pushing her people back. And then Princess charged in.

Layla and Naren came in like night blanketing the battlefield. Her squad was a shadow, set to swallow their enemies, weapons, screams, and all. Their foes never knew what hit them when Layla bashed in from the side, tearing in and forcing an opening. Ashni nodded with approval as new screams filled the battle's din. *And to think I was worried. I need to stop listening to Adira so much.*

"I can only imagine the joy on the Princess' face," Ashni chuckled and then turned her full attention back to the melee around her.

Ashni turned and received a foot in her back. The boot smacked against her sword sheaths. She wasn't hurt, but knocked off balance. Lurching forward, she spun around and put an arm up just in time to block a blade coming down. The sword clanged against the dragon-scale armor protecting her forearm and she kicked the soldier away from her. Shouting, she brought *The Golden Feather* down on him, splitting his chest open.

As more foot soldiers vanished into the void, Layla's forces closed in, but cavalry officers took note of Ashni. Horses with men in bright helmets with long tails on top rushed her. A grin tore through her face.

"Fools." Ashni rubbed her swords against each other, making them sing as a bolt sparked between them.

The mud beneath her rumbled and she howled like thunder. Swinging *The Ivory Claw*, she took a horse's head while *The Golden Feather* chopped off an officer's arm and he pulled his horse back. She dodged the third horseman with ease, stepping right into the path of the last one, and shoved her sword into the rider's chest. As the other turned to come back for her, she slaughtered a few common soldiers and then gave the rider her attention. She ducked and took the legs out from under his horse. The rider crashed into the muck and Ashni panted, breath coming out in visible puffs, body still yearning for warfare.

While taking stock of her surroundings, Ashni felled as many men as she could. Her muscles burned, and she could hear her blood pounding in her ears, but more importantly, she could smell victory in the air, despite the fact they were still outnumbered. Their enemies could overwhelm them, but she pressed on, as did her army. The dream was there. *It's there. We're here.*

Soon, the fragrance of victory was buried under the odor of death and earth. The hum of promise buzzed over the clash of metal and wood. Ashni continued to tear through people, pushing against enemy shields, cutting through their lines. She could see Layla's troops coming closer. *We will consume these fools whole and then feast on their bones.*

The last phase of Ashni's plan fell into place once Layla shoved her way into position. The enemy's numbers were dwindling. Now, Ashni's army engulfed their foes and Adira was about to complete the circle.

General Adira came in from the other side and they now had their enemies from three sides. The tide of the battle changed almost immediately. It was time to enclose these cretins who dared to stand in the way of the Daughter of the Heavens.

Before long, Ashni could hear Adira barking orders. Even with her helmet covering her ears, Ashni could hear the clash of weapons buzzing through the thick atmosphere, and shrieks of agony cluttered the air. The cold darkness on her other side told her that Layla drew closer. Her opponents probably didn't know what to make of Layla and her group and they never would.

"May the goddess Tami have mercy on their souls," Ashni muttered as she shoved several soldiers toward Layla's creeping shadows to be engulfed by the frozen darkness.

It took time, but the circle grew tighter around the enemy. Now, the superior numbers meant nothing. The burn of Ashni's muscles went to the back of her mind and she bellowed like a mighty lion, taking down even more soldiers.

In the end, Ashni stood in the bloody mud of the battlefield. She cleaned her swords, wiping them on her muck-covered pant leg, and placed her weapons in their sheaths. With a loud exhale, she removed her helmet and wiped sweat from her brow. Her amber eyes took in the scene and saw her troops stood just as strong as she, putting down any remaining resistance.

She watched as Layla waded to her, an almost deranged grin on her youthful, flushed face, which was splattered with dirt and the blood of their foes. How a teenager could wreak such havoc and not be a demigod would forever baffle Ashni, but she didn't question it. Layla obviously was given grace by some divine being.

"Did you see me come in right on time?" Layla asked, her brown eyes bright and her arms wide. Her palms were clean, but red from holding her sword, which was now sheathed on her side.

Ashni chortled, and rubbed the top of Layla's head as soon as she was close enough. She mussed her sister's short black locks done in cornrow braids, not that it mattered. Layla's hair was wild from the battle, standing on end and dripping with sweat. Layla tittered and tucked herself under Ashni's arm.

"It's good to see you didn't lose your head. Where's that idiot spouse of yours?" Ashni looked in the direction Naren should've come from, but he wasn't there. "Did I luck out and someone finally killed him? Oh, please, say someone killed him." She pressed her hands together in prayer.

Layla growled and gave her a stern glower with hard dark eyes. "Don't say that." She pointed at Ashni, wagging her finger for a second. "He's fine. He fell in some slop. I told him he was too close to the horses, but he never listens to me."

Ashni huffed. "Because he's an idiot. He's supposed to be keeping an eye on you, not falling in horse crap." She trusted that idiot to watch Layla and make sure she didn't do anything too crazy, not that anyone could stop Layla once she got a lunatic idea in her head. *Still, he should be there to save her from herself as best anyone can.*

Layla stepped away and made a face at her, gnashing her teeth, which Ashni ignored instead, she scanned the area for Adira. The dirt and soot of the battlefield made seeing any distance impossible. Adira would find her if she was still alive.

"So, now what?" Layla inquired, looking around at their handiwork. There were bodies all the way to the woods around the meadow, which was a sparkling green no longer.

"In such a vast field of men, there must be some living nobles left. We'll gather them alive, ransom who can be ransomed, enlist those we can enlist, and kill whoever's left," Ashni replied with a shrug. Any horses, dogs, supplies, and equipment would come with them.

Layla nodded, folding her arms across her black breastplate. "And the dead?"

Ashni surveyed the land once more. She had an idea as to what she wanted to happen. She would wait for Adira to get it done.

"Hey, did Adira die?" Layla put her hand up to shield her eyes from the afternoon sun, seeking the general.

"I'm pretty sure it's a lot harder to lose Adira than that. She's got a lot of nagging left in her. Besides, if she died, Saniyah would kill her."

Layla laughed and then suddenly sobered. "But, wouldn't she kill us, too, if Adira died with us?"

Ashni snorted. "Obviously."

Layla laughed again. "I can see it."

"See what?" Adira said, marching up out of the smoke from a nearby crater.

"Saniyah killing you if you die on the battlefield." Layla was now in a giggle fit.

Adira sniffed and brushed dirt from her armor. "Oh, please. She'd eat me whole if I died on the battlefield. Hell, she'd probably kill both of you for 'letting' me die in battle."

Layla nodded. "I said that."

"The end of an era at the hands of a petite engineer." Ashni shook her head.

"Isn't that the death your mother predicted for you?" Layla snickered, jabbing Ashni with her thumb.

Ashni shrugged. "Sounds like something she'd say, right?" She turned to Adira. "Make me an Orchard. One so glorious the Fire Eagle himself would praise our work. I want color and twists and bowed branches, so the gods will continue to bless our journey."

Adira's face scrunched up and she looked around. "Do we have time for that?"

"We should. We have to take stock of everything. If nothing else, we'll leave a few people behind to finish it. So, take the prisoners and make me an Orchard." Ashni made sure to make it sound like an order.

Adira took her helmet off and glared at Ashni. It was hard to take her serious, with her hair plastered to her forehead. "Really? This is what you're using me for now? You want me to hang around to make an Orchard? How about you just tattoo 'maid' across my damn forehead while you're at it?"

"I would, but I don't have the time and it would probably clash with your other tattoos," Ashni said.

Adira's gaze narrowed. "This is an utter waste of my time and talent."

"We just won a major battle and opened up the West to us. Why the hell are you so damn cranky?"

Layla chimed in. "She didn't get to kill enough people."

"I'm not cranky. I'm a general in the Roshan army. In fact, I'm the best general in the Roshan army. I shouldn't be fetching bulls or making Orchards. There are people who do that." Adira huffed, her nostrils flaring.

Ashni scowled. "So, why don't you just go order those people to do it and stop whining? Your word is as good as mine around here. Sometimes, better depending on what we're disagreeing on."

Knowing this was true, Adira threw her hands up and let loose a horrible growl of frustration. Ashni and Layla snickered as they watched her storm off.

"Well, Princess, here we are." Ashni looked around the battlefield. Inhaling, she put her chin up and let out a long sigh.

"Yeah. It's kind of ours at this point." Layla shrugged.

Ashni chuckled and threw her arm around her sister again. She pulled Layla to her, not caring about the grime of combat. Layla looked up at her and Layla's dark eyes sparkled. It was amazing how once the battle madness left her, Layla could look downright cute, even when covered in some unfortunate soul's blood. It didn't help that Layla had dimples.

"So, are we just going to stand around while Adira makes an Orchard?" Layla asked.

"Of course not. Let's rally who we have and assess everything before we get moving. No way these guys want to sit around and bask in the stench of the dead."

Layla nodded and ran off to do her part. Ashni had things to do as well, but before she started, she went to find Midnight Thunder. She owed her poor horse. He didn't even get a chance to be a part of this. Midnight Thunder found her, bumping her in the back with his snout. She laughed, turning to pet him.

"I'm sorry I teased you, boy. You know how eager I get." He snorted and nuzzled her briefly. She took it as forgiveness. "Next battle, it's you and me both, especially if Layla decides to be...you know, herself and all." He nodded.

She climbed into the saddle and rode to the top of the hill her enemies had occupied a couple of hours earlier. It gave her a good view of the West. It was green, alive, promising.

"Father, I am your legacy to this world and I will carry out your will as mine own. All of the world will be called Roshan under me and my banner. Watch me as I bring fame and glory that even you couldn't achieve," Ashni said.

"Isn't it blasphemous to taunt a god?" Adira's voice sounded taunting as she approached on her own horse.

"Not when it's your father and you're just as divine as he is."

"Are you just as divine as the Son of the Great Eagle?" Adira snorted and rolled her eye. "You forget I knew him. I rode with him."

Ashni curled her lip at Adira. "Do you deny me?"

"I merely acknowledge the gods and the Amir as they are. It's not my fault you can't take it." Adira's mouth twitched.

"What the hell do you want? Aren't you supposed to be making me a glorious Orchard of these damned souls?"

Adira shrugged. "It's being done. I delegated, like you always do, except I delegate to the right people. I just wanted to make sure you weren't planning to leave me putting together some damned Orchard when you decided to move on."

Ashni gave her a lopsided grin. "Leave behind the second-in-command?" She didn't even get to make it through the rest of her speech.

Adira pursed her lips. "Second-in-command? I thought Princess was second-in-command."

"Please, I can barely trust her to hold her sword right or not get lost in her own shadows. Besides, she is me, which means she's basically first-in-command."

Adira arched an eyebrow. "Really, two first-in-commands? Isn't that impossible?"

"And this is why I never take you anywhere."

"Oh, yeah, this is why." Adira blew out a loud breath. "Don't leave me putting together this Orchard."

"Where's the fun in that? Especially since someone needs to nag me to death."

Adira glowered at her. "If you leave me while I'm designing this damned Orchard, I'm meeting you on the battlefield myself. If there's no battle, then I'll fight you to the death in your tent."

Ashni smirked. "I'd love to see it." The latter had happened before, but not to the death. In fact, this confrontation all but guaranteed she'd leave Adira behind.

Adira gave her one hard look, which was pretty much a dare to leave her behind. Ashni would take her up on it. For the moment, she turned her attention back to the sky. "Watch over us, Father. Watch us work."

Chapter Two

"ARE YOU SURE ABOUT this?" Adira asked as she and Ashni stood on a hill, just off the road. Despite the fact that the sun was high in the sky, there was a chill in the air. They were focused on a prize in the distance, having a good view of the city of Phyllida. Scouts and spies deemed it an excellent target for plunder.

Phyllida was a large city with thick, high walls and several roads leading to several gates. Inside, there were many wealthy villas and houses, as well as open land, bustling markets, entertainment areas, and busy temples. A decadent white palace looked down on the town. Gold, ivory, and jewels decorated many places. Merchants peddled goods from other cities and even other lands. It basically begged Ashni to tear into it and take all of its treasure.

According to reports, Dorian Lysand, king of the city, was a strong-willed and clever man. He could be trouble, but he didn't have the army to cause Ashni much concern. She figured her military could overwhelm him before he managed to properly plan for her.

With an arched eyebrow, Ashni looked at Adira. "Why wouldn't I be sure? What kind of question is that?"

"The kind of question we need to ask. We have agreed to go back to Khenshu when it gets cold. We should turn around now before our desert-dwelling soldiers start freezing."

Ashni sucked her teeth. "If a little frost can scare off people riding with me, then they don't need to be riding with me. If some cold can keep them from glory, then so be it."

"Okay, fine. What about the fact that this is a little bit off of our planned attack? We've already done more than we planned and set ourselves up for a glorious return when the weather is more suitable for conquest. Why run this risk?"

"We need plunder to keep our knuckleheads riding and that city is full of it according to your spies, yes? Are you this much of a worrywart and indecisive when you're in bed? I can't imagine that's much fun for Saniyah. Unless, of course, Saniyah's the one in charge in bed, which I'm sure is the case."

Adira scowled at her. "Keep your filthy mind out of my bed."

Ashni snorted. "You probably need all the pointers I could give you. I need Saniyah to stay satisfied. Do you see the great things she came up, so we can take the West and fulfill our dreams? You make her unhappy and I will bring down the full might of the Empire on you."

Adira had the nerve to roll her eye. "Blah, blah, blah. Anyway, we could just go around."

Ashni's brow furrowed. "Why the hell would we go around? That city is sitting in a good location for trade and it's filled to the brim with proof of that. Honestly, do you think those dogs back there will be happy with hitting a more strategic target right now or one that'll bring them fortune after they watched their friends take a spear to the belly?" Ashni needed to reward her troops after they had walked through the fire with her when they crossed over.

"They've been rewarded. We've been here long enough to take enough plunder."

"More is always better."

After their first big battle since entering the West, the Roshan army had stood before several other forces. They mowed down all of their enemies, but it had not been an easy journey, not that Ashni ever expected that. Her father would never dream of something easy, after all.

A low groan escaped Adira. "So, we have a pointless battle for a city that doesn't help our true conquest and lose even *more* soldiers?"

"Do you honestly think those fools will oppose me? Do they not call me the Daughter of Death? Am I not their Blight? The Bane of Life?" Ashni beamed as she held her head high. She had heard many different names for her since they arrived.

Adira chortled. "And to think, they don't even know you personally."

"I can't wait for them to get a nickname for you. General Whiny sounds good. I might get the soldiers to start calling you that. 'General Whiny, sir.'" Ashni cackled at her own joke.

"You're not funny. This is why no one even bothers to call you The Sky Cutter, despite seeing you command lightning. You don't take things seriously."

"Well, I'm serious about taking this town." Ashni motioned to

Phyllida.

"Be sure. We have to come up with a plan."

"I have a plan. You're just questioning it because you're whiny. Let's go get the princess and we'll talk it over. I'll need her to do part of this and you can handle the heavy lifting."

Adira gawked at her. "You're trusting the princess to do the delicate part and I get the heavy lifting? Did you get smashed in the head on the battlefield?"

Ashni scoffed. "Princess can handle it. Do you honestly think you're the only person here who can do the light work?" *Does Adira really think the whole damn thing would fall apart if she wasn't here?* Well, she knew the answer to that and just how serious and not Adira was with her concern.

"You two aren't known for your 'light work.' In fact, I've seen you handle the light work. It's not with a delicate hand and she is you, is she not?"

"Yes, she is me, but she's also herself. Give her a chance to show she can do things. She is young and has to learn sometime. Besides, I have to trust her because she is me. Wouldn't you trust yourself more than anyone else?"

Adira groaned more, her shoulders slumping. "I can only wonder how the gods made two of you and then allowed you to find each other."

Ashni snickered and her golden eyes shone. "There you go worrying, again. Come on. We're in the West, we're moving forward, and we're doing something even my father couldn't do." Ashni couldn't help throwing out her arms and spreading her hands. "The gods are on our side, Adira. Join me and Princess in their grace."

Adira looked like she ate something sour, a constant with her face. Ashni wanted to tease her mercilessly, but they didn't have time for that. There was conquest to be had. Ashni enjoyed the sound of her cape fluttering behind her as she marched down the hill. Adira lingered behind for a moment before chasing after her. She fell into step next to Ashni, who held in a snicker. They mounted their horses and made their way back to camp.

"After this, do we return home?" Adira asked.

"I've got to get you back there eventually. Saniyah has probably already come up with some ridiculous torture device for me just for keeping you out this long."

"Probably."

"Besides, it is cold and we promised the troops they'd get to go home to be treated like the heroes they are. So, we'll do this one last town, if only for the treasures." They would be able to get everything else later. They would stick to the plan and it would work out. Adira nodded.

In a few short moments, they were back in camp. Guards watched as they went through the palisades. They passed tents where soldiers were gambling, fighting, or just relaxing. Despite the soldiers being rambunctious, there was no din. They knew better than to attract attention to the camp. The subtle scent of food wafted by them, but was overpowered by the horses and dogs roaming the camp, as well as the livestock pen.

Her tent was identical to her troops' lodgings in appearance. Of course, she didn't share her tent with anyone while her soldiers tended to have five to a tent. She had a few slaves and servants to attend to her, but many others had that as well. Her father had taught her to live off the bare necessities, not that it was useful at the moment. Her tent had many comforts, as her father had also taught her to enjoy the things she could.

"What the hell are you doing in here?" Ashni barked, finding Naren in her tent, curled up with her food. The little bastard was always stuffing his face.

"Layla said it was fine…" Naren replied with his mouth packed with mutton and flat bread. Gravy from the stew dotted his puffy, copper cheek.

Ashni groaned and gazed at the ceiling. She didn't want to see this guy, but he was her sister's spouse and she'd put up with him. Hopefully, he'd be gone soon or she'd lose her patience with him.

Grabbing a pillow, Ashni flopped down on a larger cushion near the table of food. She put the other pillow behind her back, rolling her shoulders to get comfortable. Adira sat down on a pillow beside her. Ashni waved a servant over.

"Go fetch the princess for me," Ashni ordered before reaching for some flat bread from the low table. Naren had the nerve to look at her. "Hey, it's my food, so don't act like I'm stealing from you. I'll throw you out on your ass and tell your spouse I did it."

Naren made a face, but he knew better than to say anything. Ashni broke off a piece of bread and dipped it into the mutton stew. Adira made no move to partake of the food while they waited for Layla to enter the tent. When she arrived, Layla sat next to Naren, making herself comfortable on a giant pillow.

"So, what's this all about?" Layla scanned the food and took a handful of mixed nuts and popped a couple in her mouth.

"Tomorrow, me and General Malcontent..." Ashni held in a laugh as Adira scowled. "Yeah, General Pouty, over here, and I are going to take formation. I'll send word to Dorian and see if he's willing to negotiate. If he is, you're going in."

Layla shrugged. "I am a royal messenger."

Ashni snorted. "You don't say."

"Don't take this so lightly," Adira said, wagging her finger at them. "This could mean the difference between peacefully taking a city or having another battle and losing thousands of soldiers."

"Yeah, because that's what I'm trying to do, get thousands of people killed." Layla huffed, waving Adira off before focusing back on Ashni. "I could just challenge a champion from the city and we can take it that way."

Ashni waved that idea off. "We know that won't work anymore. Word has spread not to fight us one-on-one." They had won a handful of battles using the champion tactic. The fighting was brutal and news traveled fast about what they had done to their opponents in single combat.

"Well, maybe if you hadn't kicked that guy's head off of his shoulders, we could've gotten away with it a little longer," Layla said.

"I'm fairly certain that when you literally walked through a man, it ended any chance we had at facing champions in battle," Adira said.

Layla gasped, daring to look affronted with her mouth agape and her hand pressed to her chest. "How was I supposed to know they'd never seen anything like that? If I walked through one of our soldiers, they'd giggle and then try to cut me in half. Besides, what about you and your..." She came up short because out of the few champion battles they had, Adira had not bothered with stepping up. Their fun had been short-lived, considering after four fights, no enemy engaged them one-on-one.

"Princess, this is the pay for most of our troops, so be sure to do this right," Ashni said. Most of their battles had been for strategic reasons, giving them a foothold in the West. The troops deserved to be showered in wealth for their accomplishments. Only a few conquered cities had that sort of bounty. Phyllida would help with that.

"Is there any other way I do things?" Layla gave her a smug look with pursed lips.

Ashni gave her a flat stare. "Do you really want me to answer that, Miss-I'm-Going-Over-The-Wall-First-Before-Every-damn-body?" Her sister's recklessness showed a lack of thought all too often when she was in a stressful situation. Most of the time, Layla's instincts carried her well, but other times—Ashni could feel her guts twist just thinking about those moments.

"It worked, didn't it?" Layla had the nerve to say that with a smile.

Adira sucked her teeth. "So, they've changed the definition of 'worked,' did they?"

"Anyway, let's work out the details for this," Ashni said. If they got off task, they would have a hell of a time getting back on it.

***

Princess Nakia Lysand was confined to her rooms in the palace, which told her something was up. She was always forced to stay in her rooms whenever something interesting was going on. She was curious. Who wouldn't be, especially when even the servants taking her to her rooms seemed so frantic?

Slipping out was easy, as she had plenty of practice. She made sure to remove any jewelry that might make noise and even took off her sandals before sneaking into the main sections of the palace. Nobles and servants hurried through the halls; heavy footsteps slapped the tiled floor. She pressed her body against the cold, stone wall and hid behind a maroon column as she came to a group of men talking.

"Those damned dirty barbarians have made it to us."

"They've wiped out at least a dozen cities already and stolen everything they could move."

"Wiped out doesn't even cover it. Those cities don't even exist anymore. They've been beyond burned to the ground. How could they bring down such ruin in a matter of months?"

"They're led by some demon who controls the darkness itself and slays dragons as well as men."

"I've heard they take the survivors as well as the dead and tie them to posts and hang them from trees, leaving them for animals to devour. The unharmed survivors, they cut them open, just enough to entice animals and insects to them. They call it a Bloody Orchard because blood and organs look like fruit on trees."

All the others gasped, their eyes wide and their mouths fell open. "Savages."

Nakia wasn't sure what to make of this. She didn't know what barbarians the noblemen referred to. These sounded like nasty, terrible people. She wanted to know more, but the men continued telling horror stories about whoever the barbarians were. They spoke of magic and spirits as well as terror, destruction, and murder. She was certain they had no real idea about the threat, especially considering one kept insisting the barbarian leader killed a dragon. Dragons were rare and only gods or true heroes could defeat them. Quietly, she moved away in search of more information.

From the rush of people, it was easy to assume these barbarians were a big deal. Clinging to the wall, Nakia skulked around for more people to eavesdrop on. They weren't hard to find, wringing their hands and whispering to each other.

"These barbarians...it's said they eat people."

"They're from the East, right? They can't even talk, just grunt."

"They have tails like wild beasts."

"How can we even begin to defeat animals then?"

"Even the women supposedly engage in savagery."

Nakia couldn't imagine women fighting. Surely, they meant something else. She wasn't sure what they meant about the barbarians being from the East. *Did they make the different from other barbarians somehow? Worse?* Of course, they didn't explain because they already knew. She was about to sneak off again, but a couple of guards got to her first.

"My Lady, you should be in your rooms. It's not safe here," one guard said.

"The King has ordered it," the other said.

Nakia had no way to protest. The guards wouldn't listen to her. So, she returned to her rooms. For the moment anyway.

***

The sky was clear, a perfect blue with only wisps of white bands streaking through it. The sun was high. There was a chill in the air, but the day still clung to the autumn's drifting warmth. It wasn't a good day to die, yet the Roshan army was lined up outside the walls as if it was. Or maybe it was a good day for barbarians to kill innocent people.

King Dorian Lysand stroked his umber beard and took a deep breath. He rubbed his massive hands together and his muscles jumped every time his sandals struck against the marble floor of his palace as he paced. He looked down from the heart of the city, past the market, past the square, past the thick walls, and to the green meadow holding the city's imminent demise. The damned Roshan army was right there.

"I thought they were myths." He punched a nearby column. Pain shot through his arm, tingling through the thick muscles. His tunic sleeves slapped against the air as he shook his hand, trying to make the agony stop. "Damn."

Reports told Dorian there were over thirty thousand soldiers at the gates. He couldn't fathom those numbers for a single army. For every four people in the city, there was a Roshan soldier who'd have no problem killing all of them and savaging their corpses. By this time tomorrow, over a hundred thousand people could be dead, or worse. And he was responsible for them all and needed to prevent that from happening. It was hard considering he could probably rally about ten thousand troops right now, and that would probably take more effort than humanly possible.

"What do they want?" he growled and shook his head. The answer was simple—blood. They only wanted to slaughter everyone, as they had been doing since showing up on the coast over five months ago. They came in like a swarm, devouring all in their path, but Phyllida shouldn't have been in their warpath.

All of the reports he had received about the Roshan army indicated they were staying near the coast. Honestly, he hadn't thought much of them. *A woman led them. How much of a threat could she be?* Then, he heard tales of this damned Daughter of the Death raising Hell all over the land, breathing fire on all that was holy and bathing in the blood of innocents.

"My Lord, what are we to do about the barbarians at the gates?" Owen demanded, marching in with a quartet of nobles in his wake. They reminded Dorian of busy bees, constantly flitting about. Once within ten feet of Dorian, Owen stopped and bowed his head.

"I'm considering our options," Dorian said.

"Surely you mean to field our army and show those barbarians and their woman what for." Owen waved a hand toward the balcony.

Dorian ground his teeth together. "I'm considering all options. They may be barbarians led by a woman, but there are still thousands of them." His voice had a slight edge to it, needing to remind this young man who was in charge.

"Then what are we to do? Open the gates and let them ravage the city?" Owen asked.

"Of course not."

"It's said their demon Queen is petting a huge, black bull she plans to sacrifice to their demon gods before she lays siege to the city. You know what happened to the last city they attacked?"

Dorian didn't respond. Of course he knew. He was more informed than every damned noble in the city. The Roshan had attacked Sapphira and lay siege to it for almost a month. In the end, the weakened city walls had been crumbled by a monstrous bolt of lightning. Within days, the city had been annihilated. It was a speck of black sand on the coast now.

In that time, other cities were able to fortify themselves and prepare in case the Roshan showed up at their door next. He hadn't bothered, believing the blood-thirsty bastards would stick to the coast. *Why did they change strategy now? Why did they head up river? Why should they show up at my city, of all places? But, why should I expect anything to make sense from beasts who follow a woman?*

A woman he heard breathed fire, that lightning shot from her eyes, and she could wipe out lines of men with a wave of her hand. Her people called her 'the Sky Cutter' and, supposedly, she commanded the Heavens themselves and could make darkness swallow men whole. He couldn't fathom this demon woman, but he needed to do something about her and those barbarians.

Before Dorian could come up with an answer, the tap of quick and steady footfalls caught his attention. For a second, he thought it might be Nakia. Damn girl didn't know how to stay where she was told, but the steps were too heavy. All eyes went to the door as a soldier charged onto the balcony. He halted fifteen feet from the king and immediately bowed his head and placed his fist to his heart.

Dorian eyed the messenger hard, as if he could force the news to be good. "You have word about those savages?" He had soldiers posted all around the wall, keeping a close eye on the Roshan and ready to report any changes. No spies he sent out made it back.

"I do, your highness. Their queen has requested you meet with her messenger and royal official, so you may be able to avoid battle," the soldier reported.

"My Lord, what if we send out a champion?" Owen said.

The soldier's eyes went wide and a bead of sweat raced down his cheek as the color drained from his face. "Have you heard what they do to champions, sir? The first champion met that demon woman on the battlefield and they said there wasn't enough of him to put in a cup."

"Impossible," Owen replied.

The soldier continued, "The second supposedly met with some waif covered in black from head to toe, who walked through the second like smoke, and there is nothing left of him." It was clear Dorian's military wanted no part of those barbarians. They weren't ready.

"You fools believe exaggerated tales meant to frighten children," Owen hissed.

The soldier swallowed loud, his throat moving. "These are tales passed on by people who witnessed the destruction. I think we should heed those tales."

Owen sucked his teeth. "Well, it's a good thing you're not the king."

With a snarl that backed up everyone around him, Dorian scowled. *Who was this woman to dictate terms to me?* Still, avoiding battle served him well. He could buy time and speak with his advisors for the best way to deal with these demons from the East. *Eventually, I'll put these dogs in their place.*

"Prepare a banquet," Dorian announced with a flourish of his hand. "Tell the demon queen I will meet with her messenger."

"My Lord?" Owen's face melted as his jaw dropped.

"It will serve us well. We can learn more of these...*people*." Dorian grimaced. Maybe they were people. He couldn't be sure, but he doubted it. "We can lull her into a false sense of power and then snap our jaws on her."

"We'll outsmart the bitch," Owen said.

Dorian's face twitched, but he held in a frown. Owen was predictable, acting as if this was all his idea. For the moment, Dorian let go. He would deal with Owen in due time, but first, the barbarians.

Dorian made a fist. "Exactly. We just have to make the right moves and put her in check."

Owen nodded and Dorian waved the soldier away. He would entertain this barbarian messenger and learn more of these Roshan. Perhaps they could be useful to him. They had eliminated some of his enemies in their bloodlust across the land. If he could turn them on to other enemies, then it could work out for him. Maybe he could even use them to rid him of some of his more annoying noblemen. *Perhaps, they can become my dogs once they're made to come to heel.*

If Dorian could not find a use for the barbarians, he would flex on them and frighten them off. The Roshan seemed to believe in gods of some kind, so he would show them the gods favored him. No one in his

24

right mind would go against the gods, even if they were savages.

***

Dorian folded his arms across his chest and tapped his fingers against his biceps, the dark linen of his long, yellow tunic sleeve scratching at his arm. The soles of his sandals sounded hollow as he paced. Barbarians apparently had less respect for time than they did for human life. The banquet he had prepared had grown cold and the nobles who had been ready to pounce on the damned savages were now bored to tears and ready to return home. Even the sun was preparing to leave.

Dorian hissed. "Where the hell is this so-called 'royal official' or whatever the hell they referred to it as?"

Just as he turned, a woman—a girl really—dropped in front of him, as if she fell from the ceiling. Taking a step back, Dorian took in the intruder to decide how to react. Clad in black from head to toe, she didn't have on shoes, only wraps around her feet. She was slight with a dusty complexion, skin much too hard for a woman. The sides of her head were shaved bald with tattoos of what appeared to be a roaring lion and a crescent moon. Feathers hung from a few odd braids in her otherwise wavy, wild hair. She watched him with a glint in dark, dangerous sepia eyes.

Before Dorian could demand to know who she was, he heard a grunt from behind her. Glancing around her, he saw a young man tangled in a thin rope. His arms flapped and his legs twisted.

"Uh...little help, sweetie?" he squeaked.

The woman groaned and rolled her eyes. Suddenly, a blade appeared in her hand. She tossed it behind her without looking, cutting the rope. The young man dropped to the floor with a thud. He grunted on impact, falling in a heap of black cloth.

"Thanks..." The tile and his cloak muffled his voice.

She merely shrugged, as if his plummet meant nothing to her. He scurried to her side, dusting himself off. He was only a little taller than the girl. His hair was also short, wavy, and decorated with feathers. He was a mess in baggy, odd garments and no shoes. It was unbelievable these two lightweights would be there for the Roshan Empire, but that was the only way to explain them. These were kids, not blood-thirsty savages. Or maybe even the youngsters of those barbarians were savage.

25

From what Dorian could see, they were strange and backwards. After all, why were a boy and a girl dressed in almost identical clothing? to him. Instead of tunics, they wore breeches, like wild hill people. For a moment, Dorian just gawked at them, unsure what to make of their wide-legged pants. The wraps around their feet went up and over the pants, stopping at mid-calf, like high sandal straps, trapping the cloth around their legs. *Why are they dressed like this? No civil society lets a man and a woman dress the same, like barbarians.* It made no sense to him.

Dorian recalled this was a Roshan official and despite their uncultured manner, he had to do something with the messenger. He turned to the young man, who wore a golden badge with a sun and half-moon symbol with wings on the side. The badge hung from a sash around his waist.

"I am Layla Akshay of Tariq and he is Naren of Tiq." The girl introduced the two of them.

"We've been waiting for you," Dorian said, stepping toward the young man. He offered his hand, but Naren didn't seem to notice. "There's a feast ready."

"Food!" Naren slapped his hands together and rubbed his palms.

"Come." Dorian motioned for Naren to follow him deeper into the banquet hall.

The nobles' chatter quieted as Dorian moved into view with the messenger by his side. All eyes were on them, but Naren didn't seem to notice. He inhaled, taking in the scent of the food. Dorian mentally patted himself on the back. *These beasts might be easier to control than I thought if they think with their stomachs.*

Naren's eyes danced as he wasted no time flopping down on a chaise and digging in. The boy ate shredded chicken and bread without a care. He didn't even seem to consider the food might be poisoned. Dorian thought the boy had to be stupid or naïve to trust the food was safe. Dorian didn't trust meals when he dined with close friends. He'd never think to eat anything prepared by an enemy.

Layla situated herself between Dorian and the Queen's messenger. Dorian made himself comfortable on the neighboring chaise and waited for Naren to say something. After some minutes, Dorian decided to break the ice, if only to call attention away from the fact that the nobles in the room were staring. *Damn fools. Can't they learn to be subtle?*

"So, how do you like the food?" Dorian asked.

"It's great." Naren's cheeks were full of pastries. Layla glanced at

Naren, but still hadn't tried any food. She seemed smarter than he was, which Dorian thought was sad. What had the Roshan done to make a girl more aware of her surroundings than someone who worked for their queen? *But, then again, these are people who follow a woman, so who knows what sort of sorry beasts they are.*

Naren didn't make an effort to introduce himself or explain his presence. He just ate. Dorian watched, at a loss for what to do. Layla watched Naren with a hawk-like gaze and occasionally she pushed Naren's hand away from certain foods. Dorian wondered if she knew those had been 'specially' prepared.

Dorian had some of the food poisoned. Not to kill the messenger, as he was certain that would start a war. No, he wanted to make the messenger sick as proof the gods weren't with the Roshan in this effort. Added to that, a sick messenger would be easier to manipulate and Dorian would be able to work things out in his favor. From this short interaction, he thought that plan would work, if only Naren ate some of the tainted food.

"Perhaps, once you've had your fill, we can discuss the matters your queen sent you here for," Dorian said.

Naren didn't even bother to look up. Dorian scowled. *What the hell was this kid playing at?*

"We can discuss matters now, if you like. I have no plans to eat," Layla replied. Her voice was low, husky, and snaked its way through the air up his spine. She spoke perfect Kairon.

Dorian fought the urge to grind his teeth. He had little desire to discuss such matters with a woman. The only reason he hadn't said anything about her presence was because she was with the representative of the Roshan queen. Now, she dared to address him, as though she would speak for the messenger. He would put her in her place to make sure she didn't interfere with their talk.

"You do not need to be his voice. He may speak when he's ready and we can work things out," Dorian said.

Layla sneered. "He'll eat until there's nothing left. But I am not here to eat. I'm here to set the Queen's terms."

Dorian was certain he heard wrong or her Kairon wasn't as good as he first assumed. "What?"

"I am here to set the Queen's terms. I am her messenger." Layla pulled out a medallion that hung around her neck. It had the Roshan royal seal on it. "Some might even say I am her."

Dorian almost swallowed his tongue, but managed not to make a sound. *This whelp is the Queen's representative? The Roshan were fools. They followed some demon woman who sent little girls to negotiate terms with me?* The element of surprise must have been the only thing that sustained them in this wave of destruction they wrought.

"These are her terms." Layla reached behind her and Dorian's heart raced. *Was this little girl here to kill me?*

Dorian was about to call for his guards, but Layla presented him with a scroll before he could utter a sound. She held the parchment up to his face, almost touching his nose with it. It was almost as thick as her arm and was locked with a royal seal.

"Jumpy, aren't you?" Layla snickered, as if she knew what he was thinking.

Dorian growled, but accepted the parchment. He balanced it in his hand. It was heavy, weighted down with some insane woman's hubris. *Does she really think I'll give whatever she wants? She's beyond mad.* He'd be sure to burn her list of demands with her body when he eliminated the mighty Demon Queen of the Roshan.

She smiled at him, her eyes sparkling with something he couldn't identify. "You have to open it and read it to see what the Queen wants."

Dorian sat up straight and was again tempted to call the guards. A night or two in his dungeon would knock the smugness out of her. Instead, he studied the scroll again.

"I'll need to review it," he said.

"The Queen wishes me back by dawn. You have until then. Should I or my companion fail to return, she will slit the bull's throat and then do the same to you," Layla replied.

He gave her a stern look, one that made people heed his words. "I need more time than that." He squared his shoulders and sat up a little straighter. He towered over the girl. He couldn't let Roshan queen dictate all things when she wasn't even present and he wouldn't let her rule him through some slip of a girl.

Layla didn't flinch and maintained eye contact. "Those are the terms." Her voice remained firm and steady.

Dorian eyed her even harder. "I'll have to sit down with my advisors."

Layla leaned back. "We'll be here." She motioned to the food. "Eating." She motioned to her companion, who didn't even glance up from his meal.

Dorian didn't bother to excuse himself as he got up and rushed off. Many of the nobles followed after him. He glanced back at Layla, who watched them go, like a cat watching mice. He hurried to escape her gaze.

Once in a private room, surrounded by guards and nobles, Dorian opened the seal. He read through the contents and shook his head. Slamming the scroll down on an oak table, his palm ached as the smacking sound bounced around room off the marble walls. The nobles scurried like rats to read the words of the Devil's Daughter.

"How does she expect us to gather so much gold within the day?" one gasped.

"We can't afford that," another cried.

"Well, we can't afford to go to war with her either," still another said.

"You men all lack imagination," Dorian said, his booming voice echoing through the room. He needed all eyes on him. He had the answers.

"What do you mean, sire?"

"We will fight them." Dorian made a fist and punched it into his palm.

"We don't have the men to fight them."

"Yes, you said so yourself, sire."

"And we can't send a champion. No one would even volunteer for that suicide mission."

"There's no way for us to fight them."

Dorian shook his head. "Not now, but we will. We just need time and we can have that. The season of war is coming to an end. They will move on, as they have done, perhaps even return home. While those barbarians sit back, following that woman, we will get to work."

"But, sire, they will return eventually. They won't simply go away, especially if we do not give them this gold."

Dorian shook his head. "Again, you lack imagination. When they return, she will panic when she sees the sights of us in the ranks with all of the surrounding city-states."

"But, My Lord, we do not have all the surrounding cities with us."

Dorian held up a finger. "If we unite and pull together, now that we see she is moving from the coast, we can stop her. I can bring us all together. I just need the time. Imagine the power we would gain if we were the leading city to stop the infection of Roshan scum!" He made two tight fists, flexing his thick biceps. This could be the dawning of a new age for Phyllida and his reign. *No, not could be. Will be. I'll play this perfectly and reign over all of Kairon. I will turn this curse into my blessing.*

"Hear, hear!" The nobles cheered, punching their fists as well.

"But, how will we buy time for that?" one man asked.

"Simple. We will give into all of her demands that we are able to and then, to beg for more time, we will offer her something precious as collateral," Dorian explained.

"What?"

"A goodwill hostage to assure her that we're working to gather the gold she demanded," Dorian said.

"And who could we send to assure her that things are going her way?"

Dorian beamed. "We'll send my daughter." He didn't want any of the nobles to volunteer members of their family for it would give them power over him. Besides, he could control her better than anyone else.

"Your daughter, sire? You would leave such a perfect young lady with those savages?"

"It will show that I trust the savage queen and it's a sign of good faith. This will be the perfect way to bide our time, gentlemen. The perfect way." He'd stop those barbarians in their tracks and become the most important king of the region. It was his time to shine.

***

Ashni could sense her little princess return before she popped her head into the royal tent. Naren was right behind Layla and went directly for Ashni's dinner. She glared at him, but it didn't stop him. It never did. He was immune to it by this point.

"So much better than that swill they served at the banquet." Naren moaned, his mouth full of her goat stew and flat bread.

"Really?" Ashni gave him a flat look. "A royal banquet wasn't as good as the slop put together in an army camp?" She looked at Layla. "What the hell do you see in this oaf?" She'd never understand why the hell Layla married Naren and part of her never wanted to understand.

Layla only smiled, like she knew some wonderful secret. "Here's the terms Dorian agreed to." She handed a scroll to Ashni.

The seal was broken. "You read it?"

Layla nodded. "Yeah. You'll be fine with it."

Ashni took Layla's word for it. "Good. Go fetch Adira."

Layla looked around. "Me?" She pointed to herself.

"Yes, go." Ashni waved her away.

Layla twisted her mouth to one side. "What? I'm not your servant."

"You're a little sister. That's essentially the same thing. Now, go." Ashni shooed her away with a flick of her wrist.

Layla made a face, but was off. By the time she returned with Adira, Ashni had read through the entire document. She flung the parchment at Adira, hitting her right in the face. She guffawed when Adira caught the document as it dropped.

Adira glowered at her. "You are such a child. What the hell?"

"Those are his terms," Ashni said. She reached for some diced apples and smacked her lips before biting into one. Nice and sweet. The flavor danced on her tongue and made her stomach giddy.

"Princess told me you had this. I'm shocked she didn't come back and say, 'oh, so, you know I accidentally killed him, right?'" Adira said.

"You put money on that, didn't you?" Ashni grinned.

"You accidentally kill one guy during negotiations and they never let you forget it." Layla threw her hands up.

Adira regarded Layla with a slight tilt of her head. "You do realize, throwing a dart into someone's head tends to lead to death and also is not an accident."

Layla huffed out a loud breath and curled her lip. "Oh, and I'm the only one who's ever done that?"

Shaking her head, Adira pointed to Ashni. "No, but since you are her, that just means you did it twice."

Ashni sucked her teeth. "That guy had it coming. He was lying to my face, after all. Anyway, back on track. Those are the terms." She pointed to the scroll.

Adira read it. "So, you want me to stick around and collect this tribute while you guys pack and head home?"

"Yes. Also, on your way back, check on the cities we've taken. Make sure all our conquests are still under our control. Appoint an official to stay here. I've already got a lot volunteers willing to stay behind. Leave a few of your spies behind, too."

"I have done this sort of thing before. Anything else?" Adira asked.

Layla spoke up. "Watch Dorian. Beyond the disrespect he showed me by acting as if Naren was the only one there in an official royal capacity and that he tried to use his size to bully me, he just made my skin crawl. He will screw us the first chance he gets."

"Well, then it's settled," Ashni declared as she clapped her hands. "Our first step into the West is over and we've accomplished more than I could ever imagine. Congratulations to me." Ashni pointed to herself.

"Me." She motioned to Layla. "And...you." She purposely grumbled as she motioned to Adira.

Adira sneered at her. Ashni simpered, feeling charged. Her claws were in the West and she'd dig in deep, never letting go. *Do you see what I've done, Dad? I know you've done it with me, but it's mine.*

Chapter Three

THE ROAD WAS ROUGH, rougher than the short boat ride Nakia had been forced to endure as she made her way into the Roshan Empire. Or maybe she was there already. She wasn't sure when the barbarian country began. It was hard to tell what they were grunting about outside, but she was certain she heard the word 'home' a few times. They might have been speaking some different, primitive language, but she wasn't sure. *Maybe it's just because I'm in the palanquin and their voices are muffled, but that doesn't sound like Kairon.*

They speak Kairon, her father told her in a long speech he gave her as he dared to hand her over to these savages. She was expected to believe him as he told her it would be all right, they wouldn't harm her, and she was helping keep the city alive. It wasn't like she had a choice in the matter. He gave an order. She obeyed it, like all of his subjects.

"You're a princess. You have a responsibility to help your people and this is a great help. They won't hurt you." He told her over and over again how they wouldn't hurt her, but these were the same people who made Bloody Orchards and scared townspeople so bad they didn't even fight, just gave the barbarians everything they asked for. These were demons with strange magic and supposedly breathed fire and devoured people. *"They won't hurt you. They wouldn't dare."* Her father had the gall to look fierce as he spoke those words.

Why wouldn't they dare? She had to be far from home. They had put her on a ship. Even before the ship, they had walked for days, taking her further and further from Phyllida with each step. *Who was there to stop them from hurting her? Certainly not her father.*

"The bastard sold me to them for time," she said under her breath. Her face had been tense ever since she walked out of the palace, escorted by strange looking men with wild hair, feathers tied in the locks and around their necks, and grunting as they took her to a palanquin for transport.

She saw the Kairon countryside for the first time with these savages. Her land was alive and green with forests, meadows, and streams. There were farms, livestock, and movement. People going to and fro, living their lives. From what she had heard of the Roshan, she had expected it to all be gone.

She thought her homeland would be torn apart, the land ripped open and on fire. It was amazing there were no rivers of blood or piles of bodies or forests of bones. The most destruction she witnessed was the broken walls of a few cities. This small comfort, however, didn't make her trust these barbarians any more than she had before leaving her home.

Now, she was so far from home, it might as well be another world. The air was dry and she wasn't even sure the road was a road. The small, two-wheeled carriage they placed her in wasn't something she was used to. It rocked and jostled as it moved, not a smooth ride at all. For a moment, she wondered how chariot racers stayed on their stands to race if it felt anything like her ride.

She leaned forward to the window on the door and opened the curtain slightly, just to see her new surroundings. Far from green, like her home and like the land where they got off the ship, it was almost the exact opposite. This place was the color of dust and clay. The rocks were nearly red. The plant life wasn't naked, but it wasn't lush. The grass stood tall, like spiked hair, and seemed more orange than grass ever should be. The trees were bent and crooked, growing at all angles, with leaves like thorns. She had never seen anything like that.

"Hey!" One of the soldiers banged against the door, causing her to jump back.

Nakia's heart raced and a bead of sweat slid down her cheek as she sat back in the seat. It was a strange seat with a cushioned back and the seat itself was a pillow on a low platform. It felt like she was on the floor rather than in a chair. *Are all of the barbarians' chairs like this?*

"Hey, what have I told you about scaring her?"

Nakia heard a familiar voice call from outside. She couldn't remember who it was, but it spoke Kairon and sounded female. There had been many females among the ranks of the barbarians. She didn't know what to make of that. She also didn't know what to make of the reprimand being said in Kairon. *Is that for my benefit? Does one of the barbarians want me to think they are on my side? Well, I'm not so gullible.*

Settling in the seat, Nakia took a deep breath and put her hand over her mouth. Her jaw trembled. *'They won't hurt you,'* he promised, *but he promised a lot of things. They had conquered her homeland. How could he say they won't hurt me?* The memory made her growl. *Of course, they would hurt her.*

"No, they need you," she reminded herself in a whisper. They needed her if they wanted the gold her father promised them. They couldn't hurt her if they wanted the tribute. "They need you."

Still, her stomach flipped each time the carriage rocked. She felt like she might vomit, but she didn't dare. She refused to allow them to open those doors and discover her covered in her own sick. She'd never give them the satisfaction. She jumped when the carriage came to a stop. She heard a din of voices outside along with animal noises. The door was yanked open. She moved to the far end of the carriage.

"We're about to enter the capital. The General wants to know if you need anything?" a soldier, a female soldier, asked.

Nakia shook her head. "Nothing you can provide."

The woman sniffed and slammed the door. Frowning, Nakia settled back on her seat and put her hand to the curtain on the window once more as carriage moved again. She wished to see what a barbarian city looked like.

There was a steady flow of people moving about, but she could just see the city gates beyond them. She had never seen gates like them, but she only had Phyllida's gates to judge them by. The road led into a canyon with high red cliff walls to the either side, but in front of them were magnificent bright blue gates. As they came closer she could make out eagles and lions carved in gold with precious gems all about them covering the walls. She was more impressed as they moved closer. The art was so detailed. Nakia wouldn't have been surprised if the images came to life, roaring, screeching, and clawing at the people as they were allowed passage into the city.

"How is this real?" she murmured, eyes wide as she tried to take in the whole scene. There were men posted on high towers, as expected, but the towers seemed to touch the sky.

The sight caused her stomach to quiver again. *How could barbarians build such a thing?* Surely they had stolen someone's wonderful city, as they would've done to Phyllida if she had refused her father's orders. There was no way people who thought a 'Bloody Orchard' was something worthwhile could create anything to leave her in awe.

Passing through the gates, there was an ocean of people inside and they blocked most of the inner gate. She could make out some more lions and eagles. *These animals are obviously important to them. Are they gods?* She wouldn't be surprised if they were. Of course, beasts would worship beasts.

A braying donkey pressed against the window, sticking its snout in. Nakia jumped away as the creature pulled back. There was shouting outside, but she decided not to see what it was all about. If there was a scuffle of some kind, she didn't want to be in the barbarians' way when they dismembered each other.

Eventually, the clamoring died down and all she heard were the usual noises of a city. She peeked out again and saw people and tall, tan buildings, so different from home. There were no columns, no white marble, no orange-tiled roofs.

The people were even more different than the buildings. They were dressed in plain clothing, no designs or mixed colors. Everyone seemed to wear pants, not just the soldiers as she had first assumed. Their hair was just as wild as the soldiers, some with braids, some with shaved heads, and there were feathers all over the place. She couldn't figure out who were the men and who were the women.

"What is wrong with these people? Are they people?" Nakia had no answers and sat back again, clutching the long sleeves of her tunic. The familiar texture helped settle her—her little piece of home in this storm of savagery.

Eventually, the carriage came to a stop again and Nakia steeled herself. She did her best not to flinch as the door opened again, a burst of odd heat coming into the carriage. The heat was dry against her face, crawling up the wide, short sleeves of her tunic. *Why is it so hot here? It's about to be winter.*

"Still alive, little princess?" a voice called as the door swung open.

The sun blinded Nakia for a moment, but she focused on the woman standing before her. She remembered her. This woman made sure she got safely into the palanquin back in Phyllida and also made sure no one touched her on the ship.

She heard people call this woman 'general,' which didn't make any sense to Nakia. Women couldn't be generals, but until meeting these people she didn't think women could be soldiers. There were many female warriors in the Roshan ranks. The general was rough-looking and was missing an eye. Nakia wouldn't have known she was a woman except for her voice.

"You look all right. It's good the journey wasn't a problem for you," the general said with a nod.

The journey was tough, but Nakia had pressed through. It wasn't like she could do anything else. She got sick on the ship, but hid it as best she could. She also got sick in the carriage, thanks to some unbearable heat, but she hid it as well. She wasn't checked on very often, only when she was brought meals, and it was easy to feign being fine for those brief moments.

"We're about to go into the palace, so I have a little gift for you," the general said.

Before Nakia could say anything, the general yanked her by the wrists and attached golden shackles to her arms. Nakia couldn't believe her eyes. The general snickered and walked away.

"Hey!" Nakia barked, leaning further into the scorching sun. The general didn't turn around as other soldiers came to Nakia and helped her out of the carriage. The soldiers stood at her side and led her into the palace.

The palace distracted Nakia for a moment. It was on a hill, bigger than her own home. As she walked, she saw parts of it were the same sandy color of all the buildings, but there were paintings and scenes on the high walls that gleamed with precious metals, coated in gold and silver. Blues and purples also adorned the palace, both clothes and images. There were people moving about, just like at home, undoubtedly trying to seem more important than they were.

"Come on. Can't keep the Queen waiting," a soldier said, motioning for her to walk faster. She gave him a look, but the sword on his hip made her do as he said.

***

Being back in Khenshu did not feel as good as Ashni assumed it would. The dry air stung ever so slightly. The heat of the day should have been a comfort after the biting cold of the West, which reminded her much too much of Helli, the capital of the Empire, in the winter. Usually, anything that made her think of the capital bothered her, but the desire for the West gnawed at Ashni. She would have to wait for the warring season to return.

She had her hands full until then. The tapestries, depicting scenes of her victories, seemed to mock her as she handled the tedious part of ruling—paperwork. *Sometimes, I think Dad had the right idea about getting out of this.* Stretching out on her throne, several fluffy pillows on a golden platform, sitting high on her three-tiered dais, she read through yet another report about how business wasn't properly handled while she was off conquering the West. She groaned.

"Why is it never good news?" she muttered. Ever since she returned, officials trickled into the Grand Hall with bad news. In between visitors, servants came in with tablets and scrolls of more bad news.

Layla slid down from the high ceiling, dangling from a thin line. "Talking to me or yourself?" she had the nerve to ask. She was upside down with her head right next to Ashni's.

Ashni looked at her from the corner of her eye. "Why talk to myself if I know you're hanging around?"

Layla flipped over and fell with a dull thud onto the main pillow of the throne. Ashni grunted as Layla hit her as she righted herself. There was more than enough space for the two of them, so Ashni assumed Layla hit her on purpose. As pay back, she pushed Layla, knocking Layla over. Layla whined and flailed a little. As soon as Layla was upright, Ashni gathered a bunch of scrolls from the table in front of her and pressed them into Layla's arms. Layla grunted and almost fell back over.

"Wow. This is a lot," Layla said.

Ashni rolled her eyes. "Thanks for pointing that out. I hadn't noticed."

"Who the hell did you leave in charge, a chicken?" Layla dared to toss the papers in the air.

"Hey! Were you raised in a barn?" Ashni shoved Layla with enough force to knock her over again.

Grunting, Layla caught herself and sneered at Ashni. "Were you? Stop pushing me. I don't need to be here, after all. And, why is there so much damn paperwork? Didn't you appoint Nasih again? He never leaves a mess like this."

Ashni sighed, shaking her head a little. "He got sick and appointed Foma. Apparently, Foma's an idiot. This is why your mother kept writing me, demanding I come back. Foma dared to try to take your parents manor from them."

Layla frowned. "They didn't tell me."

"Why should they? They know as soon as they do, you'll go have Foma piss himself at the sight of your sword."

Layla's face scrunched up. "So, you didn't tell me because you wanted to beat him to death yourself?"

Ashni chuckled. "I fed him to our brothers as soon as the courts

38

allowed it. To try to steal from me means dealing with me. But, to try to steal from the kingdom, from the Empire, from our glory, then you meet the lions and entertain the masses."

Layla didn't argue with that. Ashni knew she wouldn't, even though she undoubtedly wanted a piece of the bastard for trying to take anything from her parents. There was more to Foma's incompetence than trying to rip off beloved nobles.

They could have stayed in the West if Ashni was able to leave Nasih in charge. He was a trusted advisor and always kept things together when she was off on campaign. He had done so as a governor of this very province back when her father was Emperor. But, it seemed age caught up to him. She'd have to think of someone to replace him for the next campaign season because there would be no coming back until the world was hers.

"Where's Adira? She does this better than we do," Layla said.

"No, she does it with less complaints than we do," Ashni replied. Adira was due any day now. She could handle the bulk of the administrative work and fix the mess Foma left. "Princess, shouldn't you be training?" The all-black uniform certainly suggested that.

With a smile, Layla put her chin in the air. "I sneaked away. You're rewarded when you can get away."

Ashni shrugged. She got back to work, ignoring the fact that Layla was making faces at her. After a minute, it was too much.

"First, stick your tongue out at me again and I'm going to tear it out. Second, either read those documents and make an account of what the problem is and how to solve it or I send word to your father that you're here and not training."

Layla's face fell and she glared at Ashni. "You're an ass."

"I know. Work." Ashni pointed to one of the scrolls.

They worked quietly. After a time, a raven flew in the window and landed on Ashni's shoulder. She gently untied a note from its foot. The raven cawed and flew off.

"Adira's returned," Ashni said.

"Sound the horn," Layla called to a servant.

The servant ran off to do her bidding. Other servants appeared to clear the clutter from the table, to prop Ashni and Layla up with more pillows, and the extra fussy servants straightened Ashni's and Layla's robes. Layla batted them away while Ashni ignored them.

"Sometimes, you just have to let people do their jobs," Ashni told Layla.

"I don't need people to dress me and I don't need them to fix my clothes."

Soon, the throne room was filled with nobles, top military officials, priests and priestesses, and other people. Excited energy buzzed through the hall. Perhaps even more so than when Ashni herself returned because Adira was coming in with their final cache of treasure. In the past, there would have been a parade from the city gates to the throne, but Adira had grown tired of such pomp years ago.

A carpet was rolled out for Adira and she marched in as if she had conquered the world on her own. The cerulean cape swished behind her like a blowing banner and children reached out to touch it. Adira ignored the giggling children. She was treated to this behavior whenever she had entered the city in full uniform. She had taken this long walk many times before.

"Adira, so good of you to join us. Amuse us with tales of how you left the city of Phyllida." Ashni crowed as Adira stood before her.

Adira gave her a bland look. "Your official in the city will be sending messages roughly every two weeks to keep us abreast of any information regarding the city. Roughly a thousand troops opted to stay behind in the city and they're in contact with the other soldiers who remained in the West. I've arrived with our tribute. If you'd like..." She pulled a scroll from her side satchel.

"Please." Ashni motioned forward with her hand.

Adira read the list of gifts and tribute from King Dorian. It was a long and boring list, full of things Ashni couldn't use. The treasure would mostly go to reward the army and families who lost people in the conquest. The recitation was meant to perk up some ears, so that they would leave with more troops in the spring.

"Why did he send me a bear? Doesn't he know we have bears?" Ashni massaged her temples. Some of these gifts made no sense. If Dorian was trying to get on her good side, he needed to just give her gold, silver, and jewels.

"Our bears don't look like that." Layla motioned to the animal. It was completely black, which wasn't normal for bears in their area. Their bears were larger as well. It made for an interesting battle when a child decided to join a warrior guild and opted for the Bear Clan.

Ashni waved it off. "Send it off to my baby brothers. They might enjoy it. If not, Chandra will figure out what to do with it."

Adira nodded and waved the beast away. "Last and possibly least, the insurance that we will get the rest of our gold and can actually pay people to campaign with us this spring."

Ashni rolled her eyes at Adira's verbal melodrama. But, she should let the good general have her fun where she could get it. *How often do we get to see Adira actually has a sense of humor buried underneath her rigid exterior?*

A soldier tugged their prisoner into view, holding the struggling princess by her golden bonds. Ashni laughed. *Okay, maybe Adira's having more fun than I ever give her credit for.* Adira shot her a small smile, which let Ashni know this whole little show of dressing the princess in fancy shackles and dragging her in like a prisoner of war was for Ashni's amusement. *Adira gift-wrapped the little princess for me.*

"Let me go!" The prisoner—Princess Nakia Lysand of Phyllida— yanked at her chains. The soldier—a stout lad—didn't move.

Nakia was dressed in her native garb. It looked heavy. Nakia had to be hot. That probably added to her irritability. Of course, there was always the chance she was always like this, which would be interesting. Ashni couldn't wait to see which it was.

"Well, a spirited filly, isn't she?" Ashni cackled. Furious green eyes locked onto her. The green seemed to go on forever, like the grasses of the West.

Nakia dared to spit in her direction. The audience gasped. Ashni couldn't help grinning. *Oh, she's got fire! Fire like the belly of Hell and the Great Eagle combined!* Before Ashni could say anything, Layla snarled leaped into the fray.

"Hey, you can't do that...," Layla said.

Nakia looked Layla directly in the eye and dismissed her. "I don't take orders from filthy wretches." Nakia sucked her teeth.

The room grew so quiet Ashni thought she could hear the carpet fibers shift as Layla launched herself from the throne, jumping several feet from the dais, to stand in front of their hostage. Layla stared Nakia down and Nakia, to her credit, stood toe-to-toe with Layla.

Layla and Nakia were the same height. Ashni had seen Layla cow men twice her size with nothing more than a look. Nakia didn't flinch. Maybe her attitude was more than the heat and the fact that she was a prisoner. There might be a lion lurking in the petite foreigner.

"Why don't you say it to my face?" Layla demanded.

"I especially don't take orders from filthy wretches like you," Nakia said.

Ashni could see where this was headed and had little desire for Layla to stain her good rug with fresh blood. Layla's hand twitched in the direction of her sword. Nakia wouldn't know what hit her and then there would be a different sort of mess.

"Princess," Ashni called out, causing them both to look at her. *Oh, right. Can two princesses exist in the same space at the same time?* It didn't seem possible, but she needed to make it work. "Layla, back away."

Layla growled and eyed Nakia a moment longer before turning around. She returned to her seat by Ashni, wiggling on the throne enough to hit Ashni with her knee. Ashni stayed focused on Nakia. A ghost of a smile floated across Ashni's face.

"You are a little hellcat, aren't you? There's lava in your blood. You're lucky, you know? The only person to get a rise out of Layla like that and live is...well, me." Ashni puffed out her chest. *And Adira.*

"Barbarians afflicting barbarians," Nakia snapped.

Ashni made a fluttering motion with her fingers. "You certainly think highly of yourself for someone whose own father felt she was expendable."

Nakia winced and frowned, eyes on the floor for a moment. Her weakness wasn't hard to find, but she turned back to Ashni with as much defiance in her eyes as before. There was so much fire there, and it burned so bright it seemed like it could shine with the sun itself and even dance with Ashni's lightning. Despite it all, Nakia seemed sure of herself.

"What am I going to do with you, Nakia?" Ashni tapped her chin, as if she needed to consider it.

"*Princess* Nakia," Nakia hissed like a viper.

Ashni tapped her chin again. "Yeah, I don't know. I mean, I already have a princess and she's typically more trouble than she's worth." She glanced to her right.

Layla's nostrils flared. "You dare put me in the same sentence as this wench?" The two princesses glared at each other.

"Who do you think you're calling a wench?" Nakia demanded.

"The wench in the room, of course. Who do you think you are, commanding the Queen, as if you matter?" Layla said.

Nakia shot right back. "I matter enough to be worth my weight in gold. What could be gotten for you beyond stale bread and manure?"

"If I were you, I'd watch my tongue lest someone cut it out." Layla flipped a dagger in the air.

It was time to step in once more. Ashni snatched the dagger and gave Layla a hard look. No one wanted to deal with Layla saying, "Oops, my hand slipped" and it costing them tons of gold.

Ashni turned her attention back to their guest. "*Princess* Nakia, what should I do with you?"

Nakia mustered a sneer, as if she was in control of the whole situation. "You should make me Queen since I'm the only one around here with any semblance of civility and a measure of wit."

For a moment, the court was silent, everyone watching Ashni. They were all too aware that if her sense of humor failed her, King Dorian would never see his daughter again, except in the form of ashes Ashni would certainly send to him.

Ashni let out a howling laugh. The crowd laughed, too. Nakia turned around, glaring at everyone.

"You, my little hellcat, are something else. And you obviously like my attention, so to be close to me and gain whatever of it you can, you shall bear cups for me for your stay," Ashni said.

Rather than sighs of relief, Ashni's words caused some murmuring among the hundreds of people there. She couldn't care less about that. She was in charge and what she said went. She had made her decision.

"Now, let us celebrate the return of our Great General." She beamed at Adira.

Adira shook her head with a sigh before a smile worked its way onto her face. "We all know this is an excuse to open the dozen casks of foreign wine."

Ashni smiled back. "We all know you won't object."

Chapter Four

THE BARBARIAN CELEBRATION WAS different from than anything Nakia had experienced in her eighteen years of life. She had been to many celebrations and parties back home, but nothing like this. This seemed to be more out of control than anything she had ever attended, the very definition of a bacchanal. Voices mixed with the strange music that had too many drums and not enough flutes and created an awful din to her sensitive ears.

Dancers moved to the beat of the drums. Both men and women were barely covered and wore bells on their wrists and ankles. It didn't seem like the guests paid them any mind, but every now and then someone would snatch one of the dancers for more personal entertainment. The guests touched them, held them, tickled them, and more. It didn't seem right for a royal celebration.

There were no couches in the dining hall, only large pillows of all colors for the guests to rest on. The pillows easily fit three people, but there were only one or two people on most of them. If there were two people on a pillow, there was a guarantee they were carrying on despite having an audience. Most people didn't seem to pay it any mind.

The tables were short, shorter than the ones from home. The food was odd to her. The cooks overdid it on the hot spices and strange sauces. Fruit and vegetables were served with everything. She wasn't used to seeing fruit with evening meals. She especially wasn't used to seeing fruits with dipping sauces. Her stomach turned several times and it was a struggle not to vomit.

The smell of dinner mixed with whatever the barbarians were smoking in short pipes. They passed the pipes around, sharing them readily. Even the so-called Queen smoked when a pipe came her way.

The Queen's overall behavior was not royal, but what Nakia would expect of a savage. She looked like a child playing dress up in fancy clothes, draped in shades of teal, gold, and light blue. Odd, wide-legged trousers with golden trim covered her legs. Golden bangles with charms hung from her ankles and wrists, chiming every time she moved, which was often, especially when motioning to Nakia for wine.

Nakia, having never poured anything in her life, was careful not to spill a drop from the pitcher she held as she filled the Queen's cup. Nakia didn't want to ruin her tunic since she had a limited number of them and she didn't know how long she'd be stuck in this foreign land. Her father claimed it'd only be a short time, but she knew better than to trust him.

The thought of her father made a shot of hot lava burn in Nakia's stomach. It distracted her just enough to swish the wine jug. She righted it before she made a mistake. Though, she considered if she spilled the drink in the smoky room full of loud, drunken monkeys, they'd probably just lap it up off the floor. It wouldn't be far from what they were doing right now, shoving their faces with food, gulping wine, and groping any supple body near them.

Savages just like Father said. But, her father had freely given her to these people, so what did that say about him? Suddenly, there was a boisterous cackle behind her, much too close, and she jumped out of her skin.

"Hey! Watch it over there. You knock over my little cupbearer and spill my wine, we're gonna have us another war on our hands." The Queen shook her fist at the large man behind Nakia.

"You don't give me my split of that loot and, yeah, we will." The man let out another barking laugh.

The Queen made a rather undignified face, sticking out her tongue and cocking her head to the side. "What makes you think I won't give it all to your son? He did twice as much as you did."

"And I did twice as much as you, so what does that say about either of us?"

The Queen guffawed. "You raised a better warrior than you are, but my father raised a god. Don't forget it."

The man waved her off and went on his way, chuckling as he went. The Queen snickered and flopped back on her pillow. Her cheeks were flushed red from the wine and she didn't seem to care.

Nakia didn't understand how this inelegant creature was anything more than a buffoon. The Queen tossed back the giant golden chalice that sat by her side, downing nearly half the cup in one gulp, and went back to playing dice. Dice, of all things.

In the city of Phyllida, and the entire area of Kairon, dice was the game of miscreants and fools because it involved no skill. People who frequented brothels and drank until they passed out in their own vomit played dice. Yet, here it was the sport of kings.

"Aw, c'mon!" The Queen threw her hands up. "Princess, throw the bones for me and win back my coins."

For a moment, Nakia thought the Queen addressed her, but then she remembered there was another princess here. The hothead—Layla, if Nakia remembered correctly—sat across from the Queen. She shared a large pillow with a man who was around their age. He was curled close with a hand around Layla's slender shoulders and eating almost everything on the table in front of them. Jewels chimed between them and it was hard to tell where one outfit began and the other ended since they were dressed in the same robes and trousers. *Do men and women wear the same clothing even among the nobles or was it just them?* Glancing around, it wasn't just them. *Are all of these people backward monkeys?*

"What do I get for winning back your coins?" Layla asked with a smug tilt of her chin.

"You get to breathe another day." The Queen shook her fist at Layla.

Layla snorted like a horse. "You need me on campaign. We all know you can't kill me."

"Yet."

Layla scoffed. "Then when? The world is grand and you'll always need me for that."

The Queen made a sour face and Layla giggled. Layla shifted her body, moved to the edge of her pillow, and collected the dice. She let them fly and there were cheers. When the Queen gathered the coins, Nakia assumed Layla had won. Layla took control of the dice and again there were more cheers. The Queen collected once again.

Dragging her eyes from the lowbrow game, Nakia turned her attention to the rest of the party. She had never attended a party with hundreds of people before. Her father only allowed her to attend intimate banquets. She sneaked into some of his wilder affairs, but still this was probably the most people she had ever seen in one room, not counting the throne room earlier.

The barely clad dancers of both sexes caught Nakia's eye once more. Nakia wasn't sure what to make of them. Dancers were supposed to be women, but these backwards barbarians couldn't even get that right.

Her eyes drifted to the guest of honor, the General who brought her to the court and had paraded her around like some slave. When they first met, the General had confused her by being a woman with the highest military rank, which didn't make any sense, but this made even less sense. The General was curled up on a pillow with what appeared to be a blonde woman. Nakia guessed she was a slave because the woman fed the General several bits of fruit, but then she leaned in and kissed the General right on the mouth. The General hadn't initiated the contact and didn't get upset over it, as she should have if the woman was a slave taking liberties. Nakia almost fell over at the sight, sloshing the contents of the wine jar.

"Aw, damn it!" The Queen leaped to her feet, covered in wine. She let out an animalistic, ghastly snarl.

The banquet hall became deathly quiet. Even the music halted. The Queen locked eyes on Nakia. Nakia's heart pounded and she felt as though her soul fled her body as amber, cat-like eyes pinned her. Nakia couldn't think as she watched the Queen's fist flex.

And, then light-hearted laughter filled the air. "She got you good." Layla cackled and pointed at the Queen.

"Hey! No laughing at your big sister." The Queen focused on Layla, shaking her fist at the giggling mess of a girl.

"I am you. You can't be bigger than me." Layla said, chuckling as if this was the funniest thing of all time.

"You might be me, but that doesn't mean I can't kick your skinny butt." The Queen dived at Layla and seized her.

Layla squealed and tried to escape. The Queen gripped the smaller girl and tickled her. Layla cried out louder, doing her best to wiggle away. The music started again, the dancers danced, and conversation continued.

Nakia exhaled loudly, her shoulders slumping. She wasn't sure how she managed not to fall over or faint. She doubted intoxication would save her twice should she make another mistake. The night couldn't end soon enough for her.

***

Nakia didn't get to see her rooms until the sun was high and there was an unnatural heat to the day. She wiped her brow and rubbed her eyes. This land didn't know it was supposed to be winter. It made sense in the way it didn't make sense. The barbarian's weather was as backwards as they were.

The apartments afforded to her were what she expected as a royal guest. They were richly furnished, but not what she was used to. There weren't any couches, chaises, or chairs. Everything was pillows, rugs, and short tables. Instead of tiled mosaics, there were tapestries on the walls of historical scenes she had no knowledge of.

She wandered through three rooms before she discovered the bedroom. She collapsed in the bed, asleep before she could look around more.

***

Groaning, Ashni rubbed her face as she adjusted her body on the throne. She couldn't get comfortable, despite being surrounded by pillows. She had a headache beating against the front of her head and couldn't focus. She enjoyed the party a little too much, as was her habit.

"I really should cut my wine. A little water wouldn't kill me." Ashni scratched the bridge of her nose. Drinking uncut wine was another habit of hers and made it hard to do simple things, like keep her eyes open. She needed to get it together before officials filtered into the Grand Hall for appointments.

She looked at her breakfast tray. Everything was as it usually was, but her stomach wasn't in favor of anything in front of her. She turned away from the food. She needed to eat something, but first she needed her stomach to settle and to soothe her headache. She had already had some tea, which typically did the trick, but she had too much foreign wine last night. *It was worth it.*

Well, some of it was worth it. The few wines she liked were very sweet and tasted of the ripe fruit. There were others that were too spicy or had an odd mix of herbs. She shook the thought away. *Now is not the time to be reminiscing about wine.*

"Highness." A servant walked to the edge of the dais. He held up several scrolls. "The reports on who received what treasure last night and a few reports from captains on the proper split of treasure between their units."

"Oh, good." Ashni looked for space on her work desk only to find there was none. "Bring another tray, some tea, and my cupbearer."

"More wine, Highness?"

Ashni delighted at the boldness of the suggestion. "Nothing like last night."

The servant nodded and rushed off to do her will. Ashni didn't bother to look up at the activity going on around her. Her outside robe slid off her shoulders as her hot tea was placed at her side. She fixed the robe as best she could, but her shoulders wouldn't cooperate. It was a bit annoying, but she made sure to keep her attention on work. Nakia appeared before her, so she left the outer robe alone for a moment.

"Highness." The servant awaited more orders.

Ashni waved him away. She had no need for him and he could go do whatever the hell her servants did when she had no need of them. She imagined they had active social lives considering all of the children who ran around the palace who didn't belong to her or her inner circle. She didn't mind. She didn't need the servants every moment of the day and she didn't have enough people to occupy even a fraction of the palace.

For a while, things were quiet. She worked and sipped her hot tea, which soothed her headache. Every now and then, she heard Nakia's clothing sway as she shifted her weight. Whenever she settled, Ashni could feel Nakia eyes on her, staring at her, maybe studying her. She could hear Nakia breathing, which seemed a little rapid. Perhaps she was anxious, which Ashni couldn't blame her for.

"Why am I here?" Nakia finally huffed, undoubtedly cranky to be awake only a few hours after the celebration ended.

"To whine, apparently. You're doing an excellent job. Keep it up, kitten," Ashni said with an affirming nod.

Ashni made sure not to look at the princess. Nakia was probably dying for attention right now, not knowing what to do with herself without an army of people rushing to attend to her. The nickname probably pissed Nakia off more than being ignored. Ashni hoped this would serve to entertain her for a while. Having something fun to do would help her continue on with the drudgery of administrative work.

Nakia hissed. "Don't call me that."

"Call you what, kitten? You're a hellcat, right? Well, a hell-kitten."

"I have a name and you'd do well to use it."

"Or else what? You'll whine me to death. This I'll have to see. I've got time." Ashni motioned to her work.

Nakia snorted. "It's not like you're doing anything, so it doesn't matter."

Ashni kept her eyes on her scrolls and sipped more of her tea. "Yeah, I'm definitely not working as hard as you are."

"You're just pretending to read, anyway."

"Better than just reveling in not being able to do it like you Westerners, eh?"

Nakia growled. "You can't fool me. You don't know how to read. You're not working or ruling anything."

"So, I'm essentially doing the same thing your father is, eh?"

"Don't talk about my father." Nakia took a step, but then thought better of it.

Ashni snickered. So, Nakia was brash, but not impulsive. "Because he's such a kind, loving, and gentle man, right? That's why he sent you here instead of just giving me my gold."

Nakia let loose something that was between a scream and a sob. The sound shook Ashni's insides a little. Maybe the dig at Nakia's father was a step too far. Glancing up, she saw fire in Nakia's eyes, but they glistened as well.

"At least my father is a great man who doesn't get drunk and shoot dice like a common peon," Nakia said.

Ashni tittered. "Yeah, he loses at higher stakes games. And just so you know, I can do this all day. So, unless you're in for the long haul, I'd stop while I was ahead if I were you, even though you're not ahead at all."

"Well, you're not me. After all, I'm not some brainless monkey."

"Nah, just the offspring of one, right?"

Nakia made a frustrated noise and Ashni chortled a bit. The banter would help pass the time and get work done faster. Nakia needed to keep up.

"Better than being the daughter of a demon," Nakia sniped.

Ashni rubbed her chin in thought. "I don't know. Demons definitely beat monkeys when it comes to fighting and I think we proved that not too long ago. It's why you're here, whining like you get paid for it, right?"

Pure contempt burned in Nakia's jade eyes. "You had your demon gods on your side."

"And they obviously beat whatever the hell you Westerners pray to, therefore, they're superior."

The little back and forth continued. Servants wandered in and out, taking away scrolls and occasionally bringing new things in. Before Ashni knew it, the pile of documents in front of her had dwindled and then her stomach grumbled.

"Oh, must be lunchtime. Come, you can eat with me," Ashni said. *It'll be fine. Maybe even funny.*

Nakia's mouth fell open. Ashni chuckled as she stood and stretched. She marched down the dais, walking the few feet to a small alcove where she liked to take meals when she had a moment free of work. The servants had already set up the light meal.

"Bring another seat," Ashni called.

By the time Nakia was at the table, there was a pillow for her. A servant placed it by Ashni without needing to be told. Ashni flopped down and folded her legs underneath her. Her bangles and charms sang as she sat down.

Nakia settled with more grace, needing to move yards of cloth out of the way before she was fully down. Besides her tunic, Nakia had on a cloak that fell over only one shoulder. Surely, she was hot. Her clothing wasn't made for desert mornings, or desert days in general. Maybe this was a small rebellion along with her snaps and dirty looks.

Ashni watched with a slight tilt of her head as Nakia shifted a bit, probably trying to adjust her body to the table. Nakia couldn't be used to sitting up while eating. Ashni tended to try her best to understand other cultures, but she couldn't put together why Westerners ate reclining. It wasn't comfortable for her and Nakia seemed uncomfortable sitting up. Nakia curled onto her side as best she could and still be able to see the table. Nakia's face scrunched a little as she looked at the meal before them. She made no move to eat.

Servants had reported earlier that the grandiose princess of Phyllida hadn't touched her breakfast. It seemed Nakia had no plans to adjust to the food here, just like she had no plans to change her style of dress. Maybe she knew her father would gather his tribute quickly and she wouldn't need to assimilate. Or, Nakia was a spoiled brat. Ashni, even though she was terrible at gambling, would bet everything it was the latter.

Ashni made a show of looking around. "Well, I guess you'll have to pour for both of us."

"What?" Nakia jumped up and glowered down at her. "You have all these servants around here and you invite me to your table and then treat me like some slave."

Ashni tilted her head as she regarded Nakia. She gathered an apple slice and bit it, enjoying the sweet taste as soon as it touched her tongue. "If that's the case, get away from my table."

Nakia squinted, causing her face to scrunch up. Her offense was almost adorable. "What?"

"If that's the case, get away from my table." Ashni picked up another apple and dipped into some honey.

Nakia's eyes blazed as her face turned red. It was so notable on her fair complexion that Ashni almost laughed aloud. Nakia was frozen, like she didn't know what to do. While Nakia tried to figure out how to react, Ashni grabbed some honeyed bread and enjoyed it. Collecting her cup, she tipped it toward Nakia, who was still stuck with indignation. A second passed and nothing happened. After another second Nakia stood and poured, just as she had last night. Ashni chuckled.

Yes, Nakia seemed to have more bark than bite, but that was fine. Barking could be just as fun as biting. Nakia didn't sit with her again. She could understand that.

"You don't want any lunch?" Ashni asked.

Nakia sneered. "It's all garbage, anyway. You eat garbage, like pigs."

"No, we eat Westerners like pigs. I'm sure you noticed."

Nakia's face twitched into a scowl. "I noticed you're nothing but pigs and you'll be gutted like them eventually."

"By whom? The men we ran through like the rats they were or the cowards looking to pay us off like your dear dad?"

Nakia grimaced. She was easy to wound with remarks about her father. Sighing, Ashni turned back to the food when Nakia didn't say anything else.

Ashni went back to work after lunch and wasn't surprised when Layla showed up. Layla was probably a spider in a past life. She hung barely a foot above Ashni, waiting for acknowledgment. Ashni had tested this once and went on working and Layla had hung from the high ceiling for the whole day, no food, no water, no sound.

"If you're going to be here, what if you actually helped?" Ashni glanced upward.

"What if you stopped doing this work and put in some real work?" Layla countered, dropping onto the throne next to Ashni.

"I don't have time for that until Adira can find her way from underneath Saniyah." There were many other things she would rather do than read reports and hear from nobles, but the kingdom would not run itself.

"Do you really think she wants to?" Layla gathered some papers. "Of course, this is Adira we're talking about. She's probably trying to sneak out right now, eh?"

Ashni shook her head. "Crazy bitch." Adira probably was doing her best to get from beneath her spouse. "Speaking of spouses, where's yours?"

"Passed out in bed. He dared to try to drink with me. Well, not just with me, but from the same jar." Layla snickered.

Ashni shook her head. Naren should have known better. Layla drank pure wine, the same as she. Most needed to dilute their wine during a night of drinking. "Dare I ask why he tried to drink with you?"

A tiny smile and blush settled on Layla's face as she shrugged. "He thought it would be fun. I'm sure it was at the time, but now, he's certainly feeling the effects."

"He's an idiot. Why did I permit you to marry this moron again?"

Layla laughed again. "It's funny you think you permitted a damn thing."

* * *

Nakia watched the Queen interact with her sister and wasn't sure what to make of it. She had sisters of her own and would never call them friends. Adding to it was the ease with which Layla situated herself on the throne, sharing it with the ruler of the country as if it was normal. This was something beyond anything she could think of.

Nakia knew her father would never allow anyone near his throne, not even her own mother. The throne, the dais, the entire area was only for the ruler. Yet, Layla moved around as if it were her own and the Queen didn't seem to care. In fact, the wideness of the throne suggested the Queen might have changed it just to hold more than one body. But, Nakia might be giving these savages too much credit since the throne wasn't a chair as it should be, but a nest of some sort with pillows piled inside of it. Well, she assumed it was a nest because of the spread golden bird wings making up the back of the throne.

"Do you always act like a monkey?" Nakia snapped, cutting her eyes at the line still dangling from the ceiling.

"I dunno. Do you always act like an ass?" Layla replied. She reached up, grabbed her wire, and gave it a yank. It untangled itself from whatever it was connected to and wrapped up in her hand. She attached it to her belt.

Maybe Layla was Ashni, as she had heard Layla claim at the party. It was unnerving, but Nakia shook it off. No way would she allow someone as young and as slight as she was get the better of her.

"You're the animal here," Nakia said.

"Really? It's funny because I swore I saw a tail and donkey ears on

54

your father." Layla kept her eyes on the documents before her. She passed one to the Queen and pointed to something. The Queen frowned as she stared at it, shook her head, and put it to the side.

Nakia managed to hold in a wince, but was thrown for a moment, not expecting such a quick retort or the dismissive manner Layla used. "I think that was your husband."

"Nah, from the smell, I'm certain it was your dad. Probably you, too." Layla twisted her face up.

"At least I bathe."

Layla didn't look up. "Once a year, like all Westerners, right?"

"We're not filthy mongrels like you."

"No, actually filthy mongrel losers, right?"

Nakia gritted her teeth to the point she feared she might shatter them, but couldn't muster a comeback. Her thoughts were thrown off as the Queen caressed the top of Layla's head, and turned her attention to another document. The touch was so gentle. Nakia closed her eyes briefly and shook her head, certain she imagined the scene. Layla groaned.

"Who didn't handle that?" Layla pointed to the report.

"I think Foma was too busy stealing from the kingdom to worry about the blight," the Queen answered.

"I'll summon the doctors, surgeons, and such. I guess we need some people over there cleaning up, too. I'll have my mother take charge to make sure this is handled properly and quickly, so no one else dies."

Ashni waved her off. A servant rushed over while Layla picked up a reed to pen something. Nakia didn't have a good angle to see what it was and she didn't want to risk them assuming she was interested, so she didn't change her position. But, she was hard pressed to believe Layla could write, for writing was a sign of civility and culture. As soon as Layla was done, she sealed the note with her signet ring and handed the message to the servant, who hurried away.

Did Layla really wield as much power as the Queen? No one in all of Phyllida had the same power as my father. She heard enough tales and secreted herself away to eavesdrop enough to know how her father conducted his affairs. He had a counsel but in the end, he did what he thought was best. He never passed documents along to anyone, never let others give the orders, never allowed anyone to seal his documents, and never allowed others around him as he worked.

Nakia was certain her father never got through so much in one sitting either, but she was never afforded the chance to observe him for an entire day. Even when she sneaked around, she'd never seen her father work so much. The sisters were like a machine, but still savages nonetheless. After all, who allowed women to rule over them like this?

Chapter Five

WORK WAS DULL. ASHNI understood why her father never got into the administrative part of ruling. It was like the decrees always needed to be cried, reports always needed to be given and responded to, officials always needed to be handled and soothed, and even though there were people beneath her to handle things, tons of matters still made it to her. Conquest beat this every day of the week, hands down.

"Are you drinking my tea?" Ashni asked Layla, who shared the throne with her once more. Layla had a cup to her mouth that Ashni was certain was hers.

"And if I am? Are you willing to fight me over it?" Layla asked with an arched eyebrow and a sparkle in her sepia eyes.

Sighing, Ashni rolled her eyes. "Are you trying to pick a fight? This isn't a very subtle way to do it."

"I don't have to be subtle with you. Days of sitting here doing this has only put a lump on my butt and a cramp in my hand." Layla shook her hands out and then cracked her knuckles.

"Well, where's your spouse? You think I like sharing this already limited amount of space with you? Your elbows are pointy. Plus, you're whiny and I get enough of that from that one of over there." Ashni jabbed her thumb at Nakia, who stood by the throne, ready to pour wine if necessary.

"Hey!" The two princesses glared at her and then at each other.

Ashni chortled. *Was this what happened when Layla spent time with someone her own age?* Yes, she had her spouse, but that was extent of her time with someone her own age and that relationship was obviously quite different than this situation.

"Anyway, where is your spouse? You could spar with him and stop whining to me about fighting." Ashni would love to be able to go and burn off some of Layla's energy, but she had other things to do. She had to be responsible—for a little while anyway.

Layla dismissed the question with a wave of her hand. "He's at the races with his friends."

Ashni nodded. Racing in any form didn't hold her or Layla's attention, but was a popular pastime in the empire. For now, Layla was stuck with her doing administrative work. Until their salvation arrived. Adira staggered into the throne room. She leaned slightly to the left, as if she needed support to stand upright. There was a glow about her that had nothing to do with the glint of gold jewelry or the white of her robes.

Ashni howled at the sight. "By the Heavens, you can still walk?" She was genuinely surprised.

Adira grunted and flung her hand in Ashni's direction. "To Hell with you. I was carried here."

"I can believe it." Ashni clapped her hands and rubbed her palms together. "Well, you're here. You got this." She motioned to the papers around her. There were no pressing meetings for her to tend to, so it was safe to escape for a while. "The Princess and I are going to go bond."

Adira dismissed the sisters with a tilt of the head. Ashni wasted no time jumping up from the throne. Layla squawked as she fell over. Chuckling, Ashni moved down the dais while Layla righted herself. Servants rushed over, bringing pillows for Adira to sit on at the foot of the platform. They moved the work within arm's reach for her.

"Your spouse isn't going to come looking for you, is she?" Ashni asked, stretching her arms.

Adira rubbed the bridge of her nose with a single finger. "Uh...it's a huge possibility. She got called away for work and doesn't know I left."

"Well, Princess, you hear that. We might have a limited amount of time, so let's get going." Ashni marched off with Layla following her. She barely made it a few steps before pausing and turning to look back. "Princess Nakia," Ashni purred. Nakia stiffened. "Come."

Nakia scowled, but did as she was told. Ashni snickered and continued on with the two princesses trailing behind her. Layla settled by her side while Nakia fell behind. Ashni glanced at Nakia to find her looking around the palace as they moved.

***

Nakia wasn't sure why she was accompanying the Queen and her sister. Maybe it was because she was expected to be with the Queen. Or maybe it was because this was uncharted territory and she needed something familiar, even if it was the savage queen. She would take anything as long as it kept her from thinking about being afraid. She shook that thought away and distracted herself by taking in the sights.

The palace was so unlike the one she lived in. There were no carved columns or delicately cut pillars. Not in the sense she was used to, like the ones in her home. Instead, the support beams had pictures painted on them, showing different scenes, some battles, some celebrations, some hunting, and some outdoor scenes. It was like they told a story, one she didn't know and didn't care to know.

Servants milled about, not giving them a glance. Most of the servants weren't working. The servants here had a lot of downtime. It didn't seem to bother anyone that they weren't working. The Queen nor her sister said anything to anyone idling.

Children ran about the place as if they were in a playland and the Queen didn't seem to be irritated. Layla mussed several heads as the children ran by, stabbing at each other with wooden swords. The Queen paused occasionally to pretend to fight with a couple of small children who didn't seem to know who she was. They giggled and the Queen grinned, eyes lighting up like the sun they were colored after. Nakia had never seen anything like this. Her father wouldn't tolerate his own children coming to play with him. She shuddered to think what he would do should anyone else's children try to engage him.

"Hey! Get off that statue." The Queen shook her fist in the direction of courtyard. Several children hung off a statue of a man wearing a loincloth, wrapped in a lion's skin, and holding a sword high.

The children giggled and scattered as soon as they heard the Queen's voice. The Queen didn't chase after them, but she shook her head. Layla offered her a half smile.

"They didn't damage it," Layla said.

"They should have more respect for the Amir. Didn't their parents teach them anything?"

"I think they do it just for your attention. They know when you spot them, you'll yell," Layla said.

A devilish glint danced in the Queen's eyes. "Oh, really? I guess that easily explains the both of you."

Layla grunted and shoved the laughing Queen. They continued walking. Nakia looked back long enough to see the children returning to the courtyard and that they didn't return to the statue.

The trio descended to lower levels of the palace where there were no windows and the heat of the day was left behind, as if they were falling away from the world itself. They didn't stop until they were in the belly of the palace, but it felt like the Netherworld. Nakia wrapped her arms around herself as sunlight faded and was replaced by the glow of luminescent fish. At the top and bottom of the walls were glimmering fish, swimming a long, narrow aquarium running the length of the wall and illuminating the long corridor. In her country, glowing insects or simple fire lit dark rooms. She had never seen fish do this, never heard of fish doing this. *Is this devils' magic?*

She suspected the barbarians had demon magic. But, she didn't believe it was in the fish. It was somewhere. There were too many things off with these people for demons not to be at play.

"All right, Princess, I hope you're ready for your daily beat down." A predatory grin oozed onto the Queen's face as they stepped into an empty hall. There was no furniture and the walls were barren. The floor was covered in sand.

Nakia pressed herself against the wall, as if trying to meld with it. She wasn't sure what to expect. If the sisters planned to do something to her, no one would know. They were practically in another world. Not that it mattered, considering the Queen could have done whatever she wanted above ground. Still, Nakia tried to stay out of the way.

The Queen and Layla went to the middle of the room. Their eyes locked and suddenly the air was charged, popping with energy. Nakia's hair frizzed a little and electricity from around the room danced down her skin. She could feel power radiating from the sisters. It seemed they could bring it down by staring at each other. They tossed off their outer robes, gems and jewels jingling as they hit the floor. Nakia thought the room rumbled as the cloth landed in a heap and her nerves twitched as the noise echoed off the bare walls.

"I don't know about these delusions you're always having, sister." Layla snickered as she plucked off her rings. She pulled strips of cloth from behind her back and wrapped them around her hands.

"Oh, really? Don't you know the light cuts through the dark?" the Queen said as she slid the many bangles off her wrists. Plucking off her diadem, which looked like golden feathers dotted with sapphires, she spun it on her finger before casting it aside as if it were meaningless.

"Last I checked, darkness banishes the light." Layla took off earrings.

The Queen chortled. "I'm sorry, but have you ever noticed a shadow in the presence of the sun?"

Layla sneered. "You're not the sun."

"No, I'm worse."

Layla gasped. "Blasphemy!" She giggled.

"I think my father will forgive me. He always told me shoot for the stars and burn the sky while I was at it."

"Burn the sky, really?" Layla scoffed and hid her face in her palm briefly.

"I get it done while you hide in the shadows. After all, which one of us cuts the sky?"

"Blah, blah, blah." Layla made mocking hand movements.

The sisters stripped down to their undergarments, a band of cloth across their breasts and small loincloths around their hips. Their muscular arms and torsos were covered in tattoos. Nakia balked at the idea of women having tattoos, but seeing the size of their muscles made her think they might not be women. Maybe these barbarians were demons.

"When is that spouse of yours expecting you back?" the Queen asked.

Layla rolled her head. "We agreed to have evening meal together."

The Queen's eyes danced with demonic mirth. "Yeah, well, I hope he expects you with bruises."

Layla snorted. "You're just lucky Adira's free now, so the kingdom won't go under while you're in bed for days thanks to me."

Nakia didn't understand what was happening. It looked like the sisters—a Queen and a Princess—were about to fight. This made no sense since they were royalty and women—two reasons why they should never be near a battle, yet they went to war. Why fight each other? The whole thing made even less sense when the two ran at each other, making tight fists like this was a true battle.

And, then, they were fighting. Going after each other as if they were bitter enemies, as if the only way out of the room was to take off the other's head. Nakia's heartbeat increased and she tried to press herself closer to the wall, not sure what to expect. *Why did the Queen tell me to come? If these sisters, who seemed so close upstairs, might kill each other down here, what would the survivor do to me?*

Nakia's eyes could hardly follow the movements of their bodies, the punches, kicks, dips, and dodges. She had never seen anything like it. It was almost like a dance, until one of them struck the other and knocked her back. The sound of the blows, a sickening crunch or an obscene slam, echoed through the room. Nakia flinched with each sound and her stomach twisted. The fight went on and on. Nakia's legs grew weak and she slid to the floor, back still against the wall. It was hard to breathe, the air hot and heavy, choking her.

Every now and then, they stopped fighting, as if stopping was scheduled for that moment. They went to the fountain in the corner to drink water and pour it on themselves, and then they went back to their battle. They didn't look in Nakia's direction and she was glad. The lack of attention didn't make it any easier to breathe. Her heart rate never settled.

It seemed like a fight between beasts, predators fighting for territory, monsters fighting for everything. The occasional battle cry seemed like a roar and made her flinch each time. She didn't see an end in sight and wasn't sure how much time passed before they finally began to tire.

"Good thing...good thing...we're only here for the winter. You need the practice." The Queen panted, hunched over with her arms barely up. Her body was soaked with sweat, making her muscles gleam in the artificial light.

Layla let out a long breath. Her body bent awkwardly to the right and she looked like she was about to fall over rather than attack again. "Please...you'd be...you'd be fat and drunk by summer if it wasn't for me."

The Queen laughed, but it sounded like coughing. "I've got Adira. She does everything you do."

Layla let loose a loud wheeze that could have been a snort. "Yeah, but she isn't you."

The Queen wiped sweat dripping from her forehead. "Bath?"

Layla inhaled deeply, arching her back. "Probably need to get home. I do have a spouse to eat dinner with."

The Queen rolled her eyes. "And yet you claim to be me. I'd never abandon you for a spouse."

"Maybe because you'd never be able to keep a spouse. You'd have to marry a rabid possum filled with the most toxic magic and possessed by the darkest gods to survive a marriage."

The Queen grunted and turned to Nakia. "Well, to the bath with us." She threw a hand up for dramatic flair.

Nakia wasn't sure what that meant. *Are baths the same here? Why would she need me?* The Queen had relinquished her duties to the tired General, so she and her sister could attempt to destroy each other. None of this was expected. *What could happen in the baths?* She almost asked, but closed her mouth just in time, certain she would dislike the response.

The Queen and Layla redressed, putting on everything except their jewelry. They punched each other in the shoulder before leaving through doors at opposite ends of the room. Nakia followed the Queen. They wandered through a corridor with battle scenes on the walls. The air became thick and moist. Sweet smells from incense wafted to her nose. They came to a room with a bath the size of a small pond.

The Queen stripped off her clothing once more and left her jewelry with the discarded outfit. Servants rushed in and collected her things. One stayed and kneeled by a low platform the Queen eased down on. The servant scrubbed the Queen, rubbed her down with oil, and massaged her muscles. Her body was covered in scars and tattoos, but the servant didn't pause at any of them.

How is this normal for them? Women shouldn't have scars and tattoos and fight. How can they not understand that?

Once the servant was done, the Queen jumped into the water. "Oh, yeah." The Queen sighed and turned to Nakia. "Do you swim?"

Nakia blinked. "Swim?"

"Yeah. It's rare to find people that do. Do you?"

Nakia shook her head. There was no need to know how to swim, or so she was told. She had never been in water past her waist. She watched the Queen of these barbarians move around the water like she was a fish. Obviously, someone thought the Queen needed to know. Her sister probably knew as well.

"There's a shallow end." The Queen nodded to the end of the pool where Nakia stood. "They have baths where you're from, yes?"

Nakia nodded, moving to put her feet in the water. Gasping, she immediately yanked her feet out. The Queen snickered and Nakia glared at her.

"I like the heat. So, they have baths, but you don't swim. I don't understand that," the Queen said.

She acts like I'm the backwards one. "Our baths aren't very deep."

The Queen hummed and dived under the water. She came back up and floated on her back, her breasts just above the water like two islands. The Queen's eyes locked on the concave ceiling, which sparkled and reflected the waves of the bath. The room seemed to ripple because of it. It was an interesting effect.

"That wouldn't be much fun," the Queen muttered. "Your people seem dull. Do you spar?"

"Spar?" The word was foreign to Nakia's tongue.

"What me and Princess just did."

Nakia snorted. "Dance around and try to kill each other? Not likely. We have grander pursuits. Studying the skies, producing plays and poetry, advancing medicine and mechanics." Not that she expected a barbarian to grasp concepts of astrology, art, or technology.

"And what do you know of mechanics?"

Nakia lifted her chin at the challenge. "I know we have great engineers in my homeland. There are great thinkers everywhere. Our libraries overflow with evidence of their minds. What do you have like that?"

The Queen hummed again and went underwater for a long time. For a moment, Nakia thought the Queen drowned and she might be able to go home. The water even settled, but then the Queen broke the surface and regarded Nakia with a tilt of her head.

"Maybe..." The Queen didn't complete that thought or maybe she didn't have a response to Nakia's statement. She probably didn't know what Nakia meant by any of academics Nakia listed.

There was silence except for the swishing of the water as the Queen swam. Time went by, but eventually servants came to fetch the Queen for the night meal. Nakia was expected to pour wine once again, which she did, and then she was dismissed, free to return to her rooms.

Why had the Queen dragged me along for the sparring with her sister? Why drag me to the bath? None of it made sense and she couldn't piece any of it together once she was alone in her room. The more she reviewed the day, the less sense it made.

"I don't understand," she muttered to the air. *Is the Queen toying with me? Purposely trying to confuse me?* She didn't have much time to think about it. Just as her body alerted her to hunger that had been there all day, there was a knock at her door.

Nakia's meal was delivered to her right on time. The spread wasn't as impressive as for the Queen, but there were some foods Nakia recognized, things she could eat without forcing it down. *Who bothered to ensure I have food I know?* Like many of her other questions of the day, she didn't have any answers. She didn't ponder it, just enjoying the small comfort.

***

Another day and more administrative work that Ashni wished to

64

avoid. She had help now, so things would go faster and she'd be able to do some fun things during the day.

"We have a problem," Adira announced, holding up a paper for Ashni to see. It was hard to do since Ashni was on the throne and Adira was ten feet away from her, sitting at the foot of the dais.

"My eyes are good, but not that good. Care to read it to me, General?" Ashni raised her cup, signaling for Nakia to pour her more wine. Nakia did so immediately and Ashni smiled to herself. *It didn't take long to train her.*

Adira grumbled under her breath, but waved the document around some. A servant came over, took the paper, and delivered it to Ashni as Ashni rolled her eyes.

Ashni snorted. "Is everyone around here lazy in the winter? Next thing I know, you and Princess will start hibernating."

Adira gave her a flat look. "Really? You're questioning my work ethic? You, the person who has abandoned work for the past week to play with her sister and left the kingdom to me?"

"Blah, blah, blah." Ashni read the document. A scowl sliced its way across her face and an ungodly noise ripped its way from her throat. "Call in the eighth feathered squad right now!"

Out of the corner of her eye, she noticed Nakia jump. She realized Nakia had never heard her raise her voice. *She's not important.* She turned her attention back to the document. She was going to have to kill at least one person by tomorrow. Nakia probably had never seen that before, either. Well, time for her to see other aspects of Ashni's personality.

"You don't want the captain in here as well?" Adira asked.

"After I get the full story from the eighth. Then, I'm shoving the Ivory Claw in his belly," Ashni replied, smacking the pillow underneath her. Nakia jumped again.

Things calmed down as Ashni waited for the group to arrive. When the eighth squad filtered into the throne room, she stared down at them while Adira stood off to the side. Adira shoved the top ranked member of the squad to the front.

"Tell her," Adira barked, motioning to Ashni.

Ashni glowered down at them. "Is it true? Have none of you received a share of this year's campaign?"

The soldiers looked at each other, but the one Adira pushed forward spoke. He looked directly at Ashni with a solid gaze. "None, Highness."

"Why did you wait so long to report this?" Ashni wanted to groan, but controlled herself. It wouldn't do to lose herself in front of people who had to follow her into battle in a few months.

"It was reported earlier, Highness, but…"

Ashni sighed. "The correspondence went to the Regent instead of me." This was a huge screw up in communications. Something this stupid could give her a headache when she had the time to think about it.

"Yes, Highness."

"Of course. This is perfect. Just perfect." Ashni pinched the bridge of her nose. "Okay…" She turned to Adira. "We need the books and we need this bastard right now. If not sooner."

Within minutes, the captain was before her, but in Ashni's opinion even that took too long. He dared to march in with his head held high and he was in full uniform. His yellow cape fluttered behind him, calling her to strip him of all this ornamentation.

"Highness," he greeted her with a raised fist.

A sneer refused to leave her face and she was tempted to storm off the throne, get in his face, and ruin him. But, there would be time for that later. For now, business. She would have to do this right, as she didn't want his family later claiming he was the one who was wronged and dishonored.

"Captain Pavit, your squad claims that they haven't received payment or shares from this year's campaign. What happened?" Ashni inquired. What happened was this Captain got fancy new boots, a new horse, and was probably buying new slaves and adding to his manor house with money that was supposed to pay her soldiers. She wanted to feel his blood on her hands.

Pavit simpered at her. This bastard thought he could charm his way out of this. She hated him even more and was tempted to throw one of her hidden knives at him. She took a calming breath and focused on him with an overly sweet smile. *We will have justice soon enough.*

"Your Highness, I assure you, everything was divided properly. I think my squad is just bothered by the fact that we got such a small share compared to others," he said. He lied to her. To her face yet.

"Really? Because I've got this inventory…" She held up the paper. "Looks pretty close to what everyone else got." She made sure everyone understood how booty was divided so that everything was as fair as possible. Of course, humans were greedy creatures, no matter what. She tended to bet her troops were greedy for honor and glory, but over the years, a few surprised her.

He flinched. It was small, but enough for her. "Forgive me, Highness. I assumed others received more as the haul is usually so much larger. Either way, my troops received their share."

"But, not according to this…" She held up another document with the list of things the soldiers all claimed to receive. There were many missing items and she was willing to bet he had them.

His throat moved as he swallowed hard. "They're lying."

Not only does the bastard lie to my face, but he'll throw his own men under to save his skin. The filthy coward. "Or you are. I should hope it's them because you know how I feel about officers who steal from our fellow soldiers. We are all in this army, Pavit. *All*." She glared at him. For her to achieve her father's goals, this needed to be the greatest army the world had ever seen and she would never let anyone ruin that. No one was allowed to spit on her father's dreams.

Now, he frowned. "You sound as if you've already made up your mind, Highness."

She arched an eyebrow. "Is that your admission of guilt?"

"Never."

"Then we'll leave it up to the investigators to find out who is and who is not telling the truth. My decision will be made once all the evidence is presented to me. For now, you are dismissed." She flicked her wrist and waved her hand. Her bracelets rang out, as if a siren telling him to get out.

He wisely rushed off. He probably was going to hide his stolen goods. It was too late for that. Layla was on the job checking him out. Hardly an hour after he left, Layla was next to her.

"Are you ever just going to walk in? Use the door maybe?" Ashni asked as Layla dropped from the ceiling, onto the throne, pointy elbows and all.

Layla sniffed. "That's boring. I'm pretty sure that's how I would get my sister status revoked."

Ashni chuckled and put her arm around Layla. She yanked Layla to her, forcing the younger warrior to cuddle with her. Layla yipped and grunted as she struggled to get away. Adira glanced up from her desk, shook her head, and went back to her work.

"Maybe you two should stop flirting and get to business," Adira said, eyes on her paperwork.

"Ew!" Nakia yelped as she put her hands over her mouth.

Ashni looked at Nakia, watched her draw back and gape at the throne in horror. The expression was too much. Ashni broke into a guffaw. Layla did the same and Nakia went from being aghast and disgusted to furious. She glowered at them both as if trying to make them burst into flames. Of course, they laughed more.

"Oh, ha, ha. How am I supposed to know she's teasing you? For all I know, you filthy barbarians do things like that." Nakia huffed and folded her arms across her chest. She put her nose in the air and turned her head. This made the Queen and Layla hoot harder.

"All right, you two. It was funny. It's passed. Now, focus," Adira ordered, pointing at them.

"You are such a soul-sucking, fun-killing, sourpuss," Ashni said.

"Yes, because a captain is stealing from us," Adira replied, gesturing to the documents.

Ashni nodded. "No, yeah. Good point. Princess, report."

Layla snorted. "Are you kidding? Naren and I saw everything on the list within seconds of going in his house. His spouse was all too happy to point out things that came home from campaign with him. Personally, I think he's an asshole and she'll be very happy to see him go."

Adira arched an eyebrow. "What makes you think he's an asshole?"

"His spouse kept pointing out his favorite slaves. It didn't seem like he liked them because they worked hard at their jobs. I noticed quite a few children wandering around with similar features and they weren't his spouse's children. I talked to many of the slaves and servants and they didn't have nice things to say. Naren talked to other captains and they didn't have good things to say. It seems like everyone who knows Pavit thinks he's overconfident and entitled. They had suspicions that he was up to no good as well."

"All right. Call him back here and, Adira, make sure this shit isn't going on anywhere else. Someone stealing from us, they need to die today." Ashni growled and punched her fist into her palm. She refused to let anyone get over on her, them, or the military.

Pavit was back in her presence immediately. Guards dragged him in and flung him in front of the throne. His body made a smacking sound against the stone floor as he landed and it echoed through the hall. His eyes never left hers as he hurried to his feet, trying to look unfazed. He tilted his chin to her once he stood up.

"You stole from your squad," Ashni said.

He sneered. "You can't prove that."

"I have proven it, idiot. Tomorrow morning the judges will examine your case and we will make our arguments. Then, tomorrow afternoon,

I'll chop your head off in the arena." It was that simple. And it would taste sweet.

"They'll see you're just targeting me."

"We'll see. For now, enjoy my dungeon and maybe massage your neck a little. The Ivory Claw will go right through it," she promised.

He yanked away from the guards as they tried to take hold of him. She watched him march out as if arrows would bounce off of him. He'd learn otherwise tomorrow, in front of every soldier in the city. She'd destroy him in this life and let the gods—her father—do the same in the next.

Chapter Six

ONCE AGAIN, NAKIA FOUND herself in the middle of something she didn't understand. The Queen dragged her to court with the General and Layla, as well as other officials. It didn't make sense to her on several levels. One, why would the Queen bring her appointed cupbearer some place very unlikely to have wine? Two, why in the world was the ruler of the kingdom going to court?

"Can't she just pass the verdict herself?" Nakia mumbled, standing with the General and officials she didn't know. They were outside the courtroom, waiting for the judge's decision.

"The Queen can't argue that a crime happened and then judge herself. That wouldn't be justice," the General said.

Nakia squeaked, not expecting an answer. Taking a breath, she composed herself. "Yes, but she's in charge."

The General regarded her with a patient look. "So, your father could make a ruling on a case he brought to the courts?"

Nakia's brow furrowed. "Well, no, but this wouldn't have happened this way in Phyllida."

"And how would it have happened there?"

Nakia blinked, stunned by the barbarian's curiosity in her country. "The soldiers would've brought the matter to him and he would've heard the case."

"Does he hear all the cases?"

"I don't think that's possible. How would he have the time?"

The General nodded. "The Queen can make some decisions on matters of justice, but there's already a code in place for the whole empire. Whenever the law is broken, a panel of five judges hears the case." She motioned to the courtroom.

"Because the Queen doesn't have time for it?"

"And they've devoted their lives to studying the Empire's laws. The Queen cannot change the laws to suit her and she doesn't have the time

71

to hear everything. Besides, in cases like this, she would be biased and justice might not be served."

Nakia nodded. "But, what if the judges are biased?" Any number of things could go wrong with a panel of judges. "What if someone bribed them?"

The General shrugged. "Well, the punishment for bribing a judge is losing all your wealth, blinding, and having your hands cut off so you can't even beg. The judge is left stranded in the desert, covered in honey. How does your country handle these matters since the king cannot hear everything?"

"There is a court and we have juries. I'm told they're made up of average citizens who hear the case and then vote on it. There can be anywhere between fifty to two hundred people on a jury. It's rather difficult to bribe everyone."

"Interesting approach," the General admitted.

Nakia puffed out her chest a little. Her people could show these savages how to truly issue justice. But, it was interesting that the Queen couldn't change the law on a whim. Nakia's father had the ability to do so and she felt that was his right. The Queen, who was both royal and claimed to be divine, should have the same right. *But, what should I expect of backwards people?*

Nakia was drawn from her thoughts as it was announced the judges had come to a decision. Five judges were faster than two hundred jurors considering evidence. She suspected she knew the outcome. Despite it all, she found it hard to believe any court in any land would go against their ruler, even if they were savages.

***

As expected, Captain Pavit was judged and found guilty by the courts. Layla had easily amassed piles of evidence against him in a single day and other investigators had found more. This was a serious offense and the now former Captain knew it. When he was pronounced guilty in the open courtroom, his body shook.

Given his position in the military, he was given the chance to pick his punishment and he decided to fight in the cirque. He probably thought this would prove his innocence, winning battles, showing the gods favored him, and he'd be able to go about his life. He was in for an unpleasant surprise. The gods hated him and he needed to know that.

"Are you certain you want to go out like this?" Adira asked, pacing the tiny room in the basement of the arena.

It was a cell for fighters to prepare for their moment on the great stage, out in the cirque. It was grim with a dirt floor and dark slate walls. It held nothing beyond bare warrior necessities. It was hot to the point of being an oven for any poor soul in it, like Ashni and her lot. It wouldn't have surprised Ashni if Adira ran into the wall as she moved about the room. *She's like a caged lion when she gets this worked up.* Ashni sighed.

"What do you want me to do? Sit back and let idiots think they can steal from us?" Ashni fastened her breastplate into place. The cirque equipment was abysmal. If she dared send a soldier to fight in this piece of so-called armor, she'd have to kill herself from the shame of it all.

"The court didn't say it had to be you specifically who fought him for his honor. You could let me or Princess go." Adira gestured to herself and then to the corner by the door, where Layla stood with Nakia. They were scowling at each other and trading insults that anyone passing by the thin, wooden door could hear. If Nakia was a warrior, they would probably be shoving each other.

"Are you two finished with your mating dance over there?" Ashni snapped. The pair turned to her with wide eyes and slack jaws. "What? Stop looking so disturbed. You're pecking at each other like you need the room to yourselves."

Nakia gasped, putting her hand over her mouth. "Disgusting."

Layla glared daggers at Ashni. "You keep saying that and I'm going to punch her in the mouth." Layla pointed at Nakia.

"Why me?" Nakia shouted as she stepped back and put her hands to her chest. She was covered in a sheen of sweat as she insisted on wearing her native clothing despite the impracticality of it.

"Because that's how Layla shows she loves people." Ashni blew them both kisses. They grimaced, almost at the same time. "Hmm...maybe you two are actually sisters."

Layla shook her fist at Ashni. "Keep it up and I'll kill you for Pavit." Her voice bounced off the walls, assaulting their ears.

"Adira, take the princesses before I devour them." Ashni waved her hand, dismissing all of them. "And then I'll pick my teeth with you because I know you're going to nag me some more."

"You're going out there with a bullshit breastplate and a spear. You don't spear fight." Adira stomped her foot.

Ashni sighed. "The rules are the rules." She had been trained to use a spear. Adira was such a worrywart. She imagined Adira came out of her mother wringing her hands and furrowing her brow.

"The rules don't say the Queen has to go out there and be the kingdom's champion. Send me, send Princess. Hell, send Naren. Any of us would gladly spill his blood and watch our brothers devour him. Why should you go?" Adira asked.

"Because why should I ask any of you to do what I can?" Ashni stared Adira down. Her parents had always made it clear—she needed to be able to do anything she asked others to do. But, life taught her something a little different. "You are by my side for things that I cannot do. Why should I need you if I can do it all? You're not here to save me, Adira."

Adira hissed. "Aren't I?"

"Not in this instance." Yes, there were times when she needed Adira there, talking sense, thinking things through, seeing the other angles, but now was not the time. "I've got this. Now, take the princesses and get moving."

All three eyed Ashni before finally leaving. Ashni turned to the small wooden table at the back of the room and wrapped her hands with the thin cloth given to fighters in the cirque and then seized her spear. She wanted Pavit to taste her battle blades, but personal weapons weren't allowed for her.

She knew she shouldn't be doing this, fighting in the cirque. It was a proving ground, a moment of entertainment, or a punishment. It was beneath her and had been since she was twelve. But, she wanted to make sure everyone understood what it meant to steal from her military; she wanted everyone to see what happened if they tried to stand in the way of her father's dreams, of *her* dreams.

"I will make him pay for this trespass, Father." Ashni cracked her knuckles.

***

This wasn't Nakia's first time in an arena, but she had never been in one this size. It felt like they walked through dozens of corridors before making it to the Queen's private seating area. It was a balcony that overlooked the whole field. There were steps with pillows and rugs on them, which she suspected counted as seats since the barbarians didn't believe in or seem to know about chairs.

The General and Layla took seats that gave them a superb view of the sandy-floored open arena while Nakia stood, frozen. She gawked at the size of the crowd. She doubted she had ever seen so many people in one place. Could they all see the action on the floor? Even the ones who looked like insects to her at the top level?

"Are you going to sit or loom?" the General huffed, giving her a stern look.

Nakia looked around, thinking the General might be addressing someone else. But, Layla was in her seat and her husband was next to her. There were only servants around and they milled about the box-like space, gathering food and pouring drinks. For a moment, Nakia waited, expecting to be passed the wine jug.

"Will you sit down?" The General yanked her into the seat next to her. "People standing over me make me nervous."

Layla tittered. "Too dumb to sit down."

"Hey!" Nakia snarled at her nemesis. It seemed like Layla was always down her throat about something, even when she was just curious about something. Layla insulted her when she asked why the Queen was fighting in the first place, like she was a fool for not knowing.

"What? You're clearly the very definition of a moron. You didn't even know Ashni was fighting today. What did you think we were coming here for? It's not like we need to watch people die in the cirque," Layla said.

"And how am I supposed to know your ridiculous barbarian culture where the Queen of you monkeys actually fights criminals?" Saying it aloud made it sound even more ridiculous, yet here she was about to witness just that. *How did it not sound ridiculous to them?*

"Hey!" Layla's husband—Nakia couldn't remember his name—shook his fist at her.

"Says the monkey," Nakia snapped and glowered at him. No one asked him to speak up.

"How about you kids all cool it and watch the match?" The General took Nakia by the shoulders and turned her to look out onto the arena floor.

Nakia yanked away from the General and was about to keep going with Layla's husband, but then realized she was there to watch. She wasn't being forced to serve anyone. She was given a comfortable seat on a plush pillow with the softest fur pelt covering she'd the pleasure to touch. *Why am I being allowed to watch the match? Why am I not being treated as a servant?*

Before Nakia could figure it out, the crowd erupted into a roar of cheers. The Queen had entered the arena. She wore the plain leather breastplate Nakia last saw her in, leather gauntlets on her forearms, along with the odd, wide-legged pants these people wore. She wore boots, but no greaves, so her shins and calves were bare and unprotected. She only had a spear in her hand while her opponent held a sword and an impressive bronze shield. What was the Queen thinking? Surely this man would spill her guts all over the arena sand.

The Queen held up her spear and the crowd roared again. From her seat, Nakia could see the Queen smiling and there was that usual confidence in her stance. She looked as if she didn't believe she could lose, not to him, not to anyone. *How can any woman look like that?*

"This man thinks he can steal from the army and get away with it," the Queen shouted, her voice booming so the whole arena could hear. She pointed her spear at her opponent. "He thinks he can steal from me, my brothers, my sisters, our empire without consequence." The audience hissed. "I will show him what happens to those who steal from us. Stealing from my father's dream, standing in *our* way of glory, it's like spitting on the gods themselves!"

The audience cheered wildly. The Queen turned to her opponent and smirked at him. He scowled and held up his sword, banging it against his shield. A gong rang out and the audience cheered even louder than before.

"Why does he get real armor and weapons?" Nakia asked.

"As the criminal, and for sport, he gets to bring his own weapons and gear as a last show of mercy. After all, he'll never be able to hold them again after this," the General answered.

Nakia shook her head as she wrinkled her forehead. "What do you mean?"

"Let's say by some miracle he won this match, which he won't, he was still found guilty and will have to pay back the men he robbed. He would lose all of his possessions, but he'd at least get to keep his life."

"Yeah, but he won't even be keeping that," Layla said.

Nakia found herself nodding, even though she didn't understand. *Why should they care if a guilty man held his possessions one last time? Why would they give him an advantage over their queen? She could end up dead and they didn't seem to care. In fact, they seemed intent on helping him kill her by providing him with better weapons and armor.*

"She's going to play with him," Layla said.

"She has to punish him. A clean death is much too good for this bastard," the General said.

"I bet she feeds him to your brothers afterwards," Naren said.

The General nodded. "Oh, yes, our brothers will feast on this rotter."

Nakia wasn't sure what that meant. She couldn't understand why they thought a woman could beat a man in combat. Yes, the Queen messed around with Layla, fighting in that basement, but that wasn't real. They were playing, like children.

Everyone knew men were the warriors. Women would never compare and this sort of savage play would never be allowed back in her home. No one would sit back to watch a man fight a woman, a man kill a woman in the arena.

The Queen and her opponent circled each other for a moment before the Queen jabbed at him with her spear. Its tip collided with his shield. He swiped at her with the sword, but didn't come close to her. The crowd continued to cheer, like some great action had occurred.

Nakia leaned forward and rested her elbows on the cold stone railing. She didn't understand why the crowd was so invested in this. *Was life so boring they needed to see their Queen fight some criminal? Were they so brutal that they wanted to see a man destroy a woman? What the hell is wrong with these people?*

***

"Why would you steal from us, Pavit?" Ashni asked, her spear aimed right at him.

"Why do you think you can beat me? You haven't given me a chance at anything, no recognition for what I'm capable of. You don't know what I can do." Pavit let out a battle cry and charged her.

Ashni gave a devilish grin as she slid out of the way of his blade and slapped him with the shaft of her spear. He grunted and fell off balance. She chuckled from deep in her throat and allowed him the chance to right himself. He glared at her.

"I know what all my soldiers can do and I know you're going to die in the cirque today."

Frowning, he moved around her and studied her. "Because of your lightning?" His eyes took a quick glance at the clear sky, but his chin remained stubbornly in the air.

She snorted, throwing her head to the side slightly. "I would never waste my talent on you. I cut the sky for glory and honor. I will cut you for justice."

"You'll have to call forth everything you have if you don't want to

77

die right now." Pavit shoved at her with his shield and missed her completely.

Ashni twirled the spear and growled. She aimed her spear at his body, which he blocked with his shield as she expected. Slashing with his sword was also expected and she was out of the way in no time. Her spear slammed against his calf and he grunted at its impact against his greave.

Pavit came at her, even though he knew she had the advantage on reach. Ashni twisted and turned the spear and hit him on the shoulder with the shaft as he extended the sword again. Hissing, he pulled back. She continued to move the spear, twirling and dancing, watching him as he tried to calculate what she'd do next. Before he figured it out, she decided to teach him the next lesson.

"You're slow and you're thinking way too much." Ashni swept Pavit's feet out from under him with the heavy butt of the spear.

He grunted as he hit the sand. She tried to slam the spear down on him, wanting to bash his face in. He rolled out of the way, but as he was getting up, she smashed him in the back. He fell off balance and she cut him across the bicep with the spear tip. The crowd roared as his blood painted the white sands.

"Bitch!" He barked and jumped at her to shove her back using the shield.

She put the spear up to block and he crashed the shield against it. The wood splintered and the spear cracked in half. *Damn, it's even cheaper than it feels.* She ducked his sword as he slashed at her head. She could hear the whizz of the blade right by her ear. She jammed the spear tip into his foot, through his leather boot and deep into the meat. He screamed in pain as she hissed and pushed the metal as far into his foot as she could. Blood splashed onto her face as she yanked the spear out and rose to her full height. He swung his sword as he fell back and she dipped out of the way.

"No one steals from me." Ashni flung the spear with all of her might into his shoulder.

Pavit dropped his sword as the spear sank into his flesh. She charged him and he caught her on the chin with his shield. Her recklessness caused her teeth to click as she fell back. The crowd hissed. She quickly put her hands up and got into a defensive stance. He did the same and they circled each other, him hobbling as his foot poured blood into the sand. A grimace was set into his visage, a look he'd wear in the afterlife as far as Ashni was concerned.

"So, when you do you plan to kill me?" Ashni smirked, wanting to make him suffer. She needed to witness his agony, mock his struggle, and humiliate him in front of the masses before sending him to the gods and their punishment.

"I'll beat your face in with this." He brandished the shield as a bead of sweat ran down his cheek. His eyes weren't as confident as they had been. His fear, his worry fueled her. His concern danced down her spine and tickled her.

She snickered. "You're very welcome to try."

He took her up on her offer, coming at her, swinging the shield with precision. She dipped out of the way and gripped his arm. He yelped as she yanked him and flipped him over her shoulder. He brought the shield up in time to keep from having his face stomped in. When her foot impacted the shield, he used it to shove her.

Ashni tumbled back, taking a knee to gather herself. She landed next to his sword and watched as he climbed to his feet. Chuckling, she picked up the blade as he stalked over to her with an audacious glint in his eyes. This fool still thought he could conquer her. *Has he forgotten I am divine, that I am Chosen?*

"You can't defeat me, Highness, not on your own. Call forth your power, show me what you're really made of, so I can show them all who here the real god is," he roared.

She shook her head. "Nice dreams you have. I think I'll turn it into an ironic nightmare."

"You can't—" His words were cut off when she climbed to her feet with a battle roar and took an upward swipe with his sword.

He gasped as if his heart stopped, which it could have if she cared to end this now. The sword warped as it moved through his armor and right arm. He gawked at her as he backed away, eyes wide as his blood gushed from his body, splattering across the cirque's floor.

"You were saying something about being a god. You don't even know the strength of a god. So, tell me more how they favor you over me. Tell me more how they prefer a lowly thief to this Chosen One?" she demanded, her golden eyes molten.

He coughed, his face red and veins crawled up his forehead. "You're nothing. Not Chosen. The Amir was Chosen. You're just his bastard!"

The crowd gasped and there was dead silence before they began to boo. Ashni snickered as she stalked over to him, her blood buzzing in her ears, her nerves popping, wanting the ultimate action. She quelled that. He wasn't worth it. Like she told him, her talent was for glory and this was for justice.

"You want me to get worked up and finish you quickly, don't you? You want a death your family could boast about. They could say with my talent, I sacrificed you to the gods. I'd never allow that. You've stolen from us. You deserve the pain, the agony, and the suffering that only the Daughter of the Heavens can bring," she said, and the people cheered.

He backed away with his arm limp at his side. His retreat made her laugh more and she began to toy with him for everyone's amusement. She huffed as she jumped at him and he swung the shield wildly. The crowd cackled at his feeble attempt. Ashni shuffled in his direction a few more times, making him twitch. Sweat poured down his face, but he dared not wipe it. He couldn't chance missing her next move, not that he'd be able to keep up with her when she finally decided to end this. He limped and dodged, waiting for her. Then, she was in his face, punching him like he deserved.

A loud crunch echoed through the cirque and Ashni hoped she broke Pavit's entire skull. His cheek against her knuckles felt good. The bastard tried to cheat her soldiers and rob her. The world would know what she did to cowards like him. He tried to put the shield up, hoping to block her onslaught. She punched it, denting the metal and making him wince. He dropped the shield, his last defense. Her fists never stopped after that. She ended the flurry of punches by knocking him on the chin enough to break his jaw. He fell to his knees before her, bruised and bloody.

"Do you see this?" she hissed, standing over him and glowering at this piece of nothing. "This is where you and your kind belong. Anyone who troubles my home, who disturbs my brothers and sisters, who dares to try to stop the dream of the Son of the Great Eagle, will kneel in the dirt before me and pray that I show you mercy and cut off their head."

The people cheered and she planted her foot on his shoulder. The fool put his hand on her ankle and tried to shove her foot away. She kicked him over.

"Feed him to the lions," Ashni said, and then she spat on him.

Ashni turned her back to him and headed for the exit. She heard him struggle to his feet. *Some rotters never learn.* Turning, she snatched up the abandoned sword as he raised his shield, ready to bash her head in. The sword slid into his abdomen with ease as he gave a choked gasp and she held his wrist to prevent him from bringing down the shield.

"The lions," she repeated, staring him dead in the eye. "And you will live long enough to know my brothers have had their fill of you." She shoved him off the sword. Groaning, he hit the ground with a thud. Not satisfied, she took the sword and severed his healthy arm from his body at the elbow.

His screaming, accompanied by roaring applause from the crowd ushered Ashni from the arena. She passed the sword to the first guard she saw and made her way to her seat.

***

Nakia's mouth refused to close, even as the match ended. She couldn't believe her eyes as the Queen stabbed her opponent with his own sword. *How could a woman do that? How could a woman fight like that? Perhaps the Queen was really a man. But, she had seen the Queen and there was no mistaking her for a man. The Queen had to be a demon, a devil, something out of the darkest nightmares of any civilized being.*

Nakia nearly jumped out of her skin as someone flopped down in the seat next to her. Turning, she saw the Queen beside her, her dusty face splattered with blood. Nakia cringed and leaned away.

Before the Queen said anything, a slave came with a towel and a bowl of flower-scented water. The Queen sighed softly as she wiped her face, sounding almost like a content puppy, not like a beast at all. She sighed again once her face was clean and she discarded the towel. The servants vanished and the Queen propped her feet up on a stool.

Layla frowned at the Queen. "You were too easy on him."

The Queen cocked an eyebrow. "He's still alive and about to be eaten by our brothers. How is that not good enough for you, Princess?"

"First, they might choke on such a cad. Second, you should've put that spear in his eye," Layla said.

The Queen sneered and stuck out her tongue. "The next idiot that steals from us, you can dismantle in front of the masses."

"There better not be another idiot who steals from us after this display," the General said.

Layla sniffed. "Idiots abound. They walk the world like birds fly in the sky."

"Then, as I said, the next one is yours to do with as you please. I imagine you'll pull him into the shadows, rob him of all heat and light, and then watch him slowly freeze to death," the Queen said.

Layla smirked. "That would only be the start."

The conversation sounded like garbled gibberish to Nakia. *What shadows did the Queen mean?* Her mind reeled over how casually they discussed defeating men. *How was any of this possible?* She did not have the answers and felt like she would not have them if she lived a million years. Instead of trying to make sense of the Queen and her sister, she focused back on the arena as three lions were released.

The lions roared and went for the man, teeth and claws going through flesh. His screams tore through her as the mob cheered. While she had witnessed men die in the arena, as it was common entertainment in Phyllida, she hadn't seen them eaten alive. Wincing, she turned away, gagged, and vomited.

"Are you kidding me? You'd never last on the battlefield," Layla said.

Nakia didn't have the strength to retort. Her stomach seized again and she coughed, having nothing left in her belly to give. There was a hand on Nakia's back, but she was not sure whose it was because she couldn't lift her head.

"This is predictable and I have work to do," the Queen said.

The screams and ovations bombarded Nakia, cutting into her, making her stomach twist. Someone picked her up, cradled her close. She groaned, and her head lolled to the side enough to allow her to see who dared to touch her as her cheek encountered soft leather. The Queen held Nakia to her chest. She groaned again, considering she might be pressed against blood and gore. Nakia opened her mouth, trying hard not to throw up again. "Barbarian..." she managed before the world went black.

***

Ashni summoned Nakia for dinner. Not to join her, but to pour the wine like a good cupbearer should. She didn't have time to coddle the little princess. She had allowed the girl to hide in her rooms since they returned from the cirque, but now she had enough.

Nakia came in, dressed in clean clothes. Pavit's blood had gotten on her other outfit when Ashni picked her up. The servants told her that Nakia had torn them off when she regained consciousness. Ashni didn't get Nakia's clothing choices. She had to be hot in the middle of the desert wearing what appeared to be drapes.

"Did you eat?" Ashni asked as Nakia stood before her. She knew Nakia had been served food an hour before and she had eaten a little. The earlier activity seemed to steal her appetite, but then again, Nakia didn't eat much in the first place.

"Some," Nakia replied, her voice low.

"Can't have you waste away. I do need my gold and for that to happen, you have to at least still be alive." She gave Nakia a smirk.

"Does it matter?" Nakia grabbed the jug of wine.

Ashni's sneer quickly changed to a frown. *Why is Nakia so muted now? Had the cirque been too much for her?* If Westerners were so sensitive, she'd take over the whole world within a year.

"Don't bother, kitten," Ashni said, covering her goblet. She suddenly wasn't in the mood.

Nakia's face twitched and her eyes flashed before she stepped back. Ashni smiled. Muted, yes, but not totally off.

"So, did you like my fight, kitten?" Ashni showed her teeth, trying to look like a hungry lion.

Nakia flinched and put her hand to her stomach. If she vomited again, Ashni would ship the girl back to her father in a crate. Nakia managed not to throw up, taking a breath and releasing it. She stared at Ashni and her jaw twitched. There were words trying to get out. Ashni could practically see them in Nakia's glower. Ashni waited, wanting to pounce on whatever the insult was. But, the words never came. Was Nakia scared now? Had she not believed in Ashni's power until witnessing it in the cirque?

"I'm going to devour the West just like my brothers devoured that bastard Pavit." Ashni's lip curled into a diabolical grin.

"Our gods will protect us from you," Nakia said, her voice still lower than usual. But, at least now she had some argument in her.

Ashni laughed, throwing her head back. "Your gods? I will devour your gods, too. Am I not the Daughter of the Heavens?"

Nakia gnashed her teeth and her eyes blazed like molten jade. "They would never allow a savage like you to control us."

Ashni chortled. Apparently, while she might have lost her lunch, Nakia had not lost her fire. It needed a little fuel and Ashni would enjoy stoking the flame. She flashed Nakia a grin so wicked she could feel the evil course through her.

"And yet they allow a savage like me to control you, kitten."

Nakia growled. Her eyes erupted, shining in a way that put the sun itself to shame. Ashni sat back and sipped her stew.

"Perhaps they have placed me here to end you," Nakia said.

Ashni tittered. "End me, kitten? You couldn't even take me ending Pavit. How are you going to end me?"

"I could poison the wine." This was a real danger and why being the cupbearer was such an important job. This was the reason her court had been shocked when she appointed Nakia to the position rather than a trusted, loyal member of the court, but Ashni didn't worry over it.

"Bold. Very bold, hellcat. Let's see if you have." Ashni gathered her goblet and raised it slightly.

Nakia growled and trembled, making the wine slosh in the jar. Ashni beamed at her. As Nakia leaned forward, Ashni half-expected to be wearing her drink, but Nakia poured without missing the glass. As Nakia pulled away, she smirked at Ashni. The expression sent a little frisson down Ashni's spine and made her stomach flutter. Ashni countered with a lopsided grin as she forced her stomach to settle down.

"Bottoms up." Ashni tipped the goblet to Nakia before downing every single drop of wine. She smacked her lips together, earning a disapproving frown from Nakia. "I think you should get a refund on whatever poison you used. Obviously, it didn't work. Maybe because the gods favor me."

Nakia sneered at her and she laughed. This little slip of a girl knew that if the urge overcame her, Ashni could kill her with the goblet in her hand. Hell, Nakia knew if she felt like it, Ashni could kill her with her bare hands, but apparently that meant nothing to Nakia. *Do all Westerners have this fire? Are they all so fearless?* Ashni doubted it.

Chapter Seven

ASHNI YAWNED LOUDLY AND stretched on the throne, dropping a scroll. She heard Nakia suck her teeth, undoubtedly disgusted by the display. Ashni blew a raspberry at no one in particular and scratched her armpit, if only to disgust Nakia further. She glanced over at the princess and saw the sneer pulling at the right corner of Nakia's upper lip. Ashni groaned. "I'm so bored!" Ashni howled, throwing her arms over the side of the throne.

"Don't you have work to do?" Nakia asked. Her eyes strayed to the scroll that got away.

Ashni waved the question off. "Adira's handling it. Well, most of it. She doesn't have anything better to do, but now I don't have anything better to do."

"Where's your savage sister?" Nakia inquired.

Ashni sucked her teeth. "Spending time with her stupid spouse." She sighed. "I suppose I could go find someone to play with. Surely there are many maidens whose blood is boiling for me after that fight, even if it was days ago." The very idea put a smile on her face and she tingled a little.

Nakia's forehead scrunched up. "What do you mean?"

Ashni considered telling her, just to see her reaction, but there were only so many times she could watch Nakia be revolted over something Nakia didn't comprehend, thanks to her weird culture. *Why the hell does Nakia have a problem with people being with people?* The West seemed to have a lot of sexual taboos Ashni didn't understand. Besides, Ashni wasn't in the mood to send for physical entertainment. She had plenty of entertainment here.

"I'm going to teach you to play Bones," Ashni said. That could prove fun, especially if it frustrated Nakia enough.

Nakia's face scrunched up, her mouth pulling to one side. "Bones?"

"It's a dice game."

"Like the one you played at that party?"

"Exactly the one." Ashni clapped her hands together. Soldiers tended to play the game to pass the time and she often lost at it, going broke on some occasions if there was too much downtime. She didn't mind. It helped her stay close to her army and they all needed that connection, that bond.

Nakia's face remained twisted. "But, isn't dice a game for commoners? Are you so much of a savage?"

Ashni chuckled. "You have no idea."

Nakia's face managed to scrunch up even more as she studied Ashni. Ashni had a feeling this would be fun, so she sent for the dice and proceeded to corrupt the foreign princess. Seven dice were delivered along with two wooden cups. Servants set up a couple of pillows, wine, fruits, nuts, and other snacks in a small room off the side of the throne room. It wouldn't do to gamble in the throne room. Ashni flopped down on one pillow and motioned for Nakia to take the other. Once Nakia was sitting, the lessons began. Ashni had cake as she explained the game and they played a few practice rounds.

"This is the most confusing game ever created!" Nakia huffed several minutes later as she threw four of the dice. They clattered as they hit the wall and then settled on the floor.

Ashni brightened. "Hey, you won." She pointed to the dice.

Nakia's frown vanished as she focused on the dice. Leaning closer, her face scrunched up like before as she examined the dice. Her brow furrowed as she turned to Ashni, eyes screaming "how?" Ashni tried to explain, but Nakia's face twisted more and more. It was a little adorable.

"You throw better when you're angry, kitten." Ashni bumped Nakia with her shoulder.

Nakia shook her head and rubbed her face with both hands. "This game is stupid."

"No, you're doing good." Ashni shook her head and patted Nakia on the wrist. "Come on, throw again. Let's see what you got." Ashni gathered up the dice and passed them back to Nakia.

"I shouldn't be doing this..." Nakia sighed, her shoulders slumping. Her mouth fell into a bit of a pout.

"Why? Because it's not proper? It's not what upper class women should be doing?" Ashni snorted. "Stop being a prude, kitten. We both know you're a hellion, so stop pretending to be anything but."

Nakia scowled at her. "I'm not a hellion. I'm a Lady. I'm sure a beast like you just doesn't know what one looks like."

Ashni chuckled. *You have no idea, kitten.* "I think a beast like me knows plenty of what a lady looks like." She clicked her tongue as a wicked idea formed in her mind. "What if we played properly by adding a little wager to it?"

Nakia's eyes narrowed as she studied Ashni. "What do you want to wager?"

"If you win, you can dress me how you think a proper lady should dress and force me to act as such for the whole day," Ashni replied and Nakia's eyebrows raised. "But, if you lose, I get to dress you as a 'barbarian.'" A shiver raced down her spine at the thought of Nakia in traditional Roshan clothing. She shook it off. *Don't be a fool. This girl is worth a kingdom of gold.*

Nakia eyed her for a long moment and then turned her attention to the dice. She studied them for several seconds before picking them up, all seven of them, and weighed them in her hands. Then, she picked up one of the two small wooden cups sometimes used to throw the dice. Loading the dice inside, she rolled the cup between both hands.

"You're going to cheat, aren't you?" Nakia said as if it was a stone cold fact. The accusation wasn't off base. Maybe Nakia knew Ashni better than she pretended to.

Ashni smiled, trying her best to seem innocent, but the expression felt way too predatory. "Oh, my dear hellcat, you don't know me at all. I have no reason to cheat." *Not to say, I won't do it if it's necessary.* "I wouldn't begin to know where to cheat." *Again, not to say I wouldn't.*

Nakia's gaze narrowed. "Until I win and you change the rules."

Ashni waved the worry off. "Come on. You know the rules and how the game is played at this point, so I can't change the rules." Nakia didn't have a great grasp of how the game was played, but Ashni was certain the insane man who invented this game half a century ago didn't have a good grasp on how to play it. Ashni's father taught her how to play and he seemed to know less about how it worked than Nakia did.

Sniffing, in a rather loud, unladylike manner, Nakia left the dice in the cup. Ashni watched and waited. After a few seconds, Nakia poured the dice into her hand and took out three. She had been doing better with fewer dice as she learned the game than with all seven. She shook the dice in both hands rather than using the cups and let them fly. Their crashing against the wall echoed through the room.

Ashni's eyes watched Nakia rather than the dice. She leaned forward as she let the dice go and watched them intently. Her eyes widened as the dice hit the wall and she leaned over so far she almost fell off her pillow. The dice rattled as they landed. Her face fell, her jaw practically on the floor.

"Looks like I win, like always." Ashni tittered. *I don't get to say that often when it comes to this stupid game.*

Growling, Nakia folded her arms across her chest. "You weren't winning when you whined for your sister to throw for you at that party."

Oh, she remembered and she had fire. Ashni felt a frisson again, but managed to keep herself under control. Before the game continued and she got to see more of Nakia's beautiful fire, a servant rushed in. He was out of breath, hands on his knees, huffing and puffing. *This isn't going to be good.*

"Highness!" He panted, staring at her with wide, panicked eyes.

Ashni arched an eyebrow. "Yes?"

"Lord Amal. At the gate." He flung his arm out, roughly motioning in the direction he came.

A loud, agonized groan escaped Ashni and she slid down onto her pillow. "He comes earlier and earlier every year." *It's like a punishment from the gods. Father, tell me, what have I done to offend you so?* She sat back up and rolled her shoulders and rubbed her eyes with one hand. "Fine. Clean this up." She waved toward the snacks and game.

Ashni jumped to her feet, bangles and jewels ringing as she did so. She waved Nakia up and marched back to the throne room. Nakia jogged to keep up, her sandals echoing as they slapped against the floor. Ashni adjusted her robes and settled her diadem properly on her head before settling onto the throne. Nakia stood on the dais as usual, standing off to the left.

"Did you know this clown was arriving today?" Adira stormed into the throne room, voice loud and arms flapping. She had been working so that Ashni didn't have to, but there was no way she would stick around the palace with Amal there. Ashni wished she had that option.

Ashni sucked her teeth. "Yes, I knew he would show up exactly today, which is why I've been totally preparing for this." *Please, if I knew when this idiot was going to show up, I'd figure out excuses for all of us to leave.*

Adira glowered at her like this was all her fault. "Your sarcasm doesn't help. I'm not putting up with him, so you might as well get Princess here to do this work because I'm going home."

Ashni's upper lip curled. "Hopefully to get laid so you can stop whining."

Adira's nostrils flared and pointed at her. "I'm doing you a favor."

"No, doing me a favor would be sitting around and playing chess with Amal for the rest of his life...or killing me. Whichever." *Killing me might be the better option. I wouldn't have to deal with him ever again. There's no way we're going to the same afterlife.*

"Oh, please." Adira folded her arms across her chest. "So, the Empress can have a pike shoved through my chest and I get to die a slow death, rotting in the sun and being pecked by vultures?"

"That's why it's called a favor. You'd be taking one for the team."

Throwing her head to the side, Adira snorted. "I think I've given enough for the empire." She motioned to her eye.

Ashni's brow furrowed as she scowled. "Oh, please. The empire gave you Saniyah, so shut up."

"I don't care. I'm not staying here with him around. End of discussion." Adira made a chopping motion with her hand.

"I'm not asking you to entertain him. You keep working and you know I'll handle the entertainment. Unless, of course, you want to do me that favor." She flashed Adira a huge smile.

Adira sucked her teeth. "Not for all the territories in all the world."

Ashni groaned and rubbed her face with both hands. "Okay, can you at least keep working? The kingdom has to go on and we all know you like all the paperwork and bureaucracy for some weird reason."

"Perhaps you need to learn to like it. One of us is queen, after all."

"I can handle it, but I would just rather do other things when I can. Besides, you eat up administrative work like it was actual nourishment."

Adira didn't give an inch. "Flatter me all you like, but I can work from home."

Ashni grunted. "The hell you can. We both know the second you go home and Saniyah's there, you're not going to get anything done. She'll be in your lap, then you'll be in her, and everything else loses all importance. Use your office. There's a reason I gave you one. Get some stuff done and then go home. You don't even have to see him." *If only I could be so lucky.*

Adira eyed her for a second, which turned out to be a second too long. The announcement of "Lord Amal" echoed through the palace and Adira groaned. If Ashni could have thrown herself out a window, she would have. Unfortunately, she didn't have time for that. Amal's grand entourage appeared in the entrance hall. Adira groaned again and put her hand over her face.

"He gets worse and worse every year," Ashni grumbled. It was embarrassing.

***

Nakia watched as a parade of people marched into the throne room after servants announced the arrival of Lord Amal. This was quite different than when she came with the General weeks ago. There weren't hordes of people to see the arrival of whoever this was. The Grand Hall emptied. Officials and nobles waiting to see the Queen suddenly disappeared. Servants even made themselves scarce. Not being around seemed to be more important than being available for the Queen.

Nakia wasn't sure why everything was so lacking in pomp and ceremony for this arrival, but it obviously had something to do with this dreaded and loathed Amal person. The entrance was lavish with richly dressed people marching in, but Nakia didn't recognize them as any of the Queen's people. There were long lines of people and the last person sprinkled white flower petals near the dais. The Queen frowned at the flowers.

"Lord Amal," a servant announced. Then came a closed palanquin, which was carried to the foot of the throne. The Queen rested her chin in her hand while making a show of rolling her eyes.

Nakia's eyebrows knitted close together and she moved a little closer to see who would emerge. *Who is this?* It was obvious the Queen didn't want to be bothered, but she allowed whoever this was into her presence. It was strange. The Queen seemed like she'd never allow someone into her orbit if she didn't want them there, which explained why Layla's husband didn't spend much time around the palace. *Is this person different? Special?*

"Sister, I have told your slaves time and time again that it is King Amal." A bronze hand pushed back the purple curtain of the palanquin while the Queen rolled her eyes yet again. If she wasn't careful, she was liable to lose them.

Two legs covered in the wide-legged pants of the Roshan Empire swung out of the litter. A servant placed a step beside the palanquin and then helped a slender man out, standing on the scattered flower petals.

He was dressed in robes that were infinitely more fabulous than the Queen's clothing. His robes were dazzling green and yellow with decorative gems and jewelry and spoke loudly and clear of his status.

His face was clean and his dark hair was done in long braids with dangling feathers.

"What are you king of?" the Queen asked, rubbing her eyes.

Nakia wondered this as well. *How could he be a king if his sister was already the ruler? But, then again, why was the Queen called 'queen' if the Roshan was an empire? Why was she not the empress? Some backward barbarian logic?* Nakia shook her head, disliking the fact that she was even curious of these details.

A frown cut across his face. "I am King of all Amalia and soon to be Emperor of the Roshan Empire. You know that very well."

"Right. Amalia." The Queen deadpanned. "The kingdom with much better weather during this time of year and yet you're here."

"Isn't it best to celebrate the Festival of the Moon with family?" he said with a grin. It seemed like he wanted the expression to be charming, but there was something crooked about it.

"Yes, but most people would think you would make this holiday trip to be with our mother, yet you always spend this time with me." It sounded as if the Queen was accusing him of something, but Nakia couldn't be sure what.

He continued to smile. "Because we're so close."

The Queen waved his words off. "You have a twin. I swore there was no closer bond."

"Yes, but I want to be close to all of my siblings, especially my sister."

The Queen sighed and rubbed her forehead with two fingers, as if fighting off a headache. "I'll have servants prepare your usual apartments. Of course, Amal, had I known you would be here almost two weeks before the festival, I might have..." She didn't finish the sentence.

Nakia suspected the Queen had nothing good to say.

"I'll go supervise then and see you soon," Amal said. He slid back into the palanquin before the Queen could say a word.

And just as quickly as they appeared, the parade vanished. The Queen sighed, scowling in the direction her brother had disappeared. She shifted on the throne and turned her attention back to the General.

"Office," the Queen said.

"Today. We'll have to see about the rest. You know I have little desire to be around while *he's* here." The General turned and marched out. The Queen said nothing. This was interesting.

***

The next morning wasn't what Ashni expected, even though she should have. Nothing ever went right after Amal showed up. *How the hell did Mom actually manage to have more children after giving birth to that breathing disaster?*

Adira hadn't shown up to do the paperwork, so it was left to Ashni. It wasn't so much work that she was swamped or annoyed by it, but she had hoped Adira would finish it. Instead, Adira sent word that she was needed at home, which was utter bullshit, but for now, Ashni would leave Adira alone. No one wanted to be around Amal. *If only I could use the excuse that I'm needed at home.*

Ashni ate breakfast and went to work. The servants knew what mood she was in and brought plenty of sweet cakes for breakfast. Anything that honey or cinnamon could be added to, had it that morning. There were several pastries with baked fruits inside of them, too. It was little comfort, knowing what lay ahead of her, but she pressed on. Time wouldn't stop just because an annoyance had arrived at her door.

Nakia stood off to the left behind Ashni, yawning. Raising her cup, Ashni gave Nakia something to do. Her timing proved right because as soon as the cup was full, Amal entered the throne room. She would need more wine than usual if he stuck around. She picked up a small cake and took a bite.

"Good morning, dear sister." Amal beamed as he stood before her. Right before her. On the dais, practically at her feet. He reached over and plucked some fruit from her tray.

"Good morning, Amal," she said without bothering to look at him. If he dipped his fruit in her personal bowl of honey, they would have a problem. *No, no, no. Mom would not be happy if you stabbed Amal, especially since she knows he's here for the Festival of the Moon. Damn.*

He continued to grin before biting the apple slice. "It would be even better if we got a chance to play chess."

"I'm working." She motioned to the papers in front of her. Then, she had to brush cake crumbs from them. *Maybe I should stick to the fruit until I'm done.* It was just as sweet, but less messy.

Blowing out a breath, Amal rolled his eyes. "You don't have to work all day. Besides, there are people who can do that for you. Come on. It's about time I beat you."

Ashni sucked her teeth. "Since when do you beat me?" They had been playing chess, or games like it, since she was three and he was five. He had yet to beat her as far as she could recall. In fact, he had yet to beat her in anything if memory served her correctly.

He chuckled and darkness danced in his golden eyes. "You afraid to lose in front of your little barbarian princess?"

Her head shot up and she glared at him. *What the hell is he playing at?* Before she could say anything, Nakia stepped forward. Ashni's eyes cut to Nakia.

Nakia glowered at him with her eyes ablaze. "I'm not a barbarian. Don't confuse me with you."

Amal mirrored the burning look. "Who do you think you're talking to?"

Ashni groaned, knowing what this could and probably would, quickly descend into and that way led to madness. *I don't have the patience for this.* "Get me Adira."

Servants scrambled to do her bidding. If Adira didn't have to interact with Amal, she would be fine and she knew Ashni wouldn't summon her with him around. Now she had to keep her brother busy until Adira arrived.

"Let me finish this and we'll have an afternoon of chess," Ashni told him. *And I'll die of boredom or annoyance. Well, if the gods are merciful, I'll die.*

"Good." He grabbed another bit of fruit, a fig this time. "Have them set up a better spread." He walked off and she had to fight the temptation of throwing a bowl at his head. Their mother would never let her hear the end of it if she took this idiot's head off. *Would a bowl really take his head off? How hard must that head be?*

Ashni glanced back at Nakia and raised her cup. "Pour some for yourself, as well." It would be a long afternoon. Maybe she should just let Nakia drink the jug. It would be a kindness for sure.

Nakia must have already had enough of Amal, as she did pour herself a glass. They drank together. Nakia made a face at the first taste, probably finding it too sweet, but she finished her cup.

Adira took her time appearing at the palace. By the time she arrived, Ashni already had her office set up. She made sure Adira had everything she would need, so she wouldn't have to leave and chance bumping into Amal. With that out of the way, Ashni decided confining her brother to a small area would be best for everyone. She had the servants set up one of the smaller rooms for them.

"Come on, Nakia. Let's go suffer through a fate worse than death,"

Ashni said.

"Do you really need me?"

"You've met my brother. You should know the best way to deal with him is drunk, so yeah, I will need you."

Nakia didn't argue. She clearly understood he was a pain in the ass. He was more than that, but Ashni put it out of her mind since she couldn't do anything about it. She would entertain him and then be rid of him after the Festival of the Moon. She wouldn't have to hear from her mother about how poorly she treated her family. *Never mind the fact that Amal treats everyone poorly.*

Retreating to the lounge the servants had prepared, Ashni eased onto her side on a pillow. The seat matched her pieces on the chessboard, a polished teal, gleaming like the sky. There were trays of cakes, fruit, pastries, and bread by her pillow. There were other trays for her brother by his seat. He came in as she settled in her spot.

Amal sat across from her and looked at his trays, curling his lip at the food. Ashni managed to fight down the urge to bludgeon him with a goblet. How dare he sneer at her offerings? Instead of causing him severe head trauma, she reached for her cup and silently requested wine. Nakia wasted no time pouring.

"Are you going to go, or what?" Ashni asked, eyes on the board.

He huffed and then scowled. "Don't rush me."

She couldn't help rolling her eyes. "It's only the opening move."

"It'll set the tone."

"And you'll still lose, like you do at everything."

He scowled again, but quickly moved a piece. She managed not to roll her eyes for what she was certain was the millionth time since he arrived and countered his move just as quickly. He moved again and she countered. She could already see where the game was going and she doubted he was aware. She downed her wine and picked up a piece of cake. If he was going to repeat moves from a previous game, then she might as well gorge herself on sweets to make this afternoon worthwhile. She savored the delicious square cake while Amal definitely played a repeat game.

"Are you sure you want to move that?" she asked halfway through the game she would definitely win. After all, she had won it years ago.

Amal scowled. "Don't tell me how to play."

Sighing, she shrugged. "Fine. You're going to lose in five moves." When they played this game years ago, it would have been nine moves, but she could see her own mistakes better now. She learned from her mistakes, unlike Amal.

He gnashed his teeth to the point that Nakia flinched. Ashni glowered at him. His attention was on the board and he mucked up so bad she won in two moves. *Idiot.*

He hissed. "Again," he demanded.

"Set it up."

Instead of setting the game up, he folded his arms across his chest. Tapping her finger, Ashni considered throwing her cup at him. *It wouldn't kill him, right?* She wasn't too sure. It had been a long time since she saw him fight and didn't know the amount of punishment he could take. So, instead, she held her cup up for Nakia to pour more wine and nodded for a servant waiting in the corner to set up the board again. Amal watched as if he thought the servant could somehow cheat for Ashni.

With the board set up, Ashni waited for her brother to make the first move. Once he did, the game was on. He was easy to read and she moved less than five seconds after each of his moves. It took very little time for him to begin scowling at the board and look like a petulant child. He grunted low in his throat when it was clear he couldn't win this game either.

Ashni glanced over to check on Nakia. She was watching the game, forehead wrinkled in concentration. Ashni doubted Nakia knew how to play chess, but she obviously knew enough about the game to follow along. Amal leaned forward to move and drew her attention back to the game.

"I wouldn't move that one if I were you," Ashni said as he put his hand on a piece.

"You're just trying to psych me out. I'll have this game in three moves with this." He pushed forward.

Ashni rolled her eyes. "Yeah, but I just won." She slid a piece into place. "Checkmate."

"Bitch," he hissed under his breath.

Nakia gasped, but Ashni didn't even blink as she ate another piece of cake. He had called her worse during a simple game and even worse when he thought no one of import was around. Amal wasted no time setting the board up this time and moving a piece before Ashni could say anything. *Oh, so now he's serious. A serious brat.*

***

Nakia tried to follow the game, but she didn't see the point of it after a while. She was a little surprised the Queen played chess and it had nothing to do with her being a barbarian. In her homeland, chess was a 'thinking man's game,' emphasis on the *man* part. She knew her father played with nobles and generals, all men. She was never allowed to learn. No woman in Phyllida knew how to play as far as she knew.

Nakia used to sneak in and watch, but she never got a chance to see the game up close. From her stolen glances, she knew the winner was seen as superior in some way, like the smartest man in the room, or, at the least, cleverer than his opponent and thus better than him. Often, this 'superior' man was her father. It was amazing to see the Queen handle her brother with such ease.

"This is dull," the Queen said after winning five games in a row. Nakia was inclined to agree.

Amal snapped, slapping the pieces from the table. Nakia flinched a little. The Queen didn't even blink. She never seemed surprised by his actions, no matter how over the top. Before Nakia could contemplate why, he yanked his cup off the tray and held it up. She glanced around for the servant who would pour for him

"Wine!" He glared at her, as if she was his slave. "Are you deaf?" he snarled and his eyes turned completely black.

Nakia blinked and reeled back. She looked to the Queen. The Queen scoffed under her breath, but that was answer enough for Nakia. "What? I'm not your servant."

Amal growled, like an animal, and appeared ready to launch himself at her. Nakia fell back, expecting to be tackled to the ground. But the Queen jumped between them, staring her brother down.

"She is not your slave," the Queen said.

"She's *a* slave," he replied through gritted teeth.

"No, she's not and she doesn't serve you. Now, sit back and someone else will pour for you."

For a long moment, Amal looked at the Queen, a vein throbbing in his neck. Nakia wouldn't be surprised if he tried to pull a weapon on the Queen, but apparently he wasn't so stupid. He sat back and raised his cup for someone else to pour wine. Another servant came and put the game pieces back on the board. Once those tasks were done, the servants left the room. Nakia wished she could follow them.

"You can go first," Amal said.

"Nope," the Queen replied. She made eye contact with new servants as they entered the room. The servants bowed and settled into the positions the other slaves had vacated. It felt like a dance Nakia had just been invited to, but had gone on for a long time.

"You won't win again," the Queen's brother said, glaring at her as if she were the vilest creature to live.

The Queen sneered. "Of course not, because I won't play again." She chose another piece of cake and bit into it.

"We're playing again." It sounded like an order, which Nakia doubted the Queen would take kindly to.

The Queen smirked. "Are we? I don't think so. I think I'll only play you again if you beat…" A dark chuckle escaped the Queen and then she pointed over her left shoulder. "If you beat *her*."

Nakia gasped. "Me?" Was that a squeak in her voice?

"Her?" Amal drew back and grimaced.

"Yeah, her. If you beat her, I'll play you again and she'll pour for you. But, if you lose, you have to pour for her."

Nakia made a noise deep in her throat, sounding like she choked on air. The Queen had the nerve to look at her and smile. It wasn't malicious or mocking, just a regular look. Nakia shook her head and Amal brightened like a demon took hold of his body.

"Deal," he said.

Nakia shook her head even more. "No, I don't know how to play." The last thing she wanted to do was embarrass herself in front of this ass. Well, the Queen was an ass as well, but her brother more so.

"Come." The Queen waved her over.

"I can't play." *The Queen has just sold me down the river to this bastard, who seems to only know how to throw tantrums and objects.*

"Kitten, come." The Queen's voice was strangely patient and she patted the pillow.

"But…but…but…" Nakia wasn't sure how to say it plainer. She didn't know how to play. She didn't know the pieces of the Roshan Empire. She didn't know how they moved beyond what she learned from watching them and spying on her father.

"Come." The Queen's voice was surprisingly gentle.

Nakia found herself sitting on the Queen's pillow. The Queen moved back, so that Nakia was in front of her and in front of the board. While the Queen ate her fourth piece of cake, Amal quickly moved a piece. He then watched Nakia in a way she was certain wolves watched sheep. She examined the board, not sure what to move where.

"Move!" Amal barked and Nakia jumped, slamming into the Queen.

The Queen didn't even grunt from the impact. She placed a hand on Nakia's back, as if to calm her down, but it didn't help much. With her heart racing, Nakia picked up a piece, but then changed her mind. She set the piece back down and Amal laughed. She put her hand on another piece.

"Sorry, but once you put a piece down, that's your move. You can't change your mind once you take your hand off of it," he said.

Nakia whimpered. *How was she supposed to know that? They never spoke that rule.* But, then again, now that she thought about it, they hadn't put their hands on a piece until they seemed totally sure it was the one they wanted to move. *What is even the point of this stupid game? He just wants to pretend he's superior to me by beating me at something I don't know and I shouldn't know.*

Amal cackled as he moved. Her heart raced as she tried to figure out what to do. She didn't understand how these pieces moved or why she should move them. *Capture the king*, she recalled. *How?* Rubbing her forehead, she felt like she was going to hyperventilate. And then she felt a gentle hand on her elbow. The Queen's fingers slid up her arm to her hand. The Queen guided her to a piece and wrapped her fingers around it.

"Move that one," the Queen whispered into her ear. The sound wrapped around her, settled her enough to touch the piece with confidence.

"Hey!" Amal barked and glowered at them.

"What?" the Queen asked.

With a snarl, he pointed a crooked finger at them. "You're cheating."

"No, I'm merely tutoring. Is that a problem? You think you can't beat a first-time player with a little help from me? Well, that's rather feeble, isn't it?"

Amal ground his teeth together, the sound tearing through the air. Then, he grunted, as if giving them permission.

Nakia held in a giggle as she followed the Queen's advice. From that point on, this game wasn't so scary. When the Queen leaned against her to point at a piece, she could feel her breathing, which was soothing. She wasn't alone in this fight. Every other move, the Queen would whisper in her ear what piece to play and where to put it. Her breath tickled Nakia's ear, but in a good way. When she wasn't tutoring her, the Queen ate treats and explained the game to her. In the end, they won.

"Team work always leads to victory," the Queen stated.

"AH!" Amal kicked the table over. The board would have hit Nakia if the Queen hadn't leaned back just a little bit, pulling her along. Amal leaped to his feet and condemned them with his eyes. "This is bullshit! You cheated."

"She won. Pour for her," the Queen said.

"I won't pour anything for some barbarian bitch."

Nakia was about to scream him down, but the Queen beat her to it. "Hey! You may be my guest, but she is under my protection and I won't let you disrespect her. If you can't honor your word, then never give it."

Amal was unmoved by the words and stormed out of the room. He flipped the trays of food on his way out. The Queen sighed.

"He's good for grand entrances and exits. Hopefully, he'll storm all the way back to his stupid bit of kingdom and not ruin the festival for all of us."

Nakia wasn't sure what festival the Queen spoke of, but she wouldn't be upset should Amal decide to leave. He messed up the whole balance of the palace and he had only been there a day. She would hate to see the damage he could do over weeks.

Chapter Eight

HER BROTHER WAS ARROGANT, obnoxious, and a pest, among plenty of other negative things, but Ashni would give him one thing. Amal was persistent and consistent. He was persistent in wanting to play chess and he was consistent in losing, every single time. It was like clockwork.

Ashni gave up on placating him a few days into his very extended visit. She let Nakia handle him. The princess should learn to play chess anyway, even if she didn't think it was necessary. Chess was a good way to keep the mind sharp and everyone needed that.

Plus, it irked her brother to no end, playing against this 'little, barbarian princess,' especially since he still couldn't win. Yes, she gave Nakia tips, but with each game, she spoke a little less. Almost two weeks in and, for the most part, she just enjoyed her cake and other treats.

She was indulging her sweet tooth, nibbling a pastry, when Nakia turned to her. Ashni checked to see where Nakia's hand was. Studying the board briefly, she shook her head. Nakia shifted her hand to another piece and Ashni squinted. *No. It wasn't a bad move, but her brother would see through it too soon and he'd dominate the board after.* Ashni took Nakia's hand and jumped.

"Why are your hands so cold?" Ashni asked.

Nakia turned to glower at her. Jade eyes declared Ashni an idiot for even asking. "It's cold."

Ashni glanced at a few servants for confirmation. They shrugged. There had been a cold snap, which happened every now and then, but Nakia shouldn't be so cold. *Am I losing my mind? No, Nakia's skin is definitely cold.*

Then, it hit Ashni. "Look at what you're wearing. Of course, you're going to be cold wearing this."

Nakia's brow furrowed. She was dressed as always, in her native garb. Ashni didn't care, except now it was cold. Typically, it was chilly at night and she had no idea what Nakia did after Ashni dismissed her after dinner. But, now, the cold weather was during the day and it was obviously more than Nakia's usual clothing could handle.

"I'm usually hot," Nakia admitted what Ashni always suspected.

"I'm sure you are, but now you're exposed. Your long tunic isn't good when the temperature is normal, but it's also not good for when our temperature decides to plummet. Your clothing seems to be good for spring and autumn, but we don't have those here. You have these holes in the sleeves, which are too short."

Nakia frowned. "Those are designs."

"But they're not practical in this cold and you're only wearing this one layer."

Nakia stuck her chin in the air. "So?"

"So, when the temperature gets like this, you should have several layers covering you, keeping the cold at bay. Do you have any clothing you could layer? Any clothing without holes, even if they are there by design?"

"Hey, are we playing?" Amal huffed, calling attention back to himself. He slapped the pillow underneath him and eyed them as if they wronged him in some way.

Ashni rolled her eyes and acted without thinking. She opened her outer robe and wrapped Nakia in it. Nakia gasped, but didn't say anything. Ashni leaned in close to tell Nakia what piece to move, but noticed something for the first time. Nakia smelled sweet, like honey and apples. *So good.* Ashni just wanted to breathe her in and nothing more. Discreetly, she inhaled just enough for the scent to wash over her.

"This one?" Nakia asked.

"Hmmm?" Ashni's mind had drifted far away. What was Nakia talking about?

Nakia turned a little to look at her. "This piece?"

Oh, right, the game. Shaking her head, Ashni managed to dispel the brief enchantment, and turned her attention back to the board. Nakia picked the right piece and she directed Nakia where to move it. From that moment on, Ashni had to resist the urge to bury her face in Nakia's hair and neck to breathe this perfect aroma. She grabbed more pastries, hoping eating would distract her, but no such luck.

Has she always smelled this good? How could I not notice? Ashni was pretty sure she had never noticed because she was too busy having fun tormenting Nakia and corrupting her. Now, all she had in front of her was Nakia and this wonderful scent. It danced through her mind, jolting across nerves, making her body buzz in ways her lightning could hardly dream of. She could barely control her hands. She wanted to wrap them around Nakia's petite waist, caress her undoubtedly soft belly, and breathe in all that she was for the rest of the night.

Okay, stop thinking like that. Since her favorite pastries and cakes weren't enough to keep her mind off Nakia, Ashni paid attention to the game. She played the game in her mind. Amal was doomed, as always. She wondered how many games it would take before he threw the board across the room and cursed her and Nakia.

***

Nakia tried to focus on the chess game, but it was a little difficult. She could feel the Queen against her back. Being wrapped in the Queen's robes felt like being wrapped in the Queen herself and it was heady, intoxicating even. It was more than the feel of the Queen or even the smell of the Queen, which she was now very aware of. The Queen smelled of honey, fresh berries, a hint of smoke, and something Nakia couldn't put her finger on. It was the aroma of dangerous burning and the sky before a heavy rain.

The Queen engulfed her, like warm clouds. Nakia's heart raced a little and her chest was tight. Every few seconds, she forgot how to breathe or just held her breath, scared it might disturb the Queen and have the Queen release her. She didn't know what to make of the feeling and it was hard to focus on the game, but she managed.

Chess was still a strange game to her, despite having played nothing but chess for the past week, but she was getting the hang of it. The Queen didn't have a problem teaching her like her father did. She didn't understand why her father thought she couldn't handle it, didn't think girls could handle it. It wasn't so difficult. She doubted she would be able to beat the Queen, but she doubted even her father could beat the Queen and he tended to beat everyone.

"Hey, stop daydreaming and move," Amal said. Everything that came out of his mouth sounded like a command, even when he spoke to the Queen. His eyes made it worse, as he always looked like he believed everyone and everything was beneath him, especially when he addressed the Queen.

Nakia suspected he was the older of the siblings, but she never asked. His manner suggested it and she suspected the Queen would never take his attitude from a younger sibling. As annoying as Layla was, it wasn't to the same degree as Amal, and Layla always seemed to hold affection for the Queen, even when purposely getting on her nerves. There was none of that playful joy with Amal.

"Move," Amal said again, his tone scratchy and even more forceful than before.

Nakia shook herself out of her reverie. She studied the pieces, trying to figure out what to move. She needed not only to contemplate her move, but his counter and how she would counter that. One of the Queen's first lessons was for her to try to see three moves ahead, and once she mastered that, try to see five moves ahead and so forth and so on. Sometimes she could see it and sometimes she couldn't. Right now, she felt like she had seen it all, so she made her move.

Without thinking, she leaned back and found herself pressed against the Queen's chest. She stopped breathing, waiting for the Queen's reaction, but nothing came. Well, not nothing. For a moment, the Queen leaned in closer, almost buried in her neck. Nakia still didn't breathe, not sure what might happen. But, nothing happened. The Queen moved back a little and ate some cake, as she was wont to do. Amal finally moved a piece.

Nakia moved. "Check."

A growl got stuck in Amal's throat as he leaned in closer to study the board. While he burned his brain and probably failed to realize he was trapped, Nakia reached over and ate some grapes from the Queen's tray. The Queen didn't say anything, so Nakia helped herself to some more fruit.

"You're helping her." Amal glared at the Queen.

"Uh, yeah, three moves ago. Keep up. Since then, I've just been sitting here, enjoying my cake."

A savage snarl tore its way from Amal's mouth as he picked up the board and flung it across the room. He turned to Nakia, his eyes wild. All too often he couldn't contain himself, or his fury. He raised his hand and Nakia instinctively retreated, only to be halted by the Queen's body. She felt herself pressed against strong muscles and a strong hand fell to her hip. Her body calmed to a degree, but her heart was in her throat.

"Brother, you're obviously overtired," the Queen said in a smooth tone. He halted mid-strike and the Queen bit into her cake. "Perhaps you should retire to your rooms to ensure you're fresh for the Festival tomorrow. It wouldn't do to be fatigued before the night even begins, right?" She sounded cool, collected.

Amal's chest heaved as he focused on Nakia, but he didn't move. His hand was still posed to strike. He glanced at the Queen and Nakia watched the Queen from the corner of her eye. The Queen continued to nibble her cake, and then she glanced up at Amal again. Nakia's eyes didn't leave the Queen.

"Unless, of course, dear brother, you have other plans," the Queen said. Her eyes were steel now and there was slight tension around her mouth.

Amal took another deep breath, studying on the Queen. Nakia could feel there was a challenge here. It seemed insane for the Queen to challenge her brother, her *older* brother. He was a man and bigger than she was, but then Nakia remembered the poor, unfortunate captain who faced the Queen in the arena. He was larger than Amal and the Queen hadn't broken a sweat against him.

Amal's hand dropped and he let out a strained breath. "You're right, Ashni. I am overtired. Too much excitement." He gave a weak chuckle as a bead of sweat slid down his cheek. "I should retire. I wouldn't want to be exhausted for tomorrow night. After all, I always look forward to seeing what new things you and your people do for the Festival."

The Queen sucked her teeth and watched Amal as he exited the room. Once he was gone, the Queen sniffed, curling her top lip. Nakia breathed a sigh of relief and relaxed against the Queen's body. The Queen continued to lightly stroke her hip.

"Don't worry, kitten. My brother is both a fool and a coward. He won't try to hurt you while I'm around."

That was promising. Of course, something could happen when the Queen wasn't around. It was interesting that Amal was so frightened of the Queen, and she clearly didn't respect him. But, Nakia didn't say anything about it. She stayed where she was, not sure if she could stand on her own. The Queen didn't seem to mind, didn't say anything about their closeness.

"Have you picked out clothing for the Festival?" the Queen asked out of the blue.

Nakia frowned a little and turned to fully look at the Queen, pleased her hand didn't fall away. "Do I have to wear special clothing?" No one had briefed her about the Festival. She wasn't sure what to expect.

"I'll have you outfitted. You still owe me from when you lost at dice anyway." The Queen grinned at her and her golden eyes shone, sparkling like the noon sun. Despite the gleeful look in her eyes, her expression still held a hint of teasing and a bit of wickedness.

Nakia stiffened a bit and narrowed her gaze at the Queen. "What do you have planned?"

"It's a surprise," the Queen said in a singsong manner.

Nakia felt like she should be worried, but it was a little hard with the Queen so close. There was something about her aura, like she was wrapped all the way around Nakia and nothing could harm her. Well, nothing except the Queen anyway, who probably had very devilish thoughts dancing in her mind about how she could at the very least humiliate Nakia. *Why did I agree to that bet?*

***

Servants rushed into Nakia's rooms later that night. She met them in the first room, a sitting room, and watched as they filed in with piles of clothing. They held fabrics on top of fabrics. Nakia knew this was about the Queen dressing her. She was a little disappointed when the Queen didn't come along with the fitting party.

"My Lady, I am Daru and I am one of the royal dressers. The Queen has requested I make you presentable for the Festival," a woman said as she stood in front of all of the servants. She was dressed well with her hair done up high, in a way that Nakia hadn't seen on many people around the palace.

"Only the Festival?" Nakia studied the dozen people, holding so much clothing. It seemed like the Queen wanted her dressed for the year rather than just the night.

"Well, the Festival and perhaps if you find yourself comfortable, or if this frost remains in the air for long, you will have other clothing. I was told your native clothing isn't suited to our land."

Nakia frowned, but refused to confirm or deny that. Most of the time, her clothes left her much too warm and her poor skin felt dry often. She'd never been in a desert before, but she learned they were sizzling in general and seasons, as she knew them, didn't exist. Even at night, when it cooled down, it was hotter than she was used to. Still, she refused to surrender her clothing. She refused to surrender any more of herself than necessary to these people.

"It doesn't really matter, my Lady. The Festival is a holy day and you should be properly dressed for it," Daru stated.

"Why? I don't believe in your gods."

"No, but the day is more than just about the gods. The Festival of the Moon is about celebrating women and creativity and life itself. It's about taking pride in who you are and showing the gods how you shine."

Nakia arched an eyebrow. This was something else she didn't understand. How could a holy day not be about the gods?

"The day is also to celebrate the Queen's mother, Empress Chandra. She is connected to the Moon goddess."

"Empress?" Nakia muttered. So, there was an empress somewhere and she was considered divine. This also explained why the Queen claimed to be a divinity.

"Yes, the Empress. The Queen's mother. The Queen delights in this celebration, even if she pretends not to and even if her brother comes to spoil it for her. It would do you well to celebrate and find some solace in the comfort of a day meant to embrace all that you are."

Nakia's brow furrowed. "All that I am?" What did that mean? She was not sure who she was, beyond a princess of Phyllida. She was her father's daughter, but all that meant was that she was a subject to her king, like every other person in Phyllida. *Is that all I am?* She didn't get a chance to think on it as Daru pressed onward.

"Now, it is customary to wear white during the Festival, but you can also add colors for flair and a mark on individualism. What would you prefer?" Daru asked, eyes sparkling.

Nakia sighed and rubbed her head. This seemed like a big deal and she didn't want to ruin it. Now, she really wished the Queen had come along.

"Well, does it have to be pants?" Nakia asked. The pants drove her insane. Only barbarians wore pants. *Well, they are barbarians.* She had to remind herself of that fact.

Smiling softly, Daru tittered a little. "No, I will do away with all of the pants." She waved her hands and a few servants stepped to the back. "I think you and I shall be able to agree on things, my Lady."

Nakia smiled a little. It was nice to be addressed by a title again. Maybe she and Daru would get along. While coming up with an outfit, she might be able to learn more about the holiday. "So, everyone doesn't wear pants in the Roshan Empire?"

"Oh, no. The pants are favored by soldiers and you'll find that many people like to do things that mimic the soldiers, so many of them also wear pants. I'm sure the Queen doesn't expect that of you. I will dress you with fine gowns, but also warm cloaks. The Festival is at night, during a full moon, so there will definitely be a chill, especially with this cold gnawing at our bones."

"I have a cloak," Nakia said. She had packed some winter clothing, which seemed useless until now. Of course, this cold was worse than the winter. *How can the desert be so hot one moment and then freezing the next?*

"I will see it. It may match whatever we come up with and aid you in being yourself for the Festival. Then, we'll find you the perfect belts and jewels. We'll put makeup on your eyes and give you even more allure, allowing you to outdo the brilliance of the full moon. You will turn all heads. The Queen will find herself unable to look away." Daru put her chin in the air and beamed, her expression so bright it lit up the room.

Nakia had to laugh at Daru's confidence. She decided to let Daru dress her if for no other reason than the Festival was at night and if this cold continued, she knew she'd be cold. The nights here reminded her of winter at home.

"Makeup, you say?" Nakia asked. This was foreign to her, just as much as pants. No one wore makeup in her homeland and she thought this was normal in the Roshan Empire as well. After all, she hadn't seen the Queen or her sister wearing any makeup.

"Yes, just around the eyes. To show you're a single, but proper lady."

Nakia was sold at 'lady.' Daru would get her way a lot that night just from the use of the title. Nakia didn't realize she missed it as much as she did, but it was nice to feel respected again. *Do I feel disrespected here?* Fearing the answer, she didn't explore the idea, focusing instead on Daru.

"Is there anything I should know about this Festival? Beyond why you celebrate?" Nakia asked as Daru presented her with white outfits, wanting to start with the most important attire first.

Daru shook her head. "Nothing I can think of. It is a time of fun and to explore. There will be food from all over the Empire, as well as games. Nothing violent, as that's not allowed during this Festival. You may even witness the Queen participate in childish games."

Nakia couldn't imagine the Queen playing something a child would. Behaving like a child, yes, but playing like one, no. "I find it hard to believe the Queen was ever a child, but then again, she hasn't seemed to grow up much."

Daru smiled a little. "The Queen can be childish, yes. She likes to enjoy herself when she has the time. You should do the same. If anything catches your eye during the Festival, be sure to try it, experience it. Don't overthink anything. Just go with it. That's what the night is about."

Nakia nodded, but her forehead wrinkled slightly. Ladies didn't 'just go with it.' She supposed she'd wait for the Festival and witness it for herself before she decided on how much of Daru's advice she would follow.

***

The Festival of the Moon was by far Ashni's favorite holiday after the Day of the Golden Sun. They were two very different days in terms of what each held, beyond the usual food, games, and shows. The Day of the Golden Sun was about celebrating warriors, battle, and fighting prowess. But, the Festival of the Moon was all about inventions and arts. The Festival of the Moon showcased anything new and for this Festival, Ashni had her own little project to display.

"You're almost on time, Highness. And, look at this. You found a woman already?" Adira asked as she approached Ashni in the courtyard at the palace. Saniyah was on Adira's arm, and both were decked out in all white. They stood out against the dark blue of the night and the ethereal green glow of the lamps.

Ashni ignored Adira mocking her with the title and chuckled, throwing her own white drape over her shoulder. The 'woman' by her side was Nakia, adorned in Roshan garb perfect for the festival, complete with hair, jewels, and makeup. Nakia's white dress had a golden blouse and heavy teal robe over it to protect her from the cold that nipped the air. Her hair was done in long, thin braids with pearls threaded through the locks and tiny golden feathers hanging from a few strands. When Adira realized who the woman was, her eyes widened and her mouth dropped open.

"No," Adira whispered.

"She lost a bet." Ashni tittered while Nakia shifted on her heels beside her.

"She looks lovely," Saniyah said before going in for cheek kisses. Nakia froze when lightly painted lips touched her skin. Ashni was surprised Nakia didn't faint or fall over, but it was probably over too fast for her brain to totally comprehend what happened.

Ashni accepted Saniyah's cheek kisses and crowed, "I know a thing or two about dressing pretty girls, right?"

Adira snorted. "I think we all know Daru dressed this pretty girl. You don't know anything about fashion."

"I dressed myself." Ashni motioned down to her own white outfit and colorful outer robe.

"I rest my case," Adira said.

Ashni blew out a breath and decided to let it go. It was the Festival of the Moon, no time for arguing over silly things. "Anyway, I'm not sure you've been formally introduced. Saniyah, meet Princess Hellcat, aka Princess Nakia Lysand of Phyllida. She'll be our guest until her father comes up with mountains of gold. Kitten, this is Saniyah Gyan, chief military engineer and Adira's spouse."

Nakia's face scrunched up and Ashni chuckled. She wondered what was more baffling to Nakia, the fact that Saniyah was an engineer, worked for the military, or was married to Adira. While she was stupefied, Ashni had fun presenting her like a doll.

"The pearls in her hair are a nice touch," Saniyah said.

"Until Princess sees it anyway," Adira added.

Ashni scoffed. "The pearls complement her complexion." The pearls were meant for royal women and Layla usually was the only one to wear them during the Festival. Ashni hadn't been able to resist decorating Nakia's hair with them.

Adira arched an eyebrow and snickered. "You're just going to say everything that makes the Princess want to rip your throat out?"

Ashni shrugged. "Where is she anyway? She's usually so punctual."

Adira sniffed. "Oh, please." She jabbed her thumb off to the right and a few yards away was Layla, engaging with someone in her typical manner. "She's already over there, explaining someone else's invention for them. In fact, you might want to put a leash on her before she upsets the wrong person."

"Was she doing that or was Saniyah doing that and she's just holding Saniyah's place in the argument?" Ashni asked. She knew how these things went.

The almost mocking, girly giggle from Saniyah, complete with a hand over her mouth, told Ashni the answer to that question. She put her arm around Nakia's waist and led the princess off to retrieve the other princess. Layla stood in front of a device, telling people how it worked while the proprietor stood off to the side, glaring at her.

"Come along, Princess. You don't need to save Saniyah's place anymore," Ashni said, collecting Layla without stopping. Naren moved along with her, sighing. He had probably been bored to tears, having no head for science.

"You should find out who he is. The device is actually quite good and would help with underwater work," Saniyah said.

Ashni made a note to do that, but she didn't want to think about that right now. "I need food. Where is a moon cake stand?" Moon cake was the only way to start the Festival for her.

"Should you be eating more cake? It's all you eat when you play chess and that's all you've done since the all-powerful annoying Amal showed up. You're going to get sick," Layla said.

"Thanks, *Mom*. I'll eat what I want and it's the Festival of the Moon. You're damned right I want moon cakes. I'll eat moon cakes until I have frosting oozing out my ears if I want," Ashni said. This had been true since she was a child.

"What's a moon cake?" Nakia asked in a low voice. She seemed a little shy. It was possible she had never been around so many people before. They were in the palace's main courtyard, but it fit hundreds of people. It was open to Ashni's army as well as nobles and visitors who were friends of the Crown, Ashni, and the Empress.

Ashni gasped. "What's a moon cake? You haven't lived until you had one." Ashni guided her through the throngs of people. Nakia needed a moon cake right now or her life wouldn't be worth living as far as Ashni was concerned.

"I saw Nox's stand by the gate," Layla said.

Clapping her hands, Ashni felt light inside. "Yeah, there's a reason I keep you around, Princess."

"To keep watch for moon cakes? I think we need to discuss your priorities and misuse of my talents," Layla said.

"After cake."

Nox supplied the palace with the best cakes. Ashni needed those sweets right now. On the way to his stand, she saluted and greeted soldiers and their families. It was good for them to enjoy themselves while they had the chance. None of them stopped her for too long, knowing she was on a mission. But, there had to be the one asshole. *Damn this rotter.*

"Your highness." A familiar captain stood before her.

"Uh…" His name was on the tip of her tongue, but Ashni couldn't recall what it was. He obviously hadn't left an impression, not to mention he stood in her way of moon cakes.

"Majeed," Layla hissed into her ear. Yes, there was definitely a reason she kept Layla around.

"Right." Ashni nodded. "Captain Majeed of the Sand. How goes it? I hope you're enjoying the Festival so far." It just got underway, so it'd be hard not to enjoy the Festival, but for some reason, he'd rather stand in her way.

He beamed. "Of course." His eyes swept the courtyard before settling back on her. "I was hoping I could get a chance to discuss a matter with you."

She groaned. "This is a time of fun and for peace. There's no work tonight, my friend." *No one talks work during the Festival of the Moon unless they have a stand for it.*

"But—"

Ashni clapped him on the shoulder. "Go enjoy the night." She gestured at the revelry surrounding them and sidestepped him. She hurried away, making sure Nakia was by her side.

Layla snickered. "You always do that to him."

Ashni wrinkled her nose. "I need cake and he's in my way."

"Do you think you might have a problem? I mean, who *needs* cake?"

"I need cake and he's in my way."

"There's always something you put before him. You never listen to him."

"What's there to listen about? He's stationed down in the valley. There isn't a more peaceful region in the whole empire. Not realm, but whole empire. If he has an issue, he's doing something wrong."

Layla snickered and Adira nodded, so Ashni felt validated. Majeed wanted her attention way too often, which explained why she could barely remember his name. There was nothing worse than someone who needed attention for every little thing. She put him out of her mind.

"All right. Prepare yourself for the best cake you'll ever have," Ashni told Nakia as they stood before the stand. They were hardly there for a second before a cake was placed in Ashni's waiting hand. "I need more." She motioned to her party, drawing a circle around them with her index finger.

"No, no, no. None for this one." Saniyah patted Adira in the stomach, causing jewelry on Adira's belt to sing out.

Ashni narrowed her gaze on Adira. "How many did you eat without me?" *I wasn't even that late.*

Adira twisted her mouth up. "Don't worry about me. Enjoy the damn festival."

Ashni cackled. "Oh, someone's in trouble and that's why she's not getting treats."

Adira frowned and turned her nose up at Ashni. "Shut up. Get your stupid cake. I want to try some berry wine before the night's over."

That sounded promising. Ashni gave a slice of cake to Nakia, who inspected it like it might eat her. For a moment, an inappropriate thought eased its way through Ashni's mind. She was able to shake it off before it took root, but then, Nakia licked gooey icing from her thumb and Ashni forgot how to breathe.

"I hope you're drooling from the cake," Adira whispered with a playful spark in her eye.

"Don't think I won't kill you on this day of peace," Ashni said before taking a huge bite out of her cake. She held in a moan as sweet flavor burst on her tongue. She glanced at Nakia and then quickly looked away.

Adira chuckled. "Day of peace. You can't kill. That's the whole point to a day of peace."

Ashni sneered at her and focused on enjoying her cake. Wine was nearby, so they all indulged, trying a few different selections. Saniyah, Naren, and Nakia seemed content with the samples at the stand. Ashni, Adira, and Layla took water skins of their favorites. They scanned the area for something to do.

"Hey." Adira jabbed Ashni with her elbow.

"Hey, don't hit me with that. I have ideas as to where it's been," Ashni said.

Adira's face fell into a deadpan. "Really? You have an idea where my elbow had been? Are you drunk already?"

Ashni shook her head. "It's called a joke. Thank you for killing it on this day of peace." She turned to see what Adira wanted.

Majeed was talking with Amal. It wasn't much of a surprise. Majeed never screamed loyal to her. Sighing, Ashni shrugged. Layla turned to her, dark eyes waiting for instructions. Ashni shook her head.

"Day of peace, sister," Ashni reminded Layla.

"I know, but we all know that's not going to lead anywhere good." Layla pointed to Majeed and Amal.

"Adira," Ashni said.

"Yeah, yeah, yeah. I'll put people on it. Can we go see that game with that thing?" Adira replied.

"I hate that I know what you're talking about," Ashni said with a sigh.

"I've always suspected triplets." Saniyah motioned to Ashni, Layla, and Adira.

Adira laughed and Ashni shook her fist at her before continuing to experience as much of the festival as they could. Ashni made sure to keep Nakia by her side.

Chapter Nine

NAKIA WASN'T SURE WHAT to make of the Festival of the Moon. It was as flashy as the Queen had promised her it would be. There was so much to do and so many people. She'd seen crowds this size from a distance, but had never been elbow to elbow with the masses like this. The moon cake the Queen had given her was deliciously sweet and fluffy. She wouldn't mind trying other foods and the Queen would probably show her the best.

The Queen and her friends preferred to drink and watch displays. There were so many different little things. There were several mazes with mice running through them. There was a rabbit race. There were delicate models of cities, towns, and other places Nakia had never seen in her life. There were magicians, but none of her party were interested in seeing magic.

"We should see a show," the Queen said, eyes scanning the area.

There was no shortage of small shows held in tents instead of in theaters. It took them a few minutes to decide which one to see. Nakia tried to follow the conversation, but the words were too excited and there was so much arms and hands motion. The Roshan talked with their whole bodies when they were worked up.

"Have you been to any shows?" the General's woman asked.

Nakia yelped and shrugged, not expecting the question. She looked at the ground, wanting to avoid eye contact with the General's woman...spouse, the Queen had said. The General and the woman were married. *How?*

Nakia didn't get a chance to dwell on it as Ashni led her into the tent to watch the show. They settled into open seats rather than pushing their way to the front. Nakia looked around, wanting to make sure a stranger didn't touch her.

The show was interesting. It consisted of moving dolls with the background shifting and changing as the scenes changed. Nakia would have been curious about how it worked if it weren't for the people she was with.

"No, the background shifted too quickly," Layla said loudly.

"You didn't articulate the dolls right. Didn't you notice this jerky movement before you showed up to do this?" the Queen asked, her voice even more booming than Layla's.

"The gears are all wrong." the General's woman made a circular gesture with her index finger. "This is just shoddy craftsmanship." She frowned, as if insulted by the work.

"Come now, love, you can't expect everyone to take the same care in their work as you do. After all, people don't die if they make their dolls incorrectly," the General said, caressing her woman's side.

"Any job worth doing is worth doing right, especially if you want people to take notice," the Queen said.

"Exactly. A child could do better than this." The General's woman flung her hand out at the stage.

The heckling went on for the entire show in between sips from the wine-filled water skins. Nakia wondered how accurate the clique was in their assessments. They seemed slightly drunk, but they also sounded quite certain in their calculations. She knew the Queen was intelligent, having watched her easily defeat Amal in chess, but were the other ladies? The General, probably. She was, after all, a woman who managed to become a general. The others, she didn't know enough about, but the Queen didn't suffer fools.

"Did a puppet show deserve so much criticism?" Nakia asked as they left the tent. She hadn't followed the story much thanks to their jeering, so she didn't know if it was entertaining beyond the mechanics.

"As I said, kitten, any job worth doing is worth doing right. It doesn't matter if it's a puppet show or not. You bring your all and you shall be rewarded by the gods, always."

Nakia nodded. The Queen smiled at her and offered her a sip from the water skin. The wine was sweet, but Nakia found it good. She'd indulge a little.

"Is there anything you've noticed that you'd like to try?" the Queen asked.

Nakia shook her head. "I wouldn't know where to start."

"There's a wrestling match," Naren howled as they went in search of other activities. He pointed ahead of them at a raised platform. Nakia stood on her toes, trying to see. Was their form of wrestling the same as the form Nakia was familiar with?

"We see wrestling all the time." Layla shook her head and her husband seemed to deflate. She passed him her wine jug, as a peace offering. He merely looked at it as if he didn't know what it was and winced before shaking his head. He gently pushed her hand away.

"I think we both know I don't have your tolerance," Naren said. Maybe he didn't realize he had been sipping from her wine jug the entire time.

"Then let's find you something you can have and something that's fun."

Naren folded his arms across his chest. "But, wrestling is fun."

Nakia doubted that. If it was the same here as in her homeland, she didn't think it was fun at all. At home, it was something men enjoyed, watching one person overpower another. That was apparently the case here, too, because no one was enthused by the idea of watching it except for Naren.

"Yeah, we need something fresh," the Queen said.

"And for ladies." The General put her arm around the woman with her and pulled her close. She nuzzled her woman's neck for a moment.

Nakia held in a wince. No one else seemed to care about the display. Not just her group, but everyone around. No one stopped and stared. No one said anything. They just went on like the relationship was normal. The Queen said they were married. But, women couldn't and didn't marry other women. Marriages were supposed to strengthen friendships between families or build alliances and should result in children. The Roshan couldn't overlook those things. There was no way they could be *that* backwards

"Hey, look, your brothers." Naren pointed to a cage with lions and tigers in it. They stood on platforms, leaping through hoops.

The Queen's mouth dropped open. "What the hell am I looking at?"

"Our brothers doing tricks." Layla's mouth continued to move, but no other words came out.

"The cats are your brothers?" Nakia asked. She had wondered what the Queen meant when talking about 'her brothers' when they were at the arena.

"I will explain in a moment. Layla, Adira, with me." The Queen stepped away.

Nakia felt the Queen's absence immediately, like an emptiness inside of her. She took a breath, attempting to fill the void. It didn't work, but she tried to ignore the feeling. She stayed with Naren and the

General's woman. They watched the trio approach the big cat show and within moments people walked away from the cage. It was shut down immediately.

"Why did they do that?" Nakia wondered aloud.

"Lions are a symbol of one of the four warrior guilds. They are members of the lion guild. The lions are considered part of their family," the General's woman explained with a gentle expression.

Nakia squinted a little. "So..."

"So, they're expected to be treated in a certain manner in Ashni's territory. Really, one would think they would be treated with respect in any Roshan territory since the great Amir was a Lion as well. Oh, my."

The explanation halted. The man who ran the cat show was a mountain of a man and he wasn't eager to stop the show. He folded his arms across his barrel chest and glared at the Queen. This would probably end badly.

***

"Sir, it's a day of peace right now, but if you don't put those lions and tigers in their proper place, peace is going to have to be put on hold," Ashni said to the giant who dared to use big cats for pointless frivolity.

"I have permission from King Amal to run this show. I'm with his personal entourage," the giant replied.

"Sir, you do realize you're currently in Queen Ashni's realm and in her courtyard, yes?" Adira asked with an arched eyebrow. While her tone suggested 'moron,' she left that part unsaid. He was probably the only one unaware of what he was.

"I still have royal permission," he said.

Ashni narrowed her gaze at him. This was Amal attempting to get under her skin, she knew, but it was also a way to get her in trouble with their mother. The Festival of the Moon was a time of peace and Ashni's instinctive way to solve this type of problem was with violence. To do violence on the Festival of the Moon was like spitting in the Empress' face. On any other day, Ashni would tempt fate, but not on this important holiday.

"Yes, dear sister, he does have royal permission," Amal said, slinking in to see what disorder he wrought. She wouldn't give him the pleasure of seeing her betray their mother with violence, but she would enjoy wiping the smug look off his face.

"Yes, he has royal permission from you, a member of the Wolf guild. I shouldn't be surprised. The Order of the Wolf coming out during the Festival of the Moon makes sense as they howl and disturb the hunt of others." Ashni would need more wine after this. Amal ruined her buzz. She'd ruin his night to repay him.

Amal beamed as though he had been complimented. He stood up a little taller. "The Festival was practically made for us, yes."

"I know. Such a delight, except that lions hunt at night as well. The Moon isn't yours and the Empire doesn't bend to your will. There are laws we must all respect. Now, there's a problem with your cats," Ashni said.

"Yes, you're causing the problem," he answered.

"No, the problem is that any big cats in Khenshu have to be taken directly to the cirque. It's city law and we all know no one in the Empire is immune to the law," Adira said.

Amal blinked. "Excuse me?"

"Yes. While the Lion Guild will use the lions, the cirque still handles all big cats brought into the city. They have to be inspected properly by our cat handlers and also blessed by priests. If they're not inspected or blessed, they're here illegally and the courts then decide what to do with them. What did the courts decide last time this happened?" Adira turned to Layla.

Layla shrugged. "I recall cutting off a lot of tiger heads. It was a shame."

"But, not a waste. The meat fed the army for a time. They were all infused with the spirit of tigers," Ashni said.

The giant's face drained of color as his mouth fell open. "No, no, no. I have royal permission."

"Yes, but the law is the law after all," Ashni said.

"You can't kill his cats. I gave him permission to show them." Amal pressed his hands to his chest. Of course, by raising his voice, he called more attention to what was already an unscheduled show.

"Yes, but even if the Empress gave him permission, the law is the law." Ashni snapped her fingers. Guards came from all directions. "Seize the cats."

"No, this is my livelihood!" The giant threw his hands up.

"Yes, well, like I keep saying, the law is the law." Ashni locked eyes with Amal while her guards did as ordered. He frowned, but didn't try to stop them.

The giant fell to his knees. "Please. Please, don't do this." He argued and pled, but his words fell on deaf ears. He was a fool for listening to Amal in the first place.

"This means nothing," Amal said, giving Ashni a hard look.

"Of course it doesn't," Ashni replied. Amal stormed off. It was almost funny to watch. If it wasn't a day of peace, she'd throw something at his head, just for old time's sake.

"Yeah, because he lost, again," Layla said.

Adira sighed and shook her head. "It's always got to be a pissing contest with him. Now, he's not only ruining our regular days, but one of the best holidays. And if this was the opening act, I can only wonder what he was discussing with Majeed."

Layla gave Adira a deadpan look. "Really? You can only wonder? This is Amal we're talking about and Majeed has always had more ambition than sense."

"Put it out of your minds for now. He's always tried to ruin, well, everything. I'm pretty sure he was born ruining something," Ashni said.

Layla snickered. "Asad's chance to have his own birthday."

"It doesn't matter. We have better things to attend to." Ashni turned her attention back to Nakia, Saniyah, and Naren. Nakia and Naren watched them, but Saniyah seemed to be quite bored with the matter. Saniyah scanned the Festival, undoubtedly trying to find something else to do. Ashni felt like Saniyah had the right idea.

***

Nakia tensed when Amal arrived on the scene, but wasn't surprised when the Queen got rid of him with ease. But, for the brief moment he challenged the Queen, Nakia felt there was something more to them than a sibling rivalry. Amal looked at the Queen like she was the enemy. "Is he testing her?"

The General's woman shook her head. "Don't worry over him. He plots and schemes, but only makes a fool of himself."

Nakia didn't doubt that, but she wished she knew the full story between the siblings. Hell, she wished she knew the full story about everything. Then the Queen was back at her side and Nakia put it out of her mind. Maybe she'd get the full story of the festival.

"Well, that was annoying," Layla said as she settled in next to her husband. His arm went around her waist and she rested her hand on his.

"It also didn't solve the issue of what we're going to do now," the

General said.

Naren brightened. "Wrestling now? Less annoying than Amal."

"Being boiled in oil is less annoying than Amal," Ashni said.

"Oh, flower arrangements." The General's woman grinned and pulled the General away. The others followed. Naren groaned and tried to stay put, but Layla took his hand and tugged him along.

"Sounds like we'll be needing more wine," the Queen said before taking a swig from her wine pouch.

"You can barely walk as it is. But, flower arrangements should mean wine," Layla agreed.

Nakia didn't say anything, but she was beginning to think the festival was a big excuse to drink for at least three of the people she was with. More wine was obtained before going to see the flower arrangements. The Queen offered Nakia some of her spirits. Nakia found the drink to be sweet once again, like the wine she drank inside the palace. It wasn't awful and she accepted the water skin when it was passed a second time.

The flower arrangements were beyond beautiful. There were so many colors, which Nakia supposed many of these people didn't see since they lived in a barren desert. They were designed like living tapestries or sculptures and so vivid Nakia thought they might move. She reached for a practically dazzling display made to look like a family of deer.

"You can touch it," the Queen whispered to her. Nakia jumped a little, not expecting the Queen to be so close. Nakia's stomach fluttered a little and she had to take a breath.

"I..." Nakia wasn't sure what she should say. She wanted to touch it, but she didn't want to chance ruining the art.

"Look." The Queen nodded over to the General and her woman. Her woman ran her fingertips along one of the larger works.

The General ordered a full display, a wall of flowers, for her woman. It was a romantic gesture, but Nakia still felt it was wrong. *Women shouldn't be together like that.* The General certainly could give some men back home lessons.

For a moment, Nakia glanced at Naren, wondering if he'd take the hint. But, his wife probably didn't like flowers. Layla seemed more like a boy than a wife and Naren whined quite a bit for a husband. Nakia looked at the two couples and wondered which marriage was more abnormal.

After the flowers, they saw another show. There was more

heckling, and it was worse because this show had actors in it. The actors paused for a moment, but immediately went back to work when they saw it was the Queen and her people.

The show itself was captivating. The actors had colorful costumes, contrasting with the white outfits everyone else wore. She wasn't sure what was going on, thanks to the language barrier. After being in the palace for a couple of months, she knew some of the Roshan language, but not enough to follow along. She planned to ask, but everyone was too busy complaining. The General's woman, who would have been the easiest one to ask, was trying to keep the Queen from going on stage.

"Hey, this is a load! My father, the Son of the Great Eagle, would never blink to that shrew," the Queen called.

"Never? He did. Making the Moon greater than even the Sun," Layla said, puffing up her chest. Nakia wasn't sure if her pride came from being close to the Empress or if it had to do with Layla claiming to be darkness and shadows.

The Queen glowered at Layla. "How can my own chosen sibling be a fool?"

"Fool? It's well known that darkness defeats light every time." Layla made a fist.

The actors and the audience didn't react. They probably went through this every festival. The General's woman sighed and massaged her forehead. "Can we go to one play where this doesn't happen?"

The General shrugged. "You know Ashni thinks she knows the story of her parents better than anyone else."

Now, Nakia knew the play was about the Queen's parents, but that raised other questions. *Why would the Queen refer to her mother as 'that shrew?' Why was the Queen was so offended by her mother, yet had this amazing festival in her honor?*

"Does the Queen dislike her mother?" Nakia wondered aloud.

"Don't let her attitude fool you," the General said. Nakia wasn't expecting an answer, but nodded. The General turned to Ashni and yanked her into her seat. "Cut it out. You're drunk."

The Queen put her finger in the General's face. "Being drunk doesn't change the truth of the matter. It doesn't make it easier to accept these lies and slander either."

"May we please just enjoy the tale? I quite like it," the General's woman said.

The Queen snorted and folded her arms across her chest. "I'm surrounded," she grumbled.

"You're also drunk, making everything you say null and void," Layla said.

"You're as drunk as I am," the Queen replied.

Nakia tried to focus on the show to piece together what was going on and learn more about the Queen's parents. She found she couldn't do it, even with the Queen quiet for a moment. Her head swam a little. There was a pleasant buzz in her head.

The Queen offered Nakia more wine and then there was more heckling followed by more wine. Nakia's head drifted a little more, but she squinted at the stage and concentrated, determined to know what was going on. It seemed there was supposed to be a war and the female character was carried off. The next thing Nakia knew, the characters on stage were married, but there was a physical fight between the two characters. The Queen decided to leave at that moment, even though the play wasn't over.

"I don't trust any actor trying to play me as a child," the Queen said.

Layla sucked her teeth. "Oh, yes, that's why we're leaving. You just don't want to see the Empress put your father in his place."

The Queen frowned. "No one puts my father in his place. He owns the place. Like I said, I don't trust any actor trying to play me as a child."

"You mean, you were a child?" Naren said with a lopsided grin.

"Don't start with me, boy. You know I'll bop you." The Queen shook her fist at him.

"Day of peace," Layla reminded her.

"Damn day of peace," the Queen grumbled.

Nakia held in a laugh, but she smiled. She tried to hide the expression behind her hand, but she wasn't fast enough. The Queen noticed and squinted at her. Nakia found it even harder to hold in her laughter now and snickers escaped her. Her heart fluttered a little and the Queen leaned down, staring at her.

The Queen threw her hands up. "Oh, great, even the damned hellcat is laughing at me now."

"Laughing with you," Nakia said to placate the Queen, but her words only caused the Queen to pout.

"At you, with you. It's all a matter of interpretation," Layla said.

For the first time, something made sense to Nakia. She wasn't sure why. Nothing Layla said or did ever made sense. *That can't be a good thing.* Nakia's mind swam a little, but she shook it off.

"I'm surrounded." The Queen sighed in surrender, but put an arm around Nakia's waist and pulled her close.

Nakia curled into her shoulder, finding it easier to stay on her feet. She hadn't realized it was so hard to stand on her own until that point. It felt like the world shifted underneath her and the Queen was the only thing that could keep her up.

They wandered around the festival some more, exploring its vastness. Nakia found herself a little stuck on the change in lighting as they moved from section to section. The lamps glowed blue in some areas and green in others and white in still other places. Maybe this was by design, but she wasn't sure. *Why the hell am I so stuck on the lights? They're just lights, but they're so intriguing. Maybe it is the same reason why so many things were suddenly funny.*

"Oh! Food." Naren was off before anyone could stop him.

"I guess we're getting food," Layla said.

"Or we could leave him." The Queen beamed at the idea.

"I think I would like some food, too." Nakia had not eaten much earlier, thinking about the Festival and they had done a lot of walking tonight.

"Anything you like then." The Queen motioned around them with a sweep of her hand.

There was no shortage of food. Some was simple and easy to carry. There were grilled meats and vegetables on sticks. There were stews and fruits in bowls. There were also tables set up where people could eat full course meals. Nakia wasn't hungry enough to sit down and Naren didn't seem to have that intent either.

"Just a sample," Nakia said.

"Anything you like, kitten. Besides, we could all use something to eat."

Nakia allowed the Queen to lead her to a food stand. They all partook of what the Queen assured Nakia was grilled mutton with vegetables on a stick. It was different. It wasn't like the mutton served in the palace, not as spicy. She was able to savor it. They moved on once everyone had their food.

Nakia wasn't accustomed to walking while eating, but everyone else seemed to be doing it. The food was designed for mobility since there was so much to do. The Queen and company had so many things they could disrupt while being well fed. Nakia followed along, taking wine as it was offered to her. They moved on to another show and the bad behavior continued.

Nakia was no longer embarrassed by the antics, but found them funny. *Something's wrong with me*. It was obvious to Nakia, but no one else seemed to think there was something wrong with her. She couldn't put her finger on it and stopped caring as she snickered when an actor threw a pillow at the Queen to get her to sit down. The Queen grunted as the pillow smacked her right in the face and Nakia started laughing.

Layla guffawed, holding her stomach. "Wow, his aim is fair and true." The audience laughed with her.

"We should get that guy a bow," the General said.

"I'm already an archer during wartimes," the actor answered.

"And you're lucky I need archers." The Queen huffed and folded her arms across her chest. Nakia giggled more, but patted the Queen's knee. The Queen glanced down and then put her arm around Nakia.

"Come on, start the show already," the Queen called. The actors went back to the story.

* * *

Ashni wasn't sure how they ended up in the garden, but there they were, giggling among the shrubs at a tiny waterfall. It felt good, laughing and being carefree, forgetting any troubles for the moment. Beyond the fact that Ashni was aware they were all dead drunk, which made things funny anyway, they had also witnessed quite the hilarious sight. They watched Amal fall on his back as he tried to climb into his palanquin to continue through the festival. He was the only jerk in one, even though there were many nobles and officials there. *Idiot*.

"Hey, what's this?" Nakia asked, falling against Ashni's side.

For a moment, Ashni lost herself in the feel of Nakia. She breathed in how sweet Nakia smelled. *Yes, there is the wonderful scent of wine wafting off of her, but there is also something else that is just Nakia and it smells delicious, had smelled delicious all night.* Ashni almost bent down and nuzzled Nakia's neck, but caught herself as Nakia spoke again.

"Hey, what is this?" Nakia asked, waving food in front of Ashni's face.

"Oh!" Ashni focused on the fried meat on the skewer, squinting and trying to remember what it was called. "Oh, it's fried octopus. Loved in the original Roshan tribes."

"Why are you yelling?" Layla asked. Naren laid on her lap, his face red and his eyes almost closed, but still managing to eat several bites of meat on a skewer.

"She's eating traditional Roshan food." Ashni put her arm around

Nakia and pressed her close. A smile spread on Ashni's face and she felt a lightness inside that had nothing to do with the wine.

Nakia's pale face, flushed and bright red in the white light, twisted. "No. I'm not eating octopus."

"You'll eat mice, but not octopus?" No one in the Roshan ate mice, but Ashni knew in Nakia's culture, wild mice were fine dining.

Nakia frowned at her. "Mice are different than octopus."

"But, it's so good." Ashni wanted to see Nakia eat the octopus.

"Yeah, it is, so give it to me." Layla put her hand out.

Nakia pulled her hand back, holding her food close to her chest. "No. I'm not giving anything to you."

Layla's eyes narrowed as she stared at Nakia. "You do realize I can kill you, right?" She pulled a dagger from her ankle. Naren grunted as she shifted slightly, but he was fine when she settled again.

Nakia scoffed. "You won't."

This was true. Layla knew better than to kill the person they were holding for a large amount of gold and Nakia knew that. Maybe Nakia also understood the 'day of peace' thing they kept talking about. Ashni was impressed and then Nakia kept talking.

"She won't let you." Nakia pointed to Ashni with her free hand. This was also true, but it hit Ashni strangely. She felt some pride swell in her over the idea that Nakia trusted her to protect her from everyone, including her sister.

Layla's gaze narrowed more. "It's bad enough you dare to wear pearls today, but now you're going to defy me, too? You think Ashni could stop me if I wanted to get you? She's too drunk to do anything."

"I'm no more drunk than anyone else," Ashni said.

Layla ignored her, keeping her focus on Nakia. "Gimme the food."

Nakia stuck her chin in the air. "No."

"Hey, you either eat it or I will," Ashni said. She was partial to fried octopus. It wasn't a food they often had around these parts.

They both huffed, but Nakia put the food to her mouth and nibbled. Her eyes lit up for a moment and Ashni delighted in the look. Nakia took several bites and Ashni watched, finding it far more fascinating than any show they saw that night.

"Hey! You don't go looking at girls' mouths like that," Adira barked, glaring at Ashni from across the group.

Ashni tried her best to throw Adira a rude gesture, but found her fingers weren't working the way she wanted them to. *I must be drunker than I thought.* It didn't matter, anyway. Adira's eyes were more interested in Saniyah's cleavage than anything else, so she barely spent a second glowering at Ashni. *I'm not the only who is drunker than usual.* Of course, it didn't take much wine for Adira to openly leer at her spouse, but it took a lot to make Adira ready to jump on Saniyah with an audience in view.

"I think we all need to go home," Saniyah said, purring at the end. She was focused on Adira. She ran her hands through Adira's short black hair and played with her ear.

Adira moaned and her eyes drifted shut. "Yes." She dragged the "s," hissing like a viper.

"But, it's not even…" Naren squinted and looked around. "It's almost not sunrise." He was obviously completely out of it because the sun was peeking over the horizon and that sentence was poorly constructed even for him. The fact that he was still conscious after sharing wine with Layla all night showed he was made of stern stuff, but he probably didn't even know where they were right now.

Layla laughed, her eyes shining. "I think…I think I might need to remove my spouse." She snickered again.

"I've been telling you that for years," Ashni said. Naren was so out of it, he didn't react to the insult. He tried to focus on his food again.

Layla helped Naren to his feet while Saniyah helped Adira up. Ashni plucked Nakia off the ground and watched her wobble. She pulled Nakia close to her, steadying her.

"Everybody got…everybody?" Ashni looked around. The drunk holding up the drunker. *Thank Khurshid we only have to make it to our rooms in the palace or we'd be in trouble.*

Layla shrugged and nearly dropped Naren. If ever there was a signal to go, that was it. *Some of us might not even make it to our rooms. What was in that wine? Of course, the fact that we emptied those skins probably didn't help.* They parted ways as the sun crept higher into the sky.

With each step Ashni took, she found herself feeling dizzy. She managed to stay upright while she glanced down to make sure she still had Nakia. Nakia took a few steps and then fell against Ashni. *Hmm…probably shouldn't have given her so much wine.* But, the Festival was about having fun and wine made things fun. Nakia hadn't minded. Taking a breath, Ashni lifted Nakia into her arms so that the princess wouldn't take a tumble.

Nakia giggled as Ashni pressed her close, *for safety reasons. I wouldn't want her to hurt herself and somehow ruin our chances of getting that gold.* The giggles continued as Ashni walked on, entering the palace proper. Nakia cuddled closer and inhaled deeply, possibly breathing in Ashni, but she wasn't sure. The notion made her heart flutter. Ashni shook that thought away. *You're being ridiculous and drunk.* But, then, Nakia's scent hit Ashni and nothing seemed ridiculous. Nakia smelled sweet, like the plum wine they had drank, apples, and honey.

The aroma wrapped around her foggy brain and embraced it. Sighing, Ashni tried to focus. She narrowed her gaze and marched on to her bedchamber. She was thankful the room was empty. Sometimes she hated to be pawed at by servants. As she was about to lie down, her brow wrinkled as she realized something was off.

"Wait, I was supposed to take the kitten to her room. Damn," Ashni said. Glancing down at the still form in her arms, Ashni considered her options. She didn't feel like making the trek to Nakia's bedroom. Puffing out a breath of air, she blew a few strands of hair back. "Whatever."

Nakia was asleep and since Ashni planned on sleeping, they could share a bed. The bed was large. They probably wouldn't even realize the other was there.

Nakia groaned as Ashni eased her down and then she wrapped her arms around Ashni. Nakia simpered and her eyes were half-lidded, but her gaze was deep. Ashni froze in place.

"I've never met anyone like you," Nakia whispered.

Ashni chuckled. "That's because there is no one like me, kitten. I've always been one of a kind."

Before Ashni could put on one of her patented arrogant smirks, Nakia kissed her. Nakia's lips tasted of wine and fried octopus. Her scent flooded Ashni's senses and short-circuited her brain. *So sweet, so delicious.* Ashni wanted more, so she returned the kiss.

A short moan escaped Nakia. Ashni tilted her head slightly so she could taste all of the princess. Nakia's arm wrapped around her neck and pulled her close. Ashni groaned and her body buzzed. *I need even more. I need to feel all of my kitten.*

Ashni pulled away to claw herself out of her clothing. Nakia whined at the loss and her hands found their way to Ashni's body, wandering, gripping, clutching, and trying to pull Ashni back. Ashni was certain she tore her clothing because she had never undressed so fast. Once bare, Ashni went for another kiss and Nakia didn't disappoint.

Nakia returned the kiss with just as much passion as before, setting every nerve in Ashni's body ablaze. The kiss was sloppy and slow, but

Ashni didn't care. It gave her a chance to savor the taste of Nakia's mouth and to undress her. Once she had most of Nakia's clothing off, Ashni needed more. More sweet, delicious, creamy flesh. She placed light kisses on Nakia's cheeks and down her neck. Nakia mewled and wiggled, fingers clutching Ashni's shoulders, but didn't stop Ashni's descent.

Nakia's body was lithe, but firm, and topped with plump, perky breasts. Ashni tasted them, her tongue gliding over soft, salty skin. Nakia purred and arched herself closer to Ashni. Each sound made Ashni want to worship this scrumptious hellion. She'd devour Nakia if she could, but for now she'd do the next best thing and have as much of her as Nakia would allow.

Ashni wrapped her lips around Nakia's pebbled nipple and flicked it with her tongue. Nakia's back bowed and she pushed herself further into Ashni's mouth. Nakia ran her hands through Ashni's hair, destroying her already loose braids and pressing her close, encouraging her. Not that Ashni needed encouraging. She went from one peak to the other while her hands caressed Nakia's breasts and taut abdomen. Nakia felt as good as she tasted.

"Feels good..." Nakia breathed and hummed as Ashni flicked her nipple with her thumb.

"You taste good." Ashni licked her way down Nakia's stomach, circling her navel with her tongue.

Nakia moaned as she shifted a little. Ashni's hands went to Nakia's hips and Nakia lifted them up, so Ashni could remove the rest of her clothing. Seconds passed, it felt too long to get Nakia naked.

"By the great gods, you're lovely," Ashni muttered, taking in Nakia's petite, but curvy body. Her proportions were just right. *Proving once again that I am favored by the gods in so many different ways.*

Before going in for what she wanted, Ashni reveled in feeling their bodies touch. Nakia chirped as soon as they were skin-to-skin and Ashni purred, feeling decadent beyond all her queenly goods. She luxuriated in the feeling for a long moment, kissing Nakia's mouth once more. The feel of her body and her lips were enough to short out Ashni's brain for a second and she wanted nothing more in the world than to stay right where she was forever and always. But, with the promise of more pleasure, her mind wasn't gone for long. She slid her thigh between Nakia's legs and they both moaned into each other mouths.

Experiencing Nakia sleek, warm, and wanting against her, heat and desire rushed through Ashni's body, which moved on its own. She rocked her hips slightly and her thigh pressed against Nakia just right, causing the princess to cry out. The sound burned through Ashni in ways she'd never felt before. *And I command lightning, for crying out loud.*

"Yes," Nakia sighed, her fingernails digging into Ashni's shoulders. Even the pain felt good. The idea that Nakia was anchored to her had electricity dance down Ashni's nerves and her heart thumped to the rhythm of her movements. She wanted to make Nakia feel just as good, so she moved with more purpose. Nakia moaned and held on tighter.

Ashni could only take Nakia's moaning for so long before she needed more. She wasted no time kissing her way down Nakia's body. Reaching for Ashni, as if to pull her back up, Nakia whined, but the sound quickly turned into a long moan as Ashni took her into her mouth. *By the Great Eagle, she's sweet everywhere!*

Ashni licked and sucked, not wanting to miss a spot or lose a drop. This was the best treat she had ever had, topping all cakes, pies, pastries, and other sweets she indulged in. She doubted she'd ever be able to stop. *I've found ambrosia.*

Nakia moaned and hooked her leg around Ashni's shoulder, which Ashni took as silent begging, so she upped her effort. With her tongue busy, she allowed a finger to tease Nakia, making her buck. Ashni took a breath and then eased inside, finding the princess tight. *So beautiful, so wonderful, so amazing.* Her finger was hugged and surrounded by this magnificent, tasty treat. Moving slowly, she drew her finger in and out while her tongue, lips, and mouth remained right where they wanted to be.

Nakia filled the room with amazing sounds and her heel dug into Ashni's back as she dripped into Ashni's mouth. Her hands ended up lost in Ashni's hair for a while, trying to keep Ashni in place. Ashni enjoyed the feel of those long, delicate fingers mussing her braids. Ashni wished they could get closer. She would've told Nakia to never let go, but she refused to move her lips from where they were.

To reward Nakia for just being there, Ashni eased her free hand back up Nakia's body and gently kneaded a bouncing breast. Her thumb delighted in flicking Nakia's nipple. Nakia's moans grew and her hips chased Ashni's mouth and finger. Each movement grew more and more frantic. Ashni made sure to stay right with Nakia, wanting every last piece of her.

Suddenly, Nakia gave a scream and her body pulsed around Ashni's finger in a most enchanting way. Ashni looked up to see Nakia's face, flushed with ecstasy. *So beautiful.*

Wanting more kisses, Ashni eased out of Nakia and moved back up her body only to find her sound asleep. Ashni wasn't upset, as Nakia slept with a small, happy grin on her face. She smiled and brushed some of Nakia's hair from her glistening forehead. She kissed Nakia's forehead, tasting sweat and satisfaction, and settled in for some sleep of her own.

Chapter Ten

NAKIA'S FIRST THOUGHT WAS that her eyelids hurt and she didn't want to open her eyes. But, everything throbbed. She needed to check to see if she was physically injured. Blinking or trying to blink felt like there was sand rubbed into her eyes. Sticky sand at that.

Once she managed to open her eyes, which somehow made pain burst through her skull, she tried to assess her situation, but it was difficult. Everything was blurry and each movement of her eyes made her head hurt even more, like her head might split open. Her body pulsed with dull agony. Focusing seemed impossible, her brain barely alert despite being awake. *Why do I feel this horrible?*

Her brain offered no answers to that question. Taking a breath, she tried to remember anything from the day before. It was all a blank, so she went back to what she was doing before. *Wait, what was I doing before? Oh, right, trying to figure out what was going on.*

With a low groan, she turned onto her side, hoping the change in position would make something, *anything*, hurt less. Her shifting caused her to realize that she was nude. Then her eyes focused enough for her to notice there was a body across from her in bed.

Oh, no. No, no, no. She couldn't have shared a bed with someone. Her father would destroy her. He would have her buried alive, sealed in a tomb, left to starve to death, and never think twice about her. Her chest tightened and breathing became the most difficult thing in the world to do. She was pure. She was chaste. She'd never—and then it got worse. Her eyes focused enough for her to realize who lay across from her. She yelped and gasped for air.

"Keep it down," the Queen groused, her face buried in her pillow.

"Ke-ke-ke—" Nakia couldn't even get a word out. *What in the world is going on?* The question echoed in her mind, crashing against her skull, causing more pain.

"Don't scream." Maybe it was an order. Maybe it was a plea. It didn't matter. The Queen reached over, as if to touch her.

Nakia gasped and pushed back, retreating as fast as she could. She shot out of bed but her legs failed her. There were curtains around the bed and she got tangled in them briefly before her fall continued. She crumbled to the floor with a pained groan. *Legs, you as well? Does no part of my body work correctly anymore?*

The Queen sat up and looked over the side of the bed, squinting at her. "Are you all right?"

Nakia couldn't breathe and the room swirled. This couldn't be possible. No, this was a nightmare. This was some horrible, terrible, untrue nightmare. It couldn't be real. But, then again, the slight throb between her legs belied that notion.

"You!" Nakia cried, pointing at the Queen. "How could you?" she shrieked. Her shoulders shook as her voice caught in her throat.

The Queen flinched and closed her eyes, holding her forehead with one hand. "Don't scream," she hissed through gritted teeth.

"You monster!" Tears burned Nakia's eyes and poured down her face as she yanked one of the covers from the bed. She used it to cover her shame and hide her from this beast.

The Queen's eyes locked with hers. "I'm not a monster." Her tone was hard.

"Look what you did to me! You're a demon! You savage! You beast! You barbarian! What did you do?" Nakia screamed. Her face was hot, scorched by her tears, and her head felt like it might explode, but she didn't care.

The Queen's eyes darkened and she frowned at Nakia. "Nothing you didn't want me to do."

The words stabbed Nakia like a rusty knife. Gasping, she backed away, clutching her stomach. The Queen reached out for Nakia again. Nakia turned and bolted out of the room.

"Kitten, wait! Come back!" the Queen called, but Nakia didn't stop. She wasn't sure where she was in the palace, *if* she was in the palace, but she needed to get away before anything else happened.

***

"Damn," Ashni hissed, slapping the bed. She cut her eyes to a couple of servants trying to blend in with the wall. "Follow her. Make sure she doesn't hurt herself."

The servants took off and Ashni ground her teeth together. *I do not need this. Or the headache beating right behind my damned eyes.* She had definitely overindulged last night. Usually that wouldn't bother her, but she looked at the door.

"By the Great Eagle, I'm fucked." Ashni rubbed her forehead and realized that was putting it mildly. She took a deep breath and put her head down, counting the ways she had royally screwed up.

If anyone else had done this, she would have immediately fed them to the lions, but she couldn't very well feed herself to the lions. Someone had to carry on her father's legacy. *It isn't like I can trust my idiot brothers to conquer the West and eventually make sure the whole world is called Roshan.* Not to mention, she really wanted to do it herself. *Yeah, but it's hard to tell that when you're messing things up.*

"Damn it," she hissed again as she lifted her head. "Go." She dismissed all the servants.

"Highness—"

"Go!" she bellowed, ignoring the agony beating at her skull. A loud thunderclap echoed outside. She usually loved to be pampered after holidays, but right now she didn't want to see anyone, especially people who witnessed the morning's scene.

The servants scurried out like mice in the presence of a cat. Usually, this would have made her feel better. It was fun to scare people, but right now all she could think about were terrified emerald eyes staring at her as if she truly was a monster. Nakia thought the worst of her.

"Does she really think I could do *that* to her?" Ashni sighed and ran her hand through her mussed hair. "Okay...even if I didn't do *that*..." She shook her head. *No, I haven't done anything wrong. Nakia wanted me last night, kissed me, initiated the whole thing. This was not my fault.*

With that in mind, Ashni felt a little stronger and managed to get out of bed. Her head still hurt. Definitely overindulged on the wine, if nothing else, she mentally conceded. Making her way to her bath, which was thankfully already drawn, she settled into the scented, flower-treated water. A soft sigh escaped her and she thought back to last night.

"So sweet," she whispered to the steamy air.

When she closed her eyes, she could remember the exact way Nakia's back arched as she climaxed and the memory caused her to shiver. She could still taste sweet honey on the tip of her tongue. Best of all, she could still hear the little sounds that had come from her hellcat. *She really purrs.*

"Why did she react like that?" Ashni barked, smacking at the water. She knew the answer, but refused to acknowledge it. She hadn't violated Nakia. Nakia wanted her, she wanted Nakia, and they had each other. *So, why did Nakia freak out this morning?*

Well, she knew the answer to that question, too. Nakia was from a culture where women sleeping together wasn't sanctioned. Nakia couldn't take seeing a same-sex couple. Groaning, Ashni hit herself in the forehead. Thankfully, there were no servants around or surely they would have reported to someone that she had lost her mind. *That's all I need, Adira rushing in here to try to bring my sanity back.*

Have I lost my mind? If nothing else, she was driven to distraction. The smell of Nakia was enough to make her mind wander. Even the memory of the scent led to her thinking about sweet sounds and the inspiring rhythm of Nakia around her finger. Her body felt warm and throbbed with want. She groaned and shook her head.

"No, no, no. That way leads to madness. Stop thinking about it. Look at the trouble it has already caused." That was enough to get her mind off Nakia for the moment. To take her mind off Nakia even more, Ashni inhaled the oils and incenses around her bath. Maybe the aromas would replace the one tattooed on her brain. They were all favorites of hers. They didn't help.

Taking the bath and getting dressed didn't make her feel any more human. But, the world kept turning and she had things to do. Well, she'd find things to do. She wasn't surprised to find the throne room empty when she got there. Nakia wouldn't be joining her today, even if she summoned her.

Ashni settled on the throne and reports were delivered to her. Officials slowly filed in, waiting to be heard. Ashni didn't have the energy for them yet. She focused on the scrolls. Trying to distract herself with work, Ashni felt fine until breakfast was brought in. Apples with honey were on the tray, as always. Growling, she kicked the food away and flung the document she had in her hand across the room. Outside, thunder clapped and the servants flinched.

"Go get Adira," Ashni barked. Almost a dozen people, some not even servants, bolted out of the room to do her bidding.

It took a while for Adira to drag herself into the throne room. By then, Ashni had stewed and boiled. Adira was wet from the pouring rain. Lightning flashed through the sky as if doing battle. Ashni couldn't bring herself to care Adira was soaked, and knew that meant her rage was out of control. *You'll only hurt yourself if you don't rein in your power.*

Adira glared at Ashni. It was a look of pure hatred. "What?" Adira stomped her foot and splashed water. "What the hell could you possibly want. I got less than five hours of sleep and you've taken me away from the greatest body of all time, which was naked and pressed against me while gentle hands soothed away a headache and made me walk through your damn tantrum storm on top of that? What?"

The fury in Ashni's belly grew stronger. *Why should Adira be able to cuddle and caress her woman when Nakia thinks I am a monster? And I am not throwing a tantrum.* She kicked the table of documents at Adira, who moved out of the way in time to avoid being hit in the chest.

"What the hell?" Adira watched Ashni, on guard. The table thudded against the floor and echoed through the hall. The scrolls clattered to floor, clanking against tense air.

"Handle that shit." Ashni motioned to the documents now strewn across the floor.

"Like hell I will. You think I'm some fucking slave girl?"

Ashni roared. "You do my bidding. My will."

"In what world?"

"In this one. Now, clean it up." She went too far and Ashni knew it even in her wrath, but she didn't care. Wind howled outside and lightning blared.

"What the hell is wrong with you? Do you realize how bad my damn headache is? I should be in bed recovering from the Festival we just fucking left, which is the same thing you should be doing. Why are you being such a bitch?"

"I'm not a bitch." *And I am damn sure not a monster.*

"Then why the hell are you acting like one?" Adira stormed up to the edge of the dais, still glaring at Ashni. The wrong word or wrong move might have Adira invading the one space she never dared encroach upon. That was the one line of respect, the one area that Adira knew wasn't hers, but she wouldn't let it stop her if she felt disrespected enough. The knowledge didn't stop Ashni from pushing, punishing someone because she was hurt.

"Because you do what I say, like everyone else in this fucking place. You're my bitch, if anything," Ashni said, wishing there was something else to kick at her. Instead, she flung one of the pillows from the throne.

Adira let out a roar that usually meant she was about to take someone's head off and her hand went to her sword hilt. By the time she unsheathed the blade, Ashni was in her face with the *Ivory Claw.*

They clashed swords, gnashing their teeth at each other. The sound of the metals striking gave them pause and they eyed each other for a long moment. The pounding sound of the rain lowered and the wind died down.

Adira had a look in her eye that Ashni hadn't seen in a long time. Adira was ready to cut her down. Ashni knew she looked the same. Slowly, Adira's gaze changed, as if she recognized Ashni before her. Not the Queen, but Ashni. Just as Ashni reminded herself this was Adira, not her general, not a subject. This was the woman who would tell her the truth no matter what, who would put her in her place when necessary, and who wanted the same things as she did, wanted to help her achieve greatness.

"What the hell are we doing?" Ashni asked, her voice much calmer than before. *I can't let this get to me this much. What a fool I'd be.*

"The hell if I know," Adira answered as she glanced away. "Let's start over."

Ashni nodded and they each took one step back. They put their weapons away, Adira's on her hip and Ashni's resting on her back, on top of and across the *Golden Feather*. For a moment, they stared at each other and then stepped back toward each other.

"You want to…" Adira pointed outside.

Ashni sighed. "It's not a tantrum."

"It's not the weather either."

"I know. Let's talk somewhere else." Ashni pulled Adira away before she could protest. They rushed through the hall and slipped into a secret room.

"Now, use your words. What in the hell happened?" Adira asked, putting a hand to her temple.

"I slept with the princess," Ashni whispered through gritted teeth.

Adira took a breath and squinted for a moment. "Uh…when you say 'the Princess' I'm scared that I find myself hoping you mean Layla."

Ashni lurched back as her face twisted. "Ew! No. What the hell? You actually think it would be better if I meant my sister rather than my hellcat?"

Adira massaged both her temples and examined the floor for a second. "Hell, yeah. Because at least then I wouldn't think you've lost your mind and ruined your cause. *Our* cause." She beat her breast with a single fist. "Not to mention, ruined a huge payday for your entire army. If anyone else did that, you'd already have them slathered in honey and perched out into the desert for the fire ants to devour."

Adira waved her arms in front of Ashni, as it would suddenly make Ashni a little smarter.

"I know," Ashni hissed back. Even though she had already thought of each issue listed, hearing Adira speak them aloud made Ashni feel even stupider. *By the Sun, what in the hell is wrong with me?*

Adira groaned. "I thought you'd control your obvious attraction to her and things wouldn't go this far."

Ashni arched an eyebrow. "Obvious attraction?" Since when?

Adira let out a little puff of breath. "Uh, yeah." Adira studied her for a moment and then Adira's face fell. "You're kidding, right? You seriously have no idea?"

Ashni gnashed her teeth as she glowered at Adira. "What the hell are you talking about?" *Maybe I should have left her sleeping. She's obviously still drunk.* "I thought you held your wine better."

"Seriously? You think I'm still drunk. You're still drunk if you've never noticed."

Frowning, Ashni folded her arms across her chest. "Noticed what?"

Adira turned her head to the ceiling for a second and then held up one finger. "First, her attitude is right up your alley." She held up another finger. "You gave her two nicknames moments after meeting her."

Ashni snorted. "To annoy her."

Another finger went up. "You made her your cupbearer, a position you never gave anyone before, and you bypassed several more worthy members of court for the position."

"Again, to annoy her."

Adira made a frustrated noise as she wiped her face with both hands. "You bring her with you everywhere when you don't need to."

"To annoy her!" Ashni flung her arms in the air. She thought this was the 'obvious' part of the whole situation. Everyone knew she liked to be annoying on purpose. *No, no, no. Adira is definitely still feeling the effects of her cups.*

"You take her with you when you spar with the Princess, undoubtedly wanting her to see how well cut and defined your stupid body is."

"I take her because I know she doesn't want to be there."

Adira sighed and pinched the bride of her nose. "You share your food with her."

"Well, I can't let her starve." *Obviously.*

"You cuddle with her while she plays chess against Amal."

"Does my staff just tell you everything? I don't 'cuddle' her. She just sits in front of me."

Adira stayed her course. "You've tutored her to beat Amal in chess."

"To get on his nerves." Anything to drive Amal out of the palace quicker was always a good thing. No one needed his special brand of entitled negativity around.

Adira pressed her hands together and held them to her mouth as she sighed. "Okay, you are in some powerful denial right now. Whatever. Why the hell did you sleep with this girl? Why the hell did she sleep with you? And why the hell are we arguing about it if you slept with each other? All parties involved should be in bed right now, cuddling, like I was doing and would like to get back to doing."

Ashni rubbed her face with her hands and her shoulders slumped. "We were drunk."

Adira laughed. "Yeah, last night was amazing. So much good wine."

"No, you idiot, we were drunk when it happened. She woke up this morning and…" Ashni drew her lips back, baring her teeth in disgust.

Adira squinted as she took this in and then she shook her head. "Wait, wait, wait. You slept with her even though she was drunk?"

"I was drunk, too."

Adira gave her a sour look. "You're kidding, right? We both know you being drunk is far from the same as her being drunk. You were sharing wine with her all night. It's a miracle she was still on her feet. Hell, it's a miracle she knew who she was. You know what happens to Naren when he shares wine with Layla and you expected Nakia to be able to make an informed, sound decision after sharing wine with you? You are not *that* stupid."

Ashni wanted to blow up at Adira, but she was right. Ashni should have known better and, had anyone else pulled this stunt, she would've had them dispatched already, drunk or not. Nakia was in no shape to understand what was happening last night, but Ashni wanted her so bad.

"You have to fix this," Adira said.

Adira was right. Ashni had to fix this. She needed to do something. *But, what*? Maybe she could talk to Nakia, explain to her what happened, let her know it wasn't some horrible, brutal act. Let her know it wasn't something the gods would punish them for—well, the Roshan gods anyway, and they were the only ones who mattered.

"I do…" Ashni breathed. *I need to set this right.*

Without a thought, she ran off. She needed to see Nakia now. She hurried to Nakia's door, but a servant stopped her before she could go any further. Ashni was about to fling the elderly woman out of her way, but then she remembered Min was following orders. She was taking care of Nakia.

"I need to talk to her," Ashni said. *So, get out of my way.*

"Highness, I don't think this is the right time," Min replied, not moving an inch. If Ashni wanted, she could toss the little, old woman out of the way, but she couldn't hurt this woman for doing her job. Besides, Ashni liked Min, as did Layla and Adira. She didn't need to give Adira another reason to chew her out.

Ashni looked past the servant, trying to see inside the room. "It wasn't what she thought. I would never…" She couldn't even speak the crime aloud.

Min shook her head. "I believe you, Highness, but you still can't come in. You need to give her time. Seeing her now will only make matters worse."

Ashni grunted. *Why did Min have to be there when this happened?* No other servant would dare stand in her way like this. "But, I could explain."

Min shook her head again. "Not now, Highness. She won't hear it and the sight of you will only make matters worse."

Ashni sighed and her shoulders slumped. If she forced her way in, forced Nakia to speak with her, it would only reinforce what Nakia believed happened. *Damn.* Not seeing Nakia now would be for the best, as Ashni had no idea what she would say beyond it wasn't what Nakia thought. Now, Ashni had time to think of a better speech. Something that didn't sound weak or like an excuse.

***

Nakia curled up into a tight ball in her bed, trying to hold onto herself as it felt like she might come apart at the seams. Her body trembled and shook. She had sobbed until her abdomen hurt and her throat was sore, matching the lower regions of her body. Breathing hard, she tried to do it as little as possible. She just clutched her covers to her and tried to remember how to breathe normally. Mostly, she coughed and panted. Her lungs burned with each rapid inhale and heavy exhale.

"Princess," one of the servants said.

Nakia curled up tighter at the sound of the voice. Her eyes darted around to find the servant, needing to know where everyone in the room was. She had dismissed many of the servants because she knew she wouldn't be able to keep track of them all and she had no desire to be taken by surprise by one of these savages again.

"You need to eat," the servant said.

Her stomach lurched at the thought of food. Acid burned her throat and mouth. Shaking her throbbing head, she refused the meal. The servant bowed slightly and left the tray by the bed. If it was breakfast time, that meant the Queen was on the throne, working, or possibly avoiding work. Or, maybe she was boasting about what she had done to Nakia, like the monster she was.

How could she? Nakia didn't understand why the Queen took advantage of her. She thought they had something. She wasn't sure what that something was. But, it had seemed that the Queen respected her, considered her something of a friend or companion. She attended the festival with the Queen and her friends, took part in their silly antics, and experienced little excitements with them. Now, it seemed to have been a ploy to hurt her worse than anyone had in her entire history. No one had ever been so cruel as to pretend to want her around only to violate her.

The thought pained her chest, burned her lungs, and brought fresh tears to her eyes. No one had ever wounded her like this. Shaking her head, she blamed this place. *I let my guard down. I was foolish.* At some point, she had lowered her walls. She shouldn't be surprised that a barbarian bastard invaded her so completely. And the worst part of it was that she couldn't do anything about it.

She couldn't physically fight the Queen. The Queen would tear her apart and pick her teeth with Nakia's bones. That was no way to die. The Queen would enjoy it and she didn't want to bring the Queen any joy ever again.

She couldn't tell her father and hope for him to avenge her. He didn't care. He never cared. She, like her sisters before her, was just a pawn for him to use in his schemes. So, she was here to keep the barbarians at bay until he came up with their gold. She was supposed to be safe here. He had promised. But, his word was as worthless as he was. *Cur.*

Plus, she couldn't begin to imagine her father's reaction if he found out she had lain with a woman, even if she was forced to do so. He'd call her soiled, as well as many other names that weren't fair. She would be of no use to him. He wouldn't be able to marry her off to some ally as he had done her sisters. She wasn't sure what would happen to her if he ever found out, but she feared the worst.

Thoughts of being sealed in a tomb occurred to her. She had heard so many horror stories of such a thing happening to fallen priestesses and other women expected to remain chaste, but who had gone against the law and the gods. Her heart felt as if it would explode and her throat seized, choking her. The Queen might very well be her death should anyone ever find out. Her stomach lurched and she gagged, dry heaving. There was nothing left in her stomach to vomit. She had thrown up until her stomach was dry when she first returned to her rooms. It hadn't helped. Nothing would help.

"Just like Father. There is no help. There never will be." She gulped.

She shook her head and decided to stop thinking about him. Her thoughts returned to her physical pain. Beyond the aching in her private area, she had a terrible headache. Her screaming, hyperventilating, and crying only made it worse. It felt like her head was ready to split open.

She screwed her eyes shut, and with tears raining down her face, she wished she were dead. Death would stop the world from caving in. Since everything was falling apart, maybe it would collapse on her, crush her, and free her from this Hell.

Chapter Eleven

NAKIA SHIVERED AS SHE remained curled up in her bed. She had every blanket available piled on her. Her body was soaked with sweat, but it made her feel safe. A dry sob escaped her. She'd run out of tears some time ago. There was a pitcher of water by her bed, but she ignored it.

Eventually, her exhaustion got the better of her. She fell asleep, but woke up soon after. Jumbled images bombarded her mind. Odd sounds echoed through her brain. Even stranger sensations crept through her body and suddenly she vomited.

"My Lady!" A servant rushed to her side.

Nakia could only groan. She wasn't sure what her dream was about, but she could guess from her body's immediate reaction. Her body remembered that night, even though her mind had no idea what happened.

"Please, allow me to clean you up," the servant said.

Nakia couldn't argue. Not just because she had no desire to lie in her own sick, but also because she was too weak to do much else. She allowed the servant to clean her face, but didn't move much. The servant had to figure out how to clean the bed with Nakia lying there. Nakia refused to move, couldn't move.

A couple of servants came over to help. Nakia didn't make a sound as they gathered her and her blankets up. They made sure not to touch her. The first servant changed the bedding and then Nakia was gently placed back on the bed. *Why is it that people don't always show me this type of care? Am I not worth it?* Life seemed to suggest she wasn't.

***

"So, did you talk to her?" Adira asked as she strolled into the throne room a couple of days after Ashni told her about possibly the biggest mistake of her life.

Adira was in a better mood, which made Ashni want to punch her in the face. But, Adira was there to help with administrative work. Unfortunately, Ashni would have to put up with her attitude, such as having the nerve to act like that was a legitimate question.

Ashni glowered at Adira. Adira knew damn well Nakia didn't want to see her. No matter how many times she went to see the princess, she was always turned away. She knew better than to force her way in, as that definitely wouldn't help her argument of 'it wasn't what you thought it was' with Nakia. Nakia would only see her using brute force to get what she wanted. Still, if she couldn't get in there, then she couldn't tell Nakia it wasn't what she thought it was and explain what happened and it was driving her insane.

Ashni wasn't entirely sure what happened. Not in the sense that she didn't remember, despite how drunk she was. She wasn't quite sure *why* it happened. Yes, Nakia was adorable; a blind man could see that. But, that shouldn't have been enough to make Ashni lose her mind like she had. *What the hell was I thinking?* She doubted she'd ever be able to answer that question.

She'd been asking herself that question ever since Nakia refused to see her the first day. She got stuck on it as she tried to figure out what she'd say to Nakia when she got the chance to speak to her. But, she had no answers. She also hadn't come up with a speech to make everything right. *Do such words even exist?* The more time went by, the more she was certain there were no words. The whole situation was completely messed up and she had no one to blame but herself. It was tempting to try to blame Nakia, but Adira wouldn't allow her that escape.

Ashni thought working would distract her, but she had no idea what most of the paperwork in front of her was. Officials came and went, leaving Ashni with no idea what they discussed. Beyond the issues with Nakia and her own questions, Adira's words had been haunting her. Adira seemed to think she cared for the foreign princess. The very idea made her suck her teeth. *When did Adira get so damned stupid?*

While she was certain she had done everything Adira mentioned to irk Nakia, she was bothered by the gross misinterpretation by one of the people closest to her. If Adira, who knew her well, was dumb enough to think she felt something for Nakia, who else had come to the same conclusion? That stupid, possibly dangerous, conclusion.

She put the thoughts aside as Adira approached her worktable. Adira shook her head, undoubtedly because of the mess. Adira focused on the document right in front of Ashni. She took the document and looked it over. Ashni watched her read it, wondering what the hell it was.

"Okay, I have a solution that might work, so you can at least get your mind back in the right place before you decide to stop feeding the war horses," Adira said, waving the document around.

"Huh?" Was she really about to stop feeding their finest steeds?

"You haven't written anything on this, but did you even know it was about the horses?" Adira asked with a raised eyebrow.

Ashni sighed. *I am more distracted than I thought.* "What's your idea?"

"She's not going to talk to you because she's hurt and scared and she blames you. She's scared of you, maybe for what she thinks happened or maybe for something else. Still, first, she has to heal a little before she's ready to face you. Agreed?"

Ashni nodded. "That makes sense."

"So, we ask Bashira to talk to her."

Ashni blinked and then brightened. That was brilliant. There was no person on the planet who could resist Bashira. Bashira would be able to convince Nakia to get out of bed and listen to reason. She should have thought of that.

"Hey, stop smiling like that. This isn't for you. This is for the kingdom, your father's dreams, and our *own* empire," Adira said.

Ashni rolled her eyes. "I never said this was for me. Will Bashira go for it?" *Wait, that was a stupid question.* And further proof that she was allowing this thing with Nakia to drive her crazy.

"Of course she will. We'll have to explain the situation—"

Ashni balked at that suggestion. "We're not telling her what happened." It was bad enough that Adira and a dozen servants knew.

Adira rubbed her temples with her thumb and forefinger. "We explain as much of the situation to her as you allow and she'll make sure Nakia is returned to her father as normal as possible, so we get our gold and continue the conquest of the West."

Sighing, Ashni's shoulders slumped. "I get it!" She snorted. She had definitely screwed up and was aware Adira wouldn't let her live it down for years to come. At least Layla didn't know or that would be a headache of a different kind. But, Layla was off tracking Majeed. *Of course, I deserve this and worse. What the hell was I thinking?* "Just make sure Bashira knows to keep this to herself."

With a scoff, Adira shook her head. "I'm pretty sure that goes without saying. It does us no good for everyone to know the Queen's an idiot."

Ashni glared at Adira. "You do know one day I won't need you anymore."

Adira snorted. "Oh, so you'll be doing your own paperwork?" She rolled her eye. "I don't think so. I'll summon Bashira. You pay attention to what you're actually doing. I'll proofread what you did before I showed up when I'm done."

"I don't need a babysitter."

"That remains to be seen."

Ashni hated to admit that might be true.

* * *

Nakia was still curled in a ball on her bed. She had no idea what day it was or how long she had been there. She didn't know if the sun was out, as she had servants block her windows with heavy curtains. Light made every part of her feel raw and sound was no better. Everything tore through her like lion claws.

She couldn't even get peace in her dreams. She'd been sleeping only a few minutes at a time thanks to flashes and glimpses of the worst day of her life. She couldn't figure out those pieces, but it was enough to keep her tucked into herself.

A heavy knock on her door ripped through her and she whimpered while managing to fold in tighter. The servants would send whoever it was away. At least there were some people in this gods-awful place that she could rely on to a degree.

"Oh, my." A voice squeaked. The stupid servants hadn't sent whoever this was away. *No one in this stupid territory is worth anything.* Thankfully, it didn't sound like the Queen, but Nakia had no desire to talk with anyone.

"Go away," Nakia grumbled, hiding her face in her pillow.

"I should like to as I see you're in no state for company, but I don't think that would be the most prudent idea," the voice, female and happy, said. It had an irksome chirp, sounding much too pleased with itself.

Nakia groaned and hid deeper beneath her blankets. She didn't want to have anything to do with these barbarians. Hopefully, looking at her as a lump in the bed would get through to her unwanted guest. Unfortunately, the sound of things moving around the room suggested otherwise. *Stupid savage*. The damned barbarian made things worse by opening her curtains and letting the light in. She hissed, wishing the sound would drive away the sun.

"The sun is good for you. I know you're going through a rough time right now, but the sun heals," the voice explained.

Nakia grumbled deep in her throat. *What does this girl know of my 'rough time'?* She hadn't told anyone what happened. She had made sure the servants knew she didn't want to see anyone, especially the Queen. She was surprised the order stood, until this newcomer anyway. *Who is she and what does she know?*

Nakia lowered her cover just enough to see the room. The light stung her eyes briefly and spots danced before her eyes. She squinted, trying to find whoever was in her room. A blond blur ordered the servants around with dramatic arm movements as she zipped between them. Then, she turned to Nakia and smiled brightly, looking like the sun itself, lighting up the room. That alone made Nakia decide to hate her. *What the hell is she so happy about?*

It wasn't fair for anyone to be happy considering how she felt. It wasn't fair that the world went on while she felt like her world collapsed in on itself. She frowned at the girl, who didn't seem to notice if her continued smiling meant anything.

"Oh, you're awake. I thought you fell back to sleep. It's good you're awake. I sent out for food. I think some food will do you well. Nothing heavy, mind you. Just something to help perk you up and help you get out of bed," the blond said.

Nakia narrowed her gaze and scowled harder at the intruder. "Go away."

"I can't fathom doing such a thing," the blond replied, still smiling. She threw her hands up and waved her fingers, as if the gesture meant something. Maybe it did in this barbarian society. "You need to get out of bed, talk to someone, and experience life. Giving up and giving in never gained anyone anything, except bedsores. So, when the food comes, you should try to eat some and then I'll have the servants draw you a bath. I'm sure your body will appreciate it and a bath tends to pick up many spirits."

Nakia's lip curled in hatred for all those things. It seemed like this pest knew what happened to her. *Was the Queen boasting about what she had done? Demon.*

"Go away," Nakia commanded and seized a pillow. She flung it with all her might, which wasn't much. The pillow sailed slow and fell flat with a dull thud, hardly escaping the bed's edge. *That pillow might as well be me*. She tried to shake the thought away. She wouldn't let these barbarians defeat her.

"I'm sure you'll be able to do more once you eat and regain some strength. Then, you can throw all the pillows you want at me," the blond chirped. She was too happy.

Nakia wanted to plant an axe in her forehead. *I probably couldn't hold an axe up right now*. Considering her failure with the pillow, she doubted she could do anything. Of course, she could always go with her first line of defense. There had to be something she could say to get this invader out of her rooms.

Before Nakia could snap, a tray of food was placed in front of her. Her stomach grumbled at the sight. She hadn't eaten since she crawled into bed, so maybe food was necessary. It took an effort to lift her hand and plenty of concentration to keep her hand up long enough to grab some fruit. She steered clear of anything sweet, preferring sour berries, white grapes, several different types of nuts, and diced cheese. A few crackers helped and her body began to feel better. Before she knew it, the tray was empty of everything but the sweet fruits.

"Do you want anything heavier? I wasn't sure if your stomach would be able to handle it since the servants said you hadn't eaten in a few days," the blond said.

Nakia blinked, having forgotten the girl was there. Nakia didn't bother to answer. She still wanted this intruder gone, even if she had been right about the food. Nakia didn't feel like seeing anyone.

"I've had a bath drawn for you. I'm sure your body will like that as much as you liked the meal," the intruder said. She motioned in the direction of Nakia's private bathing room.

Nakia was about to object, but the girl had been right about the food. Maybe she should get out of bed and have a bath. Maybe it would help her feel better, even if it didn't erase the dirty feeling that clung to her like it was under her skin. She needed to be able to function. She refused to let the Queen win, let these damned people win.

The intruder smiled softly at her and Nakia sighed. Clutching a blanket, she got up and slowly made her way to her bathing room. The intruder followed her, but stopped at the sheer curtain that closed off the room from the others. The girl sat on a short stool that was usually occupied by a servant.

"I figure you don't want company right now."

That was true, but the girl shouldn't have assumed that. Having servants bathe her shouldn't bother Nakia and no one would ever think it was something that should bother her. *What did that monster say to her? Why is she here?* It seemed like the intruder knew what happened, but it didn't seem like she approved of it. Nakia wasn't sure what to think and was too exhausted to piece it together.

Nakia went into the bathroom and found it empty. Maybe the intruder sent away the servants who were usually there, making her truly alone. She was happy for that. She shrugged off her blanket and entered the water. The bath was hot, scented with oils, with flowers floating on the surface. Sighing, she eased her way into the tub, all the while watching the entrance to the room. She leaned against the wall and sighed again.

She didn't fully relax, but there was a little weight lifted off her as she settled into the fragrant, steaming water. The quiet helped. This quiet was different than the silence of her bedroom. It wasn't crushing or hopeless. The bath was slightly invigorating. Maybe, eventually, she would feel better.

"So, who are you? A servant?" Nakia spoke loud enough for the intruder to hear.

There was a light, airy chuckle. "A servant? Aren't we all?"

"No." She was a princess and she would never forget that. She wouldn't ever let anyone else forget either. "Did the Queen send you?" *What game is she playing?*

The girl made a low humming noise. "Yes, in a way, I suppose."

Nakia growled. This was some sort of trick, just as she suspected. Well, she wouldn't stand for it and she wouldn't fall for it. "What did she tell you? Did she brag about what she did to me? Told you to come and try?" The water sloshed loudly as she stood up to find a weapon.

"Nothing of the sort. I have no idea what happened between you two. I was only asked to come to make sure you're all right. The Queen didn't ask me to come."

Nakia clutched a ceramic jar with oil inside of it. She'd smash the blond in the face with it should she try to come in the room. "Then why the hell are you here?" Her voice was harsh and echoed off the tiled walls.

"To make sure you're all right. The Queen doesn't want you to suffer, but that's neither here nor there. I'm here for you, to make sure you don't allow your melancholy to overrun your life."

"Maybe I have a reason for why I am the way I am."

There was a little chortle. "Don't we all? Oh, I'm Bashira."

151

"So?" Nakia didn't care for this exchange, didn't trust this girl. *I'll never trust any of these animals.*

Another laugh. "It does you no good to stay cooped up in your rooms. I understand you're angry with the Queen—"

"Angry with the Queen?" Nakia roared, slapping hard against the jar she clutched. Angry didn't begin to cover it. If she could, she'd slit the Queen's throat with one of her damned wine cups and drink her blood from the goblet.

"It's your business. My concern is making sure you don't let your sorrow consume you."

"What do you care?" Nakia snapped as she sat back down in the water. She held onto the bottle, just in case Bashira decided to come in.

"I know what it's like to be in pain and I don't think anyone deserves that. I also know what it's like to be alone in this big wide world and no one should feel like that. Lastly, I know what it feels like to be lost in this world."

Nakia sniffed. "I'm not alone in the world and I'm not lost." Of course, that was a lie. No one on the planet cared about her. Her father had sold her, for crying out loud. She didn't fit in anywhere, didn't know how to fit in. For a moment, she dared to think of herself as part of the Queen's circle only to be proven wrong.

"No, I don't suppose you are," Bashira agreed. "But, I could use a friend." It was easy to tell she smiled while she spoke.

"Maybe I don't want to be your friend." But, her stomach flipped as the words left her mouth. *I've never had a friend and I've been fine. I'll keep being fine. It's not like I can trust this damned barbarian anyway.*

"I suppose. If you find you don't want me around, then I can easily leave. Tell me if that's your true desire."

Nakia didn't respond. She wasn't sure what she wanted. Being alone hadn't helped her feel better. In fact, it had made her feel worse, like she was worthless and shouldn't be alive. For a while, she felt like she wasn't alive. Bashira changed all of that in a few short minutes after barging in.

"If you don't mind my being around, perhaps after your bath we could spend some time together. It might do us both some good. You can come to your decision after getting to know me a bit."

Nakia still didn't respond. She wondered if Bashira would leave if she ignored her. Her heart sped up and hurt a little at the thought. She didn't hear any movement from the other room, so Bashira was probably still there. Sighing, she settled into the water once more and tried to relax. While she didn't know what Bashira wanted, she didn't seem to be there for nefarious purposes. So, Nakia tried to enjoy her bath.

It was impossible to take pleasure in the bath. Her body felt gross, dirty in many ways. Sitting in a pool of her own grime wasn't good, despite the way the water was treated. She should have washed before getting into the water, but it was too late to regret that. Besides, she wasn't ready to show her body to anyone, even a slave. *Perhaps I'll start washing myself.*

She had never washed herself. It didn't seem overly complicated. Surely she could manage it on her own. *I can manage things on my own.* She wasn't useless or incompetent, after all.

"Whenever you wish to get out, you should know I had a servant lay clothes out for you in the corner," Bashira said.

Nakia made a noise to acknowledge she heard Bashira. She looked around the room until she spotted the folded bundle in the corner closest to her. Now would be as good a time as any to get out and get dressed. She wasn't enjoying the bath anyway.

She toweled off with a nearby cloth and then inspected the clothing left behind. The clothing was of the Roshan style. She screamed as she flung them into the bath.

"Is everything all right in there?" Bashira asked.

"Everything's fine." Nakia tried to hold in a sob, but wasn't very successful.

"You sure? Should I come in?"

"No!" Another sob. Nakia wrapped her arms around herself, fell to her knees and began crying again.

"Are you sure I shouldn't come in?"

"Don't." Nakia held herself and tried to stop crying. She was so much stronger than this. She wouldn't let these savages break her. Nothing could break her. *You're fine, you're all right. Get up, carry on, and don't stop.*

She took a deep breath and put her hand over mouth to muffle her cries until she finally stopped. She held herself with her other arm, feeling like she needed to hold herself together. Eventually, she cried herself out. She pulled herself to her feet and put on a robe. She'd find her own clothing, from her own kingdom. *I can do this. I can take care of myself.* She wouldn't let these barbarians change her, mold her, or ruin her.

Marching into the other room, she walked past Bashira without acknowledging her. Bashira didn't say anything. Nakia had to look for a while before she discovered where her clothing was. Dressing without a servant or two was difficult, but she managed. Once she was in her own clothes, she took another deep breath and then returned to Bashira, who was still sitting on the stool by the bathing room. Bashira looked up at her and smiled again. *Why the hell is her smile so brilliant?*

"You said something about spending time together?" Nakia folded her arms across her chest. It would make for a good distraction until she could get herself together.

"I did, indeed. I was thinking a board game," Bashira replied.

"No chess." She would never play chess again. She had no business playing chess in the first place. She was a fool for trying.

Bashira clapped. "Very good, as I have no idea how to play."

Nakia made a noise. "I thought it was popular here." *This is a strange barbarian.*

"It is. I was never very interested. My aunt has tried many times to show me how to play, but I never took to it. There are other games. We'll find one you like."

Nakia nodded. If they found a good one, it might help take her mind off of things and help her keep it together for a few days. As they went into one of the sitting rooms, the servants rushed out.

"Wait! Bring food and games," Bashira shouted to the fleeing slaves. Giggling a little, she made herself comfortable on one of the giant pillows. Nakia had an urge to tear the pillows apart, but she resisted.

Nakia wondered why the servants obeyed Bashira. Why had they let Bashira in? Surely she had some connection to the Queen.

"So many games," Bashira said as a stack of them was placed beside her.

The servants also brought small trays of food to her and Nakia. The servants then escaped once more. Nakia kept her attention on Bashira.

"This was my favorite as a child. I'll explain the rules to you and we'll see if you like it as well," Bashira said as she plucked a game from the bottom of the pile.

Nakia didn't respond. She listened to Bashira and watched her work. Bashira went on and on as she set up the rectangular game board and the pegs. Nakia didn't pay much attention as Bashira explained how to play. She was too busy trying to figure out what Bashira was up to.

"So, who are you really? Why are you here?" Nakia asked. *Why was Bashira here if the Queen didn't send her, and why does Bashira care?*

It's not like we knew each other. She couldn't recall seeing Bashira around the palace before today.

"I'm here to help. I understand you're suspicious and all, but if you give me a chance, you'll see I'm not a spy or anything. I just want to help you."

Nakia narrowed her gaze, trying to determine if she was lying. "Did the Queen tell you what happened?"

Bashira shook her head. "I have no idea what happened to you. I just know you don't want to see her and you're handling a trauma of some kind."

"Did the servants tell you that?"

"No." Bashira sighed and then stared Nakia in the eye. "I honestly don't know what happened. I just know you're upset with the Queen and I've been told you could use a friend, nothing beyond that."

Nakia studied Bashira more. She didn't seem to be lying, but it was quite possible that a barbarian would look her in the face and lie to her. She'd be careful, but for the moment, she'd use Bashira to help her forget what happened and try to figure out what to do next.

"So, what are the rules again?" Nakia asked, eyes on the board. She didn't understand what she was looking at. The board was wooden with twenty-four cups carved into it. There were twelve cups facing her and twelve facing Bashira. In the cups, were colored rocks.

Bashira grinned and clapped. "I'm so glad you asked."

Chapter Twelve

"SO...UM...HAS BASHIRA said anything about the hellcat and how she's doing?" Ashni asked. She and Adira were sparring in one of the quieter gardens. They'd have to wrap it up soon. So many things required their attention, but Ashni needed to relax and it must have been obvious as sparring was Adira's idea.

"She hasn't and you know she won't." Adira lunged at Ashni with her sword. Most warriors practiced with wooden weapons, but she, Ashni, and Layla had ceased that nonsense years ago. If one of them lacked the control over their blades not to kill the other or if the other was too stupid or slow to avoid being killed, it was their own fault.

Ashni sucked her teeth as she slipped by the sword. "Okay, true, but is the hellcat okay?"

Adira snorted as she avoided a sweep kick. "I think she'd be more okay had a certain monarch kept her tongue to herself."

"I didn't get any complaints at the time."

"Yes, well, time marches forward and if she didn't eventually have complaints against you, she'd be a very lonely soul indeed. I'm sure she'd agree with me when I say someone here needs to learn self-control."

Grunting, Ashni glowered at Adira, but her mind flashed back to her night with Nakia. She had plenty of control then. She recalled the wonderful sounds she drew from Nakia and how sweet she was on her tongue. Her aroma alone haunted Ashni even now. *I want more.* A long, low breath escaped her.

"Ow!" Ashni hissed as she jumped back. Glancing down at her bicep, she noticed the light scratch.

"If you're going to get lost in your fuck up, what am I even here for?" Adira asked with a deadpan expression.

Ashni gnashed her teeth at Adira. "To Hell with you. I wasn't getting lost in anything."

"Oh, please. I could've cut your head off just a second ago. I know you're lost in thought about whatever the hell happened that night. Stop thinking about it. The girl probably thinks you're the evilest of creatures and it won't ever happen again."

Ashni frowned. Adira was right. Nakia thought she violated her. There had to be some way for her to get Nakia to understand she'd never do something like that. Hell, she didn't allow her soldiers to rape anyone during war and may the gods have mercy on them if any of them disobeyed her.

"I know." Ashni sighed, shoulders dropping slightly. The fact that it wouldn't happen again stung as much as Nakia thinking she was some vile fiend.

"Why the hell do you even care what she thinks?"

"Well, for one, I don't want her father to think we didn't uphold our end of the bargain. My word is my word and I shall never break it. I promised to treat her as a guest of the Empire. She thinks I have done otherwise."

"Uh...you did."

Ashni hissed. "I did not." *In fact, I treated her better than a guest. Doesn't she know how many women—people really—would love to sleep with me?*

Adira gave her a hard look, as if she knew exactly what was going through Ashni's mind. "She was drunk. She never would've stayed with you if she wasn't drunk."

Carelessly waving her sword, Ashni sniffed. "From the wine comes the truth."

With a smirk, Adira's eyebrow ticked up. "For her or you?"

Ashni snarled. There was a thunderclap and she punched Adira on the jaw. Adira stumbled back, but didn't fall. One dark eye glared at her. *She's lucky she didn't get a lightning bolt in the ass.*

"Maybe now you know how she feels. You can't take the truth and neither can she."

"You don't know what the hell you're talking about. I'll talk to Bashira myself and find out if she's gotten through to Nakia. I'm not going to be the one who costs us that much gold."

Adira chuckled. "So, this is all about your father's dream?"

"Of course." *What the hell else would this be about? We need to be able to pay our soldiers and we need that gold to do so.*

"You weren't thinking about his dream when you were between her legs, were you?"

Ashni screamed at the top of her lungs. Lightning flashed, striking a tree nearby and thunder echoed through the sky. Ashni stormed off, certain she could hear Adira cackling as she left.

Ashni had no idea where she was headed. She felt like she could go off in every direction. She wanted to lay waste to everything with her lightning, but knew that wouldn't help matters. *Damn Adira!*

By chance, as far as she was concerned, Ashni ended up at the temple of Khurshid, the Great Eagle. It had been over a half year since she was there. The realization stopped her in her tracks.

"No wonder I have lost their favor," she muttered, taking in the tall statue of the Sun god. The statue was made of gold with ivory wings spread from the god's shoulders. He held a spear in one hand and a tablet in the other. "I built you a grand temple, my Lord, but I have neglected my prayers and offerings." She made her way to the foot of the statue to light incense in the god's honor.

"Highness, would you like to consult the god through me?" Kal, one of the temple priests, offered. He had to dodge a few people who were praying to the god.

Ashni turned and smiled a little. "No, Kal. I would save that for my campaigns. No sense in bothering the god with my everyday problems."

Kal smiled back. "Your problems are as grand as the gods, my Lady. Are you not their child? Are you not the Chosen One?"

"I am, but even my father had problems that had nothing to do with his destiny."

Kal shook his head. "Would not everything placed in his path have to do with his destiny? Perhaps you should consult with your father. You do not need me for that and it has been a while."

Ashni nodded. "I haven't prayed to him like this since you blessed our campaign to the West. It eased my troops' nerves to know Khurshid had given his consent." Usually, she would dedicate more time to the gods and their temples, but she had been distracted.

"Perhaps the Great Eagle has good news for you now."

"No, I'd rather see my father."

Kal didn't hold her and she walked to a smaller room in the temple. She had built the little niche in the temple for her father. He was supposedly the son of the Sun god, so she figured Khurshid wouldn't mind sharing the temple with her father. There were people in the room, but they rushed out when Ashni stepped in. Everyone knew she preferred to speak to her father alone.

The Great Amir's statue was not as impressive as Khurshid. It stood seven feet tall, decked out in full battle armor made of gold and gems. Ashni wasted no time lighting incense. She kneeled before the statue and pressed her hands together in prayer.

"Father, your dreams have always been my dreams. I will not stray from the path you set for me. I will not be distracted," she vowed. Even as she spoke those words, she felt there was something amiss with them. She didn't feel like she lied, but there was something more. "Adira's wrong. I wouldn't do anything to put this in danger. You didn't stop. You weren't distracted. I won't be either. Watch over me, Dad. I will bring us fame and glory throughout the world. Also, if you could get rid of Amal, it might help."

Amal had made himself scarce for a few days after the Festival of the Moon. Despite everything going on with Nakia, Ashni noticed that her brother didn't need her attention. She couldn't wait for him to leave.

"So much to do," Ashni sighed. "Dad, stay with me. I'll work through this."

***

Nakia examined the game board, trying to figure out her next move. She had played over a dozen games with Bashira over the past few days. Some were better than others. Bashira was a good teacher and Nakia had beaten Bashira at some of the games.

"What if we went out?" Bashira said.

"Out?" Nakia put her hand on one piece, then changed her mind. Thankfully, this was nothing like chess and she didn't have to move the game piece.

"Yeah. Instead of us hanging out in here and not really talking about anything, what if we went shopping and didn't really talk about anything?"

Nakia blinked and looked up. "Shopping?"

"I'm sure we can find some things that interest you. Not to mention, I could use costume material anyway."

Nakia arched an eyebrow. "Costume material?"

Bashira blushed. "Never mind."

"Uh-oh. Someone has a secret. Spill." Nakia found herself genuinely curious. She couldn't remember a time she had been interested in another person's activities, beyond spying on her father and his noblemen. Of course, that was more curiosity as to what happened in the men's sphere than her caring about a particular person.

Bashira giggled. "It's not really a secret." Yet, she still blushed.

"Then you'll have no problem telling me." Nakia was able to get Bashira to do a lot of talking over their time together. Well, not really 'getting' as Bashira was a talker, but if Nakia pressed on any issue Bashira was shy about, she could get answers from her. Nakia wasn't nearly as forthcoming, but Bashira didn't seem to mind, never pressing her for information.

Bashira looked away and grimaced. She rubbed her hands together for a second. "Uh...well...I'm kinda part of this dance troop." She tried to shrug like it wasn't a big deal, but she didn't look at Nakia.

"Dance?" Nakia couldn't believe her ears. While she wasn't quite sure of Bashira's association with the Queen, she knew the blond was a noblewoman. *They can't really be so backwards that Bashira being a dancer is fine, can they?* "How can someone of your status be in a dance troop?"

Bashira shrugged. "I just am. I don't tell people and it's not like everyone in the city knows I'm a noble. It's not like I'm the Queen or her sister or something. Well, no, I suppose Layla wouldn't count." She looked up, as if she needed to think about it.

"The Queen's sister is a dancer?" Nakia was surprised, but she felt she shouldn't be. Layla was a little savage.

Groaning, Bashira rubbed her face. "I shouldn't have said that. But, yes, she dances sometimes. She likes to practice to keep her flexibility."

"I'm sure there are other ways for her to do that. She'd never be allowed to dance where I'm from."

Bashira chuckled. "You've met Layla. You should know it's hard to stop her when she's got something in mind. I get the feeling you're like that, too." She smiled.

Nakia shook her head. "So, a dancer?"

Bashira beamed, shining brighter than ever. "I honestly thought you might do something like that, too."

Nakia's brow wrinkled. "Thought I would do something like that? Why would you think that?"

There was yet another shrug and then Bashira stood up. "You're built like me." She motioned to her body with a sweep of her hand and then sat back down. "It's not exactly a warrior body, but it's definitely athletic."

Now that Bashira mentioned it, Nakia noticed it was true. Her body type was similar to Bashira's, and many other barbarians, now that she thought about it. She had always been considered thin at home. She had taken some lessons on balance and poise further than they usually went. She was agile and flexible, able to do tumbles and twists. It used to entertain her during the lonely days at home. It kept her toned in a way other people at home weren't, but seemed to be around here.

"Anyway. We should go shopping. You could help me pick out fabric for my costume if nothing else."

"I'm not sure. I don't have money." Nakia had never purchased anything in her life. She made requests and then things appeared. "I've never been shopping."

"What?" Bashira jumped to her feet, staring at her with wide eyes. "Come on. The Queen will be your money."

Nakia squinted. "What do you mean?"

"I don't know what happened between you two, but I bet the Queen owes you and she likes you anyway, so you can spend her money."

Nakia blinked hard. *The Queen what?* She was certain she heard wrong or Bashira was out of her tiny, little chipper mind.

"The Queen likes me?" Nakia managed to say. *What the hell was Bashira talking about?*

"Of course she does."

Nakia narrowed her gaze at Bashira. "She doesn't. If she liked me, she wouldn't have..." Making a fist, she took a sharp breath and almost sobbed. She swallowed it down. If the Queen liked her, she never would have hurt her. The Queen was a beast and nothing would convince her otherwise.

"I don't know what happened between you, but I do believe the Queen likes you. I mean, she lets you get away with everything."

Nakia's face tensed as she twisted up her mouth a little. "Let's me get away with everything?" *Bashira has lost whatever little mind she had.*

"I heard you talk to her when you first arrived, and I know you've spoken to everyone else around here any way you please, without consequences. Do you honestly believe everyone can do that?"

Nakia opened her mouth to object again, but as she thought about it, she realized she had been allowed to talk to people any way she pleased. She had not thought about it before, but she had even told off the Queen's brother. The Queen wasn't fond of him, but she was fond of her sister and Nakia told Layla off almost every time they saw each other. But, what did any of that matter? She was a princess. She should be able to do what she wanted.

"The Queen takes you everywhere, too. She doesn't do that with anyone else, not even her sister and I know she enjoys Layla's company. I can only imagine how much she must like you."

Nakia swallowed around a lump forming in her throat and tears burned her eyes. "She doesn't..." If the Queen liked her, she never would have hurt her, never would have violated her in such a cruel manner. *I wish...*no, she refused to finish that thought.

Bashira sighed. "I don't want to upset you. Let's go shopping. You don't have to think about it."

"I don't care about the Queen," Nakia said, holding her chin up. She didn't care about the idea of the Queen liking her, but her throat burned all the same. Her heart beat a little faster, too, but she was certain that was due to outrage over the Queen.

Bashira smiled a little. "Okay. Then, let's just forget about it and go shopping, okay?"

Nakia nodded. She'd like to see what shopping was all about and she didn't want to think about the Queen in any way, shape, or form. She didn't want to think about how she felt about the Queen liking her either.

***

Ashni sent Adira about her business with instructions to watch Amal, as he was too occupied lately, and returned to the throne room. She planned to work, but couldn't focus on anything yet again. *Come on, just do what you're supposed to do.* That little bit of coaching was useless and she sighed. Her concentration was shot. *You promised Dad you wouldn't be distracted. You promised.*

After about an hour of trying to be productive, she found herself marching to Nakia's rooms. She would speak to Nakia and explain to her what the hell happened. It wasn't that serious and she was sick of acting like it was. She was sick of being treated like she'd done something wrong. She wasn't a monster and Nakia wasn't a victim.

"Time to put an end to this crap," she muttered as she walked. She couldn't believe a little hellcat like Nakia was still locked in her rooms. She understood Nakia was traumatized, but she assumed Nakia would eat that and spit it out. She should have come out by now, wreaking havoc where she went, just like before. "Hiding doesn't suit her."

Doesn't suit her or suit your image of her? Ashni shook the thought

163

away. She didn't need things like that in her head right now. Pounding on the door, she didn't care if she knocked the damned thing down. She was about to kick the door in when Min appeared. Ashni snarled, already determined not to be told she couldn't go in. When Min stood in her way, she wasn't sure if determination would be enough. *No, to Hell with this. I'm Queen. They do what I say.*

Min bowed her head. "My Queen."

"Where's the little hellcat?" Ashni pushed her way past the servant into the front room. There wasn't much to see, but there was even less to hear. There was no noise aside from the shuffling of the servants as they tidied the place.

"She's gone out, Highness," Min said.

Ashni turned back to her. "Gone out? So, she got out of bed?" *Okay, so she's alive and kicking, just avoiding me entirely, I guess.* The news should have made her feel better, but it didn't.

"A few days ago, after Lady Bashira arrived."

Ashni blinked, but nodded. So Bashira had done the trick. "How...how has she been?"

"She and Lady Bashira have become fast friends. If I might be forthright, Highness."

"You know I never stop anyone from being honest."

"I think Lady Bashira has done your guest more good than you know. I know she was sent here to comfort the Princess, but they seem to be genuine friends now. They laugh together and talk nonstop. One day soon, I'm sure I'll walk in here to find Lady Bashira asleep on a seat or something as wild because they enjoy each other's company so much. Could you imagine such a delicate noble like Lady Bashira asleep on one of the sitting pillows? I never would've imagined the Princess allowing someone in her presence so long."

Ashni frowned. She didn't want Bashira to get that close to her little hellcat. But, then, she knew there was nothing to fear. Bashira's taste lay exclusively in men. *Wait, what do I care who Bashira is attracted to? Or Nakia, for that matter. It didn't matter.* The good news was that Nakia was up and about. Maybe they could talk soon and get everything straightened out.

"I think she will see you soon, Highness." Min smiled. It was a knowing smile that made her eyes glimmer.

Ashni decided to ignore the expression. *Why does everyone think there's more to this than me caring about getting our gold?* "Good, then we can put this whole silly matter behind us." *And I can focus on actual important things*. She couldn't rely on Adira to run the government forever.

Still smiling, Min tilted her head a little. "I suppose, Highness. She misses you, you know."

"Misses me?" Ashni scoffed. She doubted that.

"Until Lady Bashira arrives, the Princess doesn't know what to do with herself. She wakes, dresses, then paces. She mutters constantly, wondering under her breath if she should just go to the throne room."

Ashni snorted and folded her arms across her chest. "Probably looking to confront me over imagined crimes."

Min frowned and wagged her finger at Ashni. "You should not belittle the Princess' pain, Highness. If you truly wish to put this behind you, you need to acknowledge that you hurt her, even if you didn't mean to do such a thing. Your accident doesn't invalidate her agony."

Ashni flinched. The old bag was right. It wasn't in Ashni's personality or status to admit fault. She was the Queen, damn it. She was the daughter of the Eagle's Son. She was partially a god herself, their ichor following through her veins, and she always saw signs of their favor. But, none of that mattered. She had wronged Nakia and everyone could see that.

"Let me know when it's safe to return."

"Of course, your Highness." Min bowed again.

Sighing, Ashni returned to her duties.

***

The marketplace was beyond amazing and Nakia enjoyed being there, despite the return of the heat and how dry the weather made her skin. There were so many people. Sights, sounds, and smells seemed to go on forever. Nakia doubted they would be able to see the whole place before sunset, but Bashira wasn't interested in the whole place.

"The marketplace is sectioned off by item. It makes it easy to shop and it also makes sure perfumes aren't next to pets or a butcher or something else that would smell really bad," Bashira explained as they walked past stores and booths with all types of clothing.

Nakia noticed how much she stood out in her clothes, but what she noticed more was how colorful Roshan clothing was without any designs on it. The Queen and those around her wore many colors, but seeing the full spectrum of colors and the fact that not everyone wore those ridiculous pants caught her eye. There were brightly colored dresses and beautiful gems. She wanted bangles like the Queen. She enjoyed the way they rang out as the Queen moved and how they announced her whenever she entered a room.

"Is there anything in particular you want?" Bashira asked.

"Well..." Nakia looked around and started buying new outfits. Bashira was right there with her, going through a multitude of fabrics and colors.

Nakia learned several things during the trip, mostly about Eastern fashion and the marketplace. The most important thing she learned was that living in the palace made delivery easy, which she should've known from her own home, but realized here. Whatever she wanted would be sent to the palace and the Queen would get the bill. She hoped she made a considerable dent in the gold she was being held for.

No one questioned Nakia, probably because Bashira was with her. Some of the shop owners knew Bashira, but others didn't. She would talk to them for a while and they would agree to send their purchases to the palace. Nakia wanted to learn that trick.

"We should get back," Bashira said as the sun started to sink below the horizon.

Nakia nodded and they began the long walk back to the palace. She didn't mind the walk, even though she had never walked so much at home. Here, everyone walked or rode horses. The only person she had seen carried by others was Amal.

"Hey, wait a moment," Nakia said as they walked past a puppet show. There was something familiar about it.

Bashira paused. "You want to hear the story of how the Queen's parents met?"

"Is that what this is?" That explained why the Queen and Layla screamed the whole time. They must have thought the story was inaccurate, even though she knew the Queen held her father in high esteem.

"Yes."

"Is the story untrue?"

Bashira listened to the puppets for a moment. "Sounds accurate. You won't find many people willing to lie about that. It was an epic love story, after all."

Nakia arched an eyebrow. "Epic love story?" She doubted anything these barbarians did could be an epic love story.

"I can tell you on the way," Bashira offered, glancing up at the sky.

"Please."

Bashira nodded and they set off again. "So, I know the popular version of the story. It's probably the most famous story in the whole empire. The Queen always heckles whoever tells it when she's around, but I think she's teasing more than anything. The Empress has never disputed the tale."

"So, what happened?"

"It's said that the Great Amir Khalid, son of the Great Eagle, met his wife Chandra in the wilds of the frontier north. He sought to extend the Empire to the mountains and rode in with his whole army. He was still a boy, really, roughly seventeen summers old. But he had already conquered enough for the Roshan kingdom to be called an empire."

"Wait, so he conquered everything?"

"Well, his grandfather united the Roshan tribes of the eastern plains and started the conquest. Amir Khalid carried on when he was old enough. Now, do you want to hear the story or not?"

Nakia grimaced. "Hey, I have questions. This is the first time I've heard the story, after all."

"True enough, but let me get through the story and then you can ask what you want, okay?"

"Okay."

"Now, where was I? Oh, right..."

Amir Khalid Akshay was upon his mighty steed, his cape bellowing behind him, as he marched up a grassy hill, his mind set on the village below. The plan was to bend this valley to his will and add it to his father's kingdom. The mountains surrounding the area, the protection for these people, seemed so far away, as if the mountains left this space open just for him. And then, someone stood in his way, literally. At the top of the hill stood a willowy girl, Chandra. She wasn't any older than he was. She was dressed simply and didn't seem like much of anything, yet there she stood as if mountains moved from her path.

"What is your business here?" Chandra demanded of him. She stared at him as if she could stop the gods themselves. He stared back.

The most fearsome men of the Roshan Kingdom were at the Amir's back while Chandra's villagers stood behind her. No one moved. No one blinked. No one even dared breathe too loud. The tension reached the sky and parted the clouds. A rumble of thunder clapped and it clearly wasn't going to rain. The sky was charged, making hair stand on end.

Khalid and Chandra continued to watch one another, neither giving ground. Then, the impossible happened. The Amir blinked.

"Who are you?" Khalid asked, his voice low, as if she awed him.

Chandra regarded him with a tilt of her head, before turning away, flipping her long, flowing ebony hair as she did so. Khalid watched her walk away, his golden eyes wide and his mouth agape. No one had ever turned their back to him before and lived.

A general rode up beside Khalid. "Highness, shall we raze this village to the ground for such insolence?"

Khalid shook his head. Urging his horse on, he chased after Chandra. She didn't turn around, but disappeared behind a cluster of huts. He scanned the area for her, but she was gone.

Growling, he hunted to find out who she was. He interrogated everyone he could, wanting to know everything about her. It wasn't hard. Chandra was the daughter of the village's chieftain. Khalid set up a meeting with him.

Khalid sat with the chief in his hut, but the chief did not speak. His wife did the talking. The Amir felt he was in the presence of one of the scariest women ever to live, but he had already blinked once. He'd never blink again.

"They tell me you're interested in the offspring of my flesh and the fire of the underworld," she said.

He arched an eyebrow. "The fire of the underworld?"

"My daughter, Chandra, is the daughter of the great fire god."

Khalid glanced at the chief, doubting this man was a god of any kind. None of the villagers spoke of the chief being a god, but they spoke of his wife being a demon. Seeing her pale skin, he could understand how she could be confused for a corpse destined for the underworld.

The villagers didn't speak of Chandra in the same way. They held her in high regard. They considered her a blessing, but felt her mother was a curse. Chandra kept their fields bountiful, healed the sick, and kept invaders at bay. But, they also whispered that they could see dark fire in Chandra when she was rubbed the wrong way. He was certain he saw that dark fire and wanted to know it intimately.

"You do know my daughter is the true bringer of death and destruction, unlike your title," she said.

Khalid chuckled. "You think my title is all talk, witch?" He was known by many names, including Son of the Great Eagle, the God of War, and best of all, the God of Death. He earned each and every title with his actions.

She snickered. "Witch? I see my people talk too much."

"Your people?" He glanced at the chieftain again, who said nothing.

Maybe she was a witch and had him under a spell. It didn't matter. The wife wasn't much of a concern for Khalid. He had only one desire at the moment. "I would like to marry your daughter."

She laughed again. "Marry my daughter? You, a lowly warrior, would marry the daughter of a god?"

He held his head high. "I am the son of a god, am I not? No one will ever be more worthy of her."

His claim silenced the witch for a moment. Khalid was well known for being the son of the Sun. It was said that he wasn't born of a human, but of the sky and the earth. Lightning struck a rock and he came from the stone. His father found him and claimed him as the prince of the Roshan kingdom. Khalid never told the tale, but he never disputed it either. Let others sort out the truth once he was dead.

No one knew what else was said in the conversation, as it never seemed important. What was important was the witch agreed to allow Khalid to marry Chandra. Khalid didn't raze the village, but Chandra almost did when she learned she was betrothed to the outsider. It was said she had to be held down by a dozen men during the marriage ceremony. Khalid almost didn't survive the wedding night.

Chandra went to her new spouse's tent armed with a dagger and tried to slit his throat. Khalid was no easy target. They ended up getting into a huge tussle, and not in the proper manner. The whole camp heard the struggle and the new couple had to be separated before one of them killed the other. In fact, they had to go to the surgeons for stitches and be treated for multiple bruises.

No one knew if Khalid and Chandra consummated their marriage by the time they returned to the capital of the Roshan kingdom. The King wasn't happy to greet his new daughter-in-law and it was believed it was the only time the King showed displeasure with his son. How dare the Crown Prince, the Great Amir, marry some lowly, savage northern hill woman? And, the King said as much to Khalid and Chandra.

Khalid didn't react, but Chandra moved as soon as the King finished speaking. She had a dagger to his throat before the King's guards could move. Khalid smirked while amusement danced in his eyes.

"How can I not love her, Sire? Not when we are so clearly cut from the same cloth," Khalid said.

"Son..." The King trailed off and swallowed hard. He glanced down at the hand threatening him.

"Sire, meet my one and only, my future Queen, Chandra Akshay. She is of our house now and you should treat her as the daughter she is,"

Khalid said.

The King nodded slowly. "Yes, of course. Greetings, my daughter."

Chandra eased the dagger from his throat and returned to Khalid's side. From that point on, they were always together. When Khalid rode off for the warring season, she was by his side and together they conquered. They made the army beyond unstoppable. Nothing halted their war machine—no wall, no body of water, no army—nothing could stop them. They shared everything. He gave her all his power, commands, and shared tactics with her. She gave him something even bigger.

It was through Chandra that the Amir learned how to govern. Before, he conquered and moved on. She was the one who made sure people knew they were now part of the Roshan. The people began the Roshan Empire and they were all Roshan.

By the time Khalid came to the throne, he was ready to be an emperor. He still preferred the title 'Amir,' and used it on the battlefield. But, at home, he was 'Emperor.' Chandra was his empress and he made sure that everyone understood she was him and he was she. They were the same, equal. Her word was his will.

People still gossiped about her. She and Khalid had been married for two years and Chandra hadn't given him a child. It wasn't from lack of trying by that time. They had come a long way from their wedding night. When they went on a campaign together, they spent every moment together, but Chandra never became with child.

There had always been talk that Chandra was a witch and she had enthralled Khalid, but now the talk was worse. Nobles and servants alike whispered that she had bewitched Khalid and the dark magic blinded him to the fact that she couldn't give him what he needed, namely an heir. Some nobles tried to convince him to take another spouse, which was well within his rights. As long as he could give the other spouses equal attention and care, he could have as many spouses as he wanted, just like any other citizen of the Empire. He exploded with rage and almost cut one man down for saying so.

Chandra heard the rumors and each of them felt like hot metal poking her flesh. There were times she thought Khalid should take another wife, someone to bear him the mighty children he deserved. She once sneaked off and returned to her mother. She asked her mother to read bones and entrails for her. She was promised children, children like she and Khalid, children to be feared, envied and loved, children of the gods. Chandra had to be patient.

Chandra returned to Khalid feeling secure in their legacy, beyond the growth of their empire. The rumors slid right off of her. But, it would take another year to prove her mother's reading correct. From the birth of their first son, Chandra made up for lost time. Khalid was overjoyed when Chandra gave birth to their first son, Jay for victory. Victory not only over those who wanted to see her reputation soiled and see her downfall, but also victory for the Empire as there was now a proper heir.

Chandra would bear Khalid six sons in total. In the middle of the six sons came their only daughter, Ashni. The sons were like their father, but Ashni was the perfect mix of both parents. Her parents loved her best of all.

Khalid loved his family with all his heart, but still went to war when the season arrived. Chandra stayed behind and managed their ever-growing empire. Khalid promised the world would one day be called Roshan and he took his children with him on campaigns once they reached their twelfth year. Some took to it better than others. Until the children could ride with their father, Chandra taught them how to govern. Again, some took to it better than others.

For twenty years, Khalid and Chandra were the most powerful couple on the planet. And, then, one day, just before he was to turn thirty-eight, Khalid went to rest by a river to escape a budget meeting. He lay down under a tree and never woke up. Chandra is said to still be in mourning to this day.

***

"That is a love story," Nakia said. She and Bashira were tucked away in her sitting room when Bashira ended the tale. There were snacks waiting for them, which they nibbled. Nakia still avoided anything sweet.

"It is pretty amazing. It's something many people now strive for in the Empire, but it's not easy to achieve. Such a powerful love only happens between the gods."

Nakia nodded. "And is this why the Queen wants to conquer the West? Because her father wanted the world to be under the Roshan Empire?"

Bashira nodded. "Yes."

This level of devotion to a parent surprised Nakia. Neither of her parents had ever inspired her to carry on their dreams, not now and not once they died. Her mother had already died. She wasn't sure she'd mourn her father beyond what was considered proper. How could she mourn someone she wasn't even sure saw her as a person? She had no idea what his dreams were and she had no desire to find out.

"How did the Queen...how did she take her father's death?" Nakia asked. *Why do I care?*

Bashira scratched her head. "She's trying to keep his legacy alive. There's always this feeling like she didn't have enough time with him. She was barely sixteen when he passed and she rode with him from the second she turned twelve until the moment he died. Some like to say she was the one who found him, which would make it hard. She was definitely there when his body was discovered. She joined his warrior order, the order of the Lion. Maybe the conquest makes her feel closer to him."

Nakia sighed and her heart thumped heavy in her chest. She wasn't sure why. Maybe she was envious. She had never had a relationship with her father because she was a girl. But, that hadn't mattered to Amir Khalid. It sounded like he loved his family, loved his daughter, and his daughter loved him.

"She's not completely heartless, you know?" Bashira said.

Nakia swallowed hard. "I don't care about her." But, for some reason, she wanted to know more about her, but she swallowed down any questions.

Chapter Thirteen

SIGHING, ASHNI SCRATCHED HER forehead and tried to focus on the reports in front of her. As usual, it was impossible. They all blurred together. Only one thing stayed on her mind—Nakia. She wanted to talk to Nakia and she wasn't sure when she'd get a chance. It was driving her out of her mind.

"Layla," Ashni said as her sister slid down next to her.

Layla sighed dramatically as she flipped over, so she was right side up. She fell onto the throne and tucked in close to Ashni. Ashni threw an arm around her.

"What do you have for me?" Ashni asked. Maybe what Layla found out would get her mind off Nakia, if only for a few minutes.

"Amal and Majeed are still palling around. Adira wanted me to tell you that she noticed Amal's men wandering around the market. One visited our dear friend, Hati."

Nodding, Ashni rubbed her chin. Hati was an apothecary she often hired to prepare medicines and poisons for her military campaigns. "My brother never ceases to amaze me. None of them really."

Layla shrugged. "They're all pretty stupid."

"I can't argue that with you, even though the twins are at least cute."

Layla curled her lip. "You mean the little twins, right?"

Ashni scoffed. "Well, definitely not Asad and Amal. Could you imagine?" She was certain those two had never been cute, even when they were babies. Her younger brothers, the other twins, were cute. She hoped they grew out of the stupidity that seemed to infect her brothers.

Layla rolled her eyes. "Definitely not. What do you think is going on?"

"I can guess. Amal's nothing if not predictable. We need to be alert. This might be the year we get to send him back to Mom without having to worry about proving what he's up to." Ashni shook her head. Her brother was annoying, but her mother was more so. Her mother knew what Amal was like, but still let him roam the globe like he didn't deserve an axe to the forehead. Of course, Ashni felt like that about most of her brothers, so maybe she was a little biased.

Layla snorted. "I'm sure she knows."

"You just like giving her credit because she's an outsider like you. So much love for the outsider."

"You're partial to outsiders yourself." Layla held her head up high.

Ashni pursed her lips. "I'm partial to disemboweling them."

Layla shrugged. "Yeah, but you're also partial to letting them get close." She dared to snuggle against Ashni.

Ashni rubbed her knuckle in the middle of Layla's head. Layla jumped back just enough to not crowd Ashni. Layla glowered at her and Ashni grinned.

"I heard the high and mighty princess went out shopping with Bashira today," Layla said.

"She did. I'm already getting the bills." From what she saw of the orders coming in, her hellcat had excellent taste in Roshan garments. She'd happily shower Nakia in all the fine cloth she desired if she could just talk to her.

Layla studied her for a long moment. "Anything you want to talk about?"

Ashni cut her eyes at her sister. "You know I don't."

With a huff, Layla threw her hands up. "Okay, but you know you can talk to me. I am the perfect sibling, after all." She had the nerve to give an adorable smile, showing her dimples and loving eyes.

Ashni blew a raspberry. She wasn't affected by the look. "You don't have much competition in the area for me. Now, don't you have other things you should be doing? Majeed isn't going to watch himself."

Layla had the nerve to wag her finger. "You're avoiding."

Ashni glared at her sister. "Anything I have to say about the hellcat needs to be said to her, not to you. Mind your business and go do your business."

Layla groaned. "You're no fun when you're cranky."

"I'm always cranky."

"Not to this degree and, usually, you're cranky with a purpose."

Ashni continued to glare, hoping Layla would get the signal to leave it alone. Layla giggled and climbed back up her line, disappearing from the throne room. Ashni sighed and ran her hand through her hair.

She should be focused on Amal and Majeed. They were up to something dangerous. She couldn't be bothered with worrying about it. She wanted to blame it on the fact that Amal was always up to something dangerous and just too incompetent to put something together. She knew that wasn't why she didn't dwell on it.

Her mind was stuck on Nakia. The shopping trip seemed to go well. Nakia wasn't just out of her room, but was out of the palace, so she had to be feeling better. Ashni would give her the rest of the day and then try again tomorrow. Maybe she'd be open to listening and talking then. She wasn't sure how Nakia would react if they did talk.

Rubbing her palms together, Ashni's mind couldn't wrap around not knowing something. She was good at predicting, reading situations, and acting accordingly. Nakia threw off her usual instincts.

"What if she doesn't understand?" Ashni tried not to think about that, but it was possible.

Nakia wasn't from a culture where people loved people regardless of gender. Ashni didn't understand, but she was aware of it, and she could respect it since it was connected to Nakia. She wasn't sure if Nakia was capable of returning the favor. Nakia didn't have the vast experience with other people and cultures like she did to know that different didn't have to mean wrong.

"But, my hellcat might surprise me yet," Ashni said. Nakia was full of surprises, after all. Besides, her behavior hadn't followed her cultural norms. "But, does she realize that?"

She doubted Nakia noticed how much she didn't follow her own beliefs. After all, if she really thought society knew best, Nakia wouldn't be a hellcat. She would be demure and defer to authority, defer to men. Nakia probably didn't know what the word 'demure' meant.

***

Nakia crawled into bed and sighed as her head hit the pillow. She was tired from walking around in the hot desert sun. The comfort of her bed was even better than the soothing bath she had earlier with the luxurious scented oils used to moisturize her skin and relax her. She barely closed her eyes before she was haunted by visions that had been with her for days. Flashes of sandy blond hair, alluring, cat-like golden eyes, and an almost devilish smile caused jolts through her body. She had to press her legs together for a moment, but got little relief from that action. It passed, as it always did. But, this time, it came back after she fell asleep.

Sound accompanied the second set of dreams. She heard moaning, maybe even purring, definitely cooing. The noise danced down her nerves. She didn't know what to think of it, especially when she woke with a moan spilling from her lips. Her body was burning, but in a good way. She sat up, took a deep breath, and tried to shake it off.

"It was wrong, it was wrong, it was wrong," she chanted until she calmed down. She needed to make sure she understood that. Once her heartbeat returned to normal and her skin cooled down, she settled on her pillow again.

She took a deep breath and rubbed her face. She doubted she'd get used to the dreams. She didn't want to get used to the dreams, especially since they seemed to change each time she had them. The dreams didn't really change, but her reactions to them changed. It was wrong, even if her mind and body seemed to be trying to convince her otherwise. She managed to fall asleep a third time and hoped it'd be for the rest of the night.

The next morning, Nakia sat down for breakfast and waited for Bashira. If patterns held, Bashira would show up before she was done. Before she had a chance to start eating, there was a knock at the door and then a servant stood before her.

"You have a visitor," the servant said.

"Let Lady Bashira in."

The servant shook her head. "My Lady, it is not Lady Bashira."

A stone sank into Nakia's stomach. "Not Lady Bashira? Then who?"

"The Queen, my Lady. Should I send her away?"

Nakia froze and her heart thumped heavy in her chest. *Should I send the Queen away?* She knew if she decided not to see her, the Queen would respect her wishes and leave. The Queen had done that since the incident. Maybe it was time to face the Queen and hear her out. Maybe it would help her move on.

Move on? I have moved on. Well, she felt like she had moved on when she was awake. She could interact with people again. She had gone out and hadn't flinched over anything. In fact, she hadn't looked at anyone outside with a suspicious gaze. She no longer moved away from the servants when they approached her. She allowed one servant to help bathe her. This was progress, right? She didn't need any help from the Queen to get herself together. She was together.

"You can send her in," Nakia said. The Queen needed to see she hadn't won. She hadn't broken Nakia.

The servant nodded and rushed off. Nakia took a deep breath and ate some eggs, hoping to settle her stomach and give herself some strength for what she was about to endure. She regretted it as soon as the Queen stepped into view. She smelled the Queen's scent and her stomach flipped. She almost threw up, feeling the burn in her throat, but she managed to avoid it. *Be strong. She can't hurt you.*

"Princess," the Queen's voice was low, but not small. Her eyes were on the floor and she bowed ever so slightly.

"Highness," Nakia said. "Please, sit." She motioned to the pillow across from her.

"Thank you." The Queen sat down. Her eyes remained on the floor and she wiped her palms on her knees.

"So, you barbarians do have some manners." Nakia didn't mean to sound as playful as she did. "You wanted to talk." She put some bite in her tone. She didn't want the Queen to believe everything was fine between them because it wasn't. It might never be again.

Sighing, the Queen rubbed her palms together and took a deep breath before she looked up. Her amber eyes glistened. She swallowed before she managed to speak. "I need you to know...to understand...what you think happened isn't exactly what happened."

Nakia's insides twisted and her jaw clenched. "Well, I think we both know I wouldn't do something like that on my own." What happened was wrong, disgusting, and could get her killed. Nakia would never do something so stupid on her own.

The Queen licked her lips. "No, of course not. I know where you're from this isn't done, isn't considered proper. You probably didn't even think something like this is possible."

"And yet, here, it's something done."

"Well, here, and all over the Empire and in other cultures. We find it acceptable to love whom you love. People are people. Gender doesn't matter. The same thing that allows us to love a person no matter the gender is also the same thing that allows people to feel confident in following me regardless of my gender."

Nakia nodded, even though none of it made sense. She had observed the lack of gender roles around the palace. She hadn't looked when she was in the marketplace. Was the entire Roshan Empire really like that? It was so backwards, so it was hard to imagine the entire Empire was this way.

"That doesn't explain what you did to me," Nakia said through a tense jaw.

Sighing, the Queen scratched the back of her head. "No, it doesn't. I didn't do what you think I did."

Nakia glowered at the Queen. "Oh, so you didn't have your way with me? Force yourself on me? At least take responsibility for it." She slapped at the table, rattling the dishes. She was tempted to slap the Queen, but at best the Queen would avoid it and at worst the Queen might kill her.

The Queen flinched and clenched her knees briefly. She looked Nakia in the eye. "I know what I did. I had my way with you while you were drunk and, for that, I apologize. While you didn't object at the time, I should've known better. It was wrong to take you in that state. But, I didn't force myself onto you."

Nakia blinked. "This is your apology? 'It was wrong to take me in that state?'" Nakia jumped to her feet, narrowing her eyes. "You think I'm just some toy here for you to play with." It was more and more tempting to hit the Queen.

The Queen was on her feet, too. "That isn't what this is about."

"Isn't it?" Nakia screamed as tears gathered in her eyes. *No, don't cry in front of her. Don't let her know you're hurt because you're not hurt. You're over the pain and now you're angry.* Her tears didn't seem to know that. "I'm just some toy, some pawn. You're no better than my father!"

Before Nakia realized it, the Queen was in her face. She didn't have time to process what it meant as the Queen took her into her arms. It took more than a few seconds to figure out that the Queen embraced her. Nakia struggled to get away. Unable to do so, she began sobbing. The Queen held her tighter, which only made her weep more.

"How could you do this to me?" Nakia wailed, tiny fist slamming against the Queen's abdomen. "I thought you cared."

The Queen inhaled sharply. "I do. Kitten, you are precious to me."

"You don't do that to someone precious. You don't."

"I didn't do what you think I did, kitten. We were both drunk and I know it's not a good excuse, but you smelled so sweet. I couldn't resist and when you...you were so open with me. You never...you never said stop," the Queen whispered.

Nakia just cried on. She couldn't stop, no matter how much she wished to. She shouldn't be crying on the Queen. She should be furious and she should give the Queen the cold shoulder, but she couldn't bring herself to do so. So, she just cried more.

***

Ashni looked at Nakia as she wept, her tears soaking Ashni's teal, silk shirt. Ashni didn't care about her clothing. She wanted to make Nakia feel better, to understand she hadn't meant to hurt her. *I didn't mean to hurt her.* For some reason, this was a revelation, but it was also a club to her head. Regardless of what she meant to do, what she had done was reduce this amazing and strong creature before her into a bawling mess. Maybe she was a monster.

Cradling Nakia in her arms, Ashni held her close and settled onto the nearest seat. Nakia buried her face in Ashni's collarbone. Ashni brushed some of Nakia's silky, black hair out of her face and caressed her cheek.

At the moment, it felt like everything was wrong with her. Each of Nakia's sobs cut through her like a serrated blade and took a piece of her that she doubted she'd ever get back. Maybe she didn't deserve it back. She clutched Nakia a little tighter each time a sob escaped her. Ashni needed to be careful or she'd crush the princess, but she couldn't let Nakia go. After long minutes, the sound of Nakia's weeping tapered off.

"Kitten, I'm so sorry," Ashni said, knowing how inadequate the words were. She could never make up for what she did and she understood that now. *Damn it. How could I mess things up this much?*

Nakia only shook her head. Her face was red and puffy. She probably wouldn't be able to say anything for a little while. Ashni checked the breakfast tray and located a teapot. She had to motion for a servant to pour the tea, as her hands were full, but she managed to grab the cup.

"Have some tea, kitten. It'll help soothe your throat." Ashni placed the cup to Nakia's lips.

Nakia took a small sip of the hot liquid. Ashni made sure to keep a good grip on the cup, not wanting any of it to accidentally slip out on either of them. Nakia took a few more sips and then nodded to indicate she had enough. Her face settled into a slightly more relaxed state, but a frown remained.

"I truly am sorry. I had no desire to violate you or treat you as if you were less than what you are," Ashni said.

"Why did you do this to me?" Nakia asked, her voice low and hitching.

"I didn't mean for it to happen. I know it doesn't matter, but I didn't want things to go like this."

"So...did you... do *that* because you were drunk, too?"

Ashni sighed. She feared this conversation wouldn't go the way she liked. But, she owed it to Nakia. She had done major damage and she needed to set things straight as best she could. She doubted things would ever be the same after this.

"While I have been known to do a lot of stupid things while drunk, this was more a lapse in judgment. I let my desire convince me that it was all right to sleep with you because you didn't object."

Nakia licked her bottom lip and Ashni had to suppress a shudder. For a moment, she dared to wonder what that lip tasted like. Shaking the thought off since she would probably never know the taste of that lip or soft skin again, she focused on Nakia.

"I didn't mean to hurt you," Ashni said, stroking Nakia's cheek. She was pleased that Nakia didn't pull away.

"But, you did."

For some reason, this made Ashni feel a little better. *I'm sick.* Knowing she meant enough to Nakia that she could hurt her had to mean something. Of course, she might have ruined that out of her usual selfishness. *No, no, no. I am favored by the gods and the Chosen One. I can fix this.*

"I know I did. I didn't mean to, kitten."

For a long moment, there was silence. Ashni occupied the time enjoying Nakia's soft skin. Feeling Nakia under her fingertips, only made her want to feel more and she had ruined that. *Damn my decisions.*

Nakia looked at her and Ashni almost couldn't breathe. Nakia took her hand, the one on her cheek. Ashni wasn't sure what to think of how it made her feel. The feeling was different, new, not unpleasant, though unsettling and overwhelming in its subtlety.

"Did I...did I..." Nakia took a deep breath and let it out through her nose. "Did I like it?"

The question made Ashni's heart stop for a second. This was curiosity, not repulsion. Maybe she hadn't completely ruined everything. She had to swallow before she trusted her voice to sound normal.

"Well, as I said, you didn't object."

"But...did I..." Nakia's voice hitched and seemed to be stuck in her throat.

"I can't tell you if you liked it or not. I can tell you that it seemed that way to me. You made so many cute noises and you put your leg on my shoulder…" Ashni felt her mouth water as she remembered and she had to take a second to get herself under control. Now wasn't the time to think of sex, even if they were discussing it.

Nakia blinked. "I…what?"

Ashni shook her head. Nakia was probably an innocent maiden with little idea of what took place during sex, especially sex between two women. *I'd enjoy nothing more than teaching her everything there is to know.* "It's not important. It seemed like you enjoyed yourself if the noises you made meant anything. You seemed to like it."

Nakia looked away and Ashni was bewildered. Nakia had once been predictable, entertaining but predictable. Now, Ashni couldn't figure her out. It was intriguing.

"I've had dreams," Nakia whispered.

"Dreams?"

"That night…it haunts me as I sleep." Nakia turned back to her. "I don't know what to think of the dreams. I mean I don't know what's real. I don't know how to take it. Women don't do those sorts of things. Ladies don't do those sorts of things." Tears welled up in her eyes again as she shook her head. Ashni couldn't begin to imagine how lost Nakia must feel.

"Shh. Shh. Shh." Ashni cupped Nakia's cheek and gently caressed it, smoothing out worry lines etched into Nakia's forehead. She brushed Nakia's hair out of her face. "It's okay. It's okay. You don't have to worry about that. Here, ladies do it all the time. You've even seen it up close. Adira and her spouse, Saniyah. In the Roshan Empire, they're legally married. There are many others like them."

Nakia shook her head again and buried her face in Ashni's shoulder. "No, no, no."

"Yes. It's fine. You didn't do anything wrong. If you did enjoy it, you didn't do anything wrong. Pleasure is pleasure. I know that idea is present in your culture, right?" Ashni knew enough about the West to know men did plenty of things that was considered inappropriate for women, but in Roshan culture it was fine for either gender.

"This is…this is beyond…" Nakia shook her head, as if that would make the right words come out.

Ashni gently moved Nakia's face so they were looking at each other. "No. Listen to me. You haven't done anything wrong. If you were a man and you had lain with me, you wouldn't be beating yourself up like this."

"But, I am not a man. I can't…I can't…" Nakia let out a long breath and looked down. Her body shook and Ashni held her tight again.

"Listen to me. You're fine. No, you are not a man, but you haven't done anything wrong. Why should a man be allowed to do these things and not you? Are you less than a man?" Ashni asked. Gender inequality was something she could not wrap her mind around. Not just with the West, but also in some of the conquered territory. What made a man greater than a woman? Greatness was measured with actions, abilities, achievements. Someone had to do something to be great, not just be born in a state of grace.

"No, but everyone has their place in society to make sure things go well."

Ashni shook her head. "And your sex determines your role? If that's the case, would Adira be a successful general? Would I have survived the battlefield? Would Layla be my most trusted guard? Everyone has their place, but you make it for yourself. You don't let someone tell you where you belong, especially based on something like what parts are between your legs."

Nakia stared at her with wide, red eyes. The wheels were obviously turning in her head. Did Nakia notice how well she fit in around the Roshan? Did she realize how well she could do with the Roshan, with Ashni?

"Do you like me?" Nakia asked. Her voice was lower than before, as if she feared the response.

"You are precious to me."

"Because of the gold?"

"Because of who you are." Ashni caressed Nakia's cheek with her thumb. "You have no idea, do you?" Ashni smiled just a little as she realized that. "All that fire and bite and you have no idea."

Nakia's brow furrowed as her eyebrows bent in and she eyed Ashni as if she had turned into a two-headed dragon right before her eyes. "No idea?"

"Of how amazing you are. You think it's because of the princess status and maybe that gives you your claws, but that's not all. You burn bright, so bright I'm sure even the Sun watches you. You are second to no one, not because they're male or royalty or anything. You're second to no one because you're you."

Before Ashni could muster any more words, Nakia sat up. There was that delicious taste of honey again. Nakia pressed her lips to Ashni's mouth. Nakia was kissing her. Ashni, not being a fool despite past actions, kissed back..

Chapter Fourteen

NAKIA WASN'T SURE WHAT she was thinking when she kissed the Queen, but when her lips touched the Queen's she no longer cared. For the first time in days, her body and mind felt like they could settle, calm down, and just be. Feeling the Queen kiss her back made her mind and body settle even more. It was like the world tilted back to its proper place. Eventually, she pulled away enough to look at the Queen.

"Was that...was that all right?" Nakia sounded shy even to her own ears and her nerves returned. After all the trauma she had been through, she wasn't sure why she kissed the Queen, but now she wanted to do it again and again. As the Queen said, men were allowed their pleasure, why not her? But, she needed to be sure it was all right. She couldn't go around stealing kisses because it felt good, even though she knew there were men who did such a thing.

The Queen smiled. "If you're asking was it all right for you to kiss me, you can do that whenever you like. If you're asking if the kiss itself was all right, it was sweet and you know how I am with sweet things." The smile transformed into a wide grin.

Nakia chuckled, but it sounded more like a sob. She beamed, which seemed to assure the Queen. The Queen stroked her cheek with her thumb. It felt pleasant. The caressing was relaxing and she realized the Queen had the tactile power to calm her. In fact, she'd been using that power since she came in and Nakia was suddenly grateful for it.

"May I?"

Nakia's heart jumped. She doubted she'd be brave enough to initiate a kiss again unless she was overwhelmed again. Her throat was dry from the thought of the Queen doing it. She couldn't even muster a nod to give the Queen permission. Her stomach was unsettled despite the Queen's soothing touch.

"Do you want me to leave?" the Queen asked after long moments of silence.

"No," Nakia squeaked. Her face burned with embarrassment and she put her hand over her mouth and took a breath. "No, don't leave."

The Queen smiled. It wasn't exactly cruel, but it was teasing. Her eyes danced as if she knew some wonderful secret. "Then what about kissing you? May I kiss you?"

Nakia wanted nothing more than that, right now. This time, she could, at least, nod. The Queen didn't disappoint. The Queen caressed her cheek again and then slowly leaned down, as if giving her time to change her mind. The Queen's lips touched hers and sunshine flowed through her. Nakia whimpered when it seemed like the Queen was pulling away, but then the Queen's mouth was back on hers and everything was right in the world.

Nakia wasn't sure how much time passed, but she didn't care. The only things that mattered were the soft kisses and the Queen caressing her cheek. She wasn't even sure if she could compare the feeling to anything. *This must be what happiness feels like*. It was the only thing that made sense.

Nakia adjusted her body a bit and felt more of the Queen against her. A sigh escaped her. She felt like she should be doing something with her hands, but she didn't know what. Another squeak escaped her and she pulled back as she felt the Queen's tongue race across her lips.

"Oops. Sorry." The Queen apologized again.

How often does the Queen apologize to others? Nakia very much doubted it was this much. "What was that?"

The Queen snickered and wiggled her eyebrows. "Oh. Well, fair maiden, I wanted a different sort of kiss."

Nakia narrowed her gaze. "Don't mock me, barbarian. Where I'm from a maiden's innocence is of the utmost importance."

"I truly can't imagine why."

"You're kidding, right?"

The Queen laughed. "No, I'm not. I can't imagine why and don't care to know. After all, this is nice, right?"

Nakia had to swallow before she could answer. "It is." But, still, her innocence was important. Whoever she married needed to believe she was pure. "My husband has to know any children I bear him are his." *Why did I say that?*

The Queen groaned. "Like I said, I didn't care to know, but here I am knowing. Do you really want to have this conversation right now?"

"How is this not important to you?"

"Well, for one, you can't get me pregnant and I can't get you pregnant unless the gods really are in a playful mood. This is about pleasure. If you want to talk about families and legacy, we can do that later. Let's focus on making you feel good, okay?"

Nakia swallowed hard. She should object, should remind the Queen about why this was a bad idea, but she couldn't bring herself to it. She wanted to experience this pleasure. Besides, like the Queen said, she couldn't get pregnant from it.

"I want to feel good." Nakia's voice shook as her heart beat quickly in anticipation. She wanted to know what the Queen would do to her, wanted to know what this thing was that haunted her dreams.

"Then, trust me?" The Queen looked at her with her big eyes that made it impossible to say no.

Nakia nodded and the Queen kissed her again, caressing her cheek, to help keep her calm. It was as gentle as the others, but then came the Queen's tongue again. It ran lightly against her lips and didn't feel bad at all. Opening her mouth, she thought she might try it, but got a pleasant surprise. The Queen's tongue slipped into her mouth and, although it should have been disgusting, it was better than the other kisses. The Queen's tongue slid against hers and she moaned.

Before Nakia realized it, her confused hands found their way around the Queen's neck and her fingers played with the hair at the nape of the Queen's neck. The Queen mewed and the sound sent tingles down Nakia's spine. She pulled the Queen closer, wanting more of her, wanting to take more of her in, and experience more of this new type of kissing. Unfortunately, she also needed to breathe. She pulled back for air, but the Queen didn't seem to need to breathe.

The Queen's lips fell to Nakia's cheek and neck, placing wet kisses and sending wonderful shivers through Nakia's body. The hand she didn't have pressed against Nakia's face fell to her hip. She caressed Nakia's hip with the same care she stroked Nakia's face. Nakia's body hummed, demanding more, but she wasn't sure more of what exactly.

Nakia clutched the Queen a little tighter and whimpered. "Ashni…"

The Queen tensed for a moment and pulled away to look at her. *Did I do something wrong?* If she had, she would do a million penances and sacrifice to every god if it meant the Queen could go back to kissing her.

"My name sounds so good on your lips," the Queen said before kissing her again.

Nakia moaned again as the Queen's lips and tongue contacted hers. It was amazing. Nakia never wanted it to end.

As the kiss continued, Nakia was aware the Queen's hands were wandering. They were both on her hips now, turning her body. She ended up with her legs on either side of the Queen, her tunic pushed to her knees, and her arms still around the Queen's neck. Now, she felt even closer to the Queen. And, then, damn it, she had to breathe.

The Queen didn't let breathing stop her, going right back to Nakia's neck as Nakia took in some air. Now, along with heated kisses, there were also nips. At the first graze of teeth, Nakia whimpered and bucked against the Queen. The Queen moaned and held Nakia a little tighter. She kissed a trail up to Nakia's ear.

"This time, I'm asking and you're not in your cups. May I?" the Queen asked.

"May you...?" Nakia barely understood words. There was no way she'd get any hidden meanings.

"I want you, kitten. I want to feel your bare skin under my hands. I want you in my mouth. I want to hear my name dripping from your lips as I taste you again, and again as I bring you pleasure you haven't even had a chance to dream about," the Queen whispered.

The Queen's voice struck Nakia in parts that had never felt so alive. The proposal made her throb in a way she never had before. And the words conjured up enough of a memory to make her buck against the Queen, her body trying to relieve some of the pressure building.

"Is that a yes?" the Queen asked.

Nakia managed a teasing smirk. "Does a maiden not deserve a bed? A princess at that?"

"My princess deserves all she desires." The Queen gripped Nakia's hips and then rose to her feet.

Nakia yelped in surprise and held onto the Queen tighter. Apparently, the Queen was strong enough to pick her up with no problem, not that she weighed much, but still this was a display of raw power. Of course, she didn't need the display. She knew what the Queen was capable of. This woman who could possibly conquer the whole world wanted her. She felt dizzy.

***

Making it to Nakia's bed was a little trickier than it should have been, but Ashni had to kiss Nakia the whole trip. Nakia's mouth was so sweet and Ashni wished her tongue could live in there, tasting and befriending Nakia's tongue. But, there'd be little time for that as she

186

eased Nakia onto her bed.

Nakia looked up at her and Ashni almost asked if she was sure once more. She didn't want there to be any misunderstandings this time. She couldn't bear the thought of hurting Nakia again, of ruining whatever this was between them.

"Well?" Nakia dared to say. The fire was coming back and it burned its way through Ashni, dancing across every nerve in her body.

Ashni purred, deep in her throat. It took all of her self-control not to tear their clothes off and explore every inch of Nakia with her hands and mouth. Settling above Nakia without putting any weight on her, Ashni kissed her with vigor. Nakia's arms went around her neck again, as if they belonged there and pulled her closer.

Ashni propped herself up on her elbows while making sure her mouth didn't lose Nakia's. It was obvious this was Nakia's first time kissing, but Ashni didn't care. It was sloppy and delicious and she wanted more and more. She could only imagine the things she'd get to teach Nakia, all the things she would get to *show* Nakia.

Nakia broke the kiss for need of air. Ashni would have been upset if there wasn't so much of Nakia to taste. Her lips and tongue wandered Nakia's neck and then she decided to go lower. Once she reached Nakia's tunic, she wanted all clothing to go immediately. She pulled away, earning a whine from Nakia.

"I just need..." Ashni trailed off, running her hands along Nakia's outfit. "I need to feel you, all of you." *How the hell does this stupid thing come off?*

Nakia swallowed so hard it seemed to echo across the room. "Yes..." she breathed.

That was all Ashni needed and she rid them of their clothes before Nakia had a chance to change her mind. It was also all she needed to figure out how to get Nakia's tunic off. There were two belts around her waist, one on top of the tunic and one underneath. There were ties at the shoulders. Ashni undid everything within the blink of an eye. Nakia moaned as her tunic was slid from her body.

The Queen's clothing was gone in seconds. Her robes and shirt were thrown off. The belt keeping her pants up fell away with a flick of her wrist. As Nakia watched, a blush burned her cheeks, but she never looked away. She licked her lips as soon as Ashni was nude and that was all Ashni needed.

She leaned over Nakia, kissing her again as soon as possible. Their skin pressed together felt incredible. Ashni's body sang out in ways that it never had. Nakia moaned so loud, it hit Ashni right in her core. She could only imagine the sounds Nakia would make when they really got started. Until then, she enjoyed the new feel of them together, skin-to-skin, bodies sharing heat and bringing each other joy.

The next time Nakia needed to breath, Ashni began her journey down Nakia's body. Open mouth kisses went to Nakia's neck and then her collarbones. One hand caressed Nakia's perky breast while her mouth latched onto the opposite nipple. Nakia called out and arched against Ashni enough to make her groan, but she didn't release her bounty. By the Great Eagle, all of Nakia was sweet. Ashni might never get enough.

Nakia's hand slid from around Ashni's neck to her back and she dug her nails into Ashni's shoulders as Ashni delighted in her sweet, pink nipples. She licked and sucked at each of them, spending a few seconds with one before going to the other and then back. Her hands palmed and kneaded each breast, loving how they seemed to fit perfectly in her hands. The gods must have made Nakia just for her, so therefore Nakia was divine. She would have to treat her as such.

Each time Ashni touched one of Nakia's nipples, Nakia moved against Ashni. She felt hot desire against her and she needed it now. She released Nakia's breast from her mouth, but her hands refused to move. She kissed her way down Nakia's abdomen, taking a lick at her bellybutton. Nakia let out a cute little whine.

"Are you...?" Nakia moaned.

"Do you remember this? Remember my head here?" Ashni whispered. She was tempted to flick her tongue against the source of sweet flavor, but controlled herself. She wanted to know if Nakia truly remembered this part of their night. This was what haunted her more than anything else.

Whimpering, Nakia only nodded. Maybe the anticipation made her mute. Ashni wouldn't let either of them wait any longer. She needed this as much as Nakia did. With a light taste, a gentle flick of Ashni's tongue, Nakia's back arched off the bed with a surprised yelp. It wasn't enough for Ashni, who barely got anything to savor there. Using the flat of her tongue, Ashni's slow lick made Nakia coo and melt. One of her hands fell into Ashni's hair and lightly scratched her scalp.

With each movement of her tongue, Nakia's hand shifted in her hair. Sometimes she pulled Ashni closer, but other times she caressed Ashni. The sensation coupled with the smell and taste of Nakia was more than enough for Ashni to never want to leave this position. She needed to make Nakia feel the same way.

As she gave Nakia's clit a little kiss, her fingers also rolled the gem atop Nakia's breast. Nakia cried out and suddenly her leg was on Ashni's shoulder and her heel dug into Ashni's back. She rolled her hips into Ashni's mouth.

"Yes," Nakia groaned and Ashni sucked on her for a moment.

Nakia's hips moved with Ashni's mouth. Ashni doubted it'd be long before Nakia got to experience an amazing orgasm. She would remember this one beyond her dreams. As Nakia's moans became louder, Ashni's hands kneaded her breasts with more energy and she licked faster, with broader strokes, drinking in Nakia's essence. Nakia's hips chased her tongue faster and faster with each movement.

The moment Nakia went over the edge, Ashni was blessed with more nectar on her tongue, but also nails in her scalp and a kick to her shoulder. Chuckling into Nakia, she didn't mind. She kissed Nakia's thigh, making Nakia's hips buck.

"By the gods, Ashni..." Nakia sighed as her body calmed down. She left her leg over Ashni's shoulder, but her hands fell to the bed.

Resting her head on Nakia's hip, Ashni grinned up at her. "Well, it's about time you realized I'm more than a queen. Now, do I have to do that every time I want you to say my name? Because I will." And enjoy every second of it while she was at it.

Nakia gave a tired smile, but there was a mischievous twinkle in her jade eyes. "Is that a promise, Ashni?"

Oh, she was in for it now. Ashni went back in for seconds. Maybe even thirds. She would see how things played out, but she felt like Nakia had the stamina for thirds at the least.

Nakia moaned and arched into Ashni. Her hand went back to Ashni's head. Ashni was very confident thirds were in her future. *I am definitely favored by the gods.*

***

Nakia wasn't sure when she fell asleep, but she woke up to Ashni caressing her hip. She was a little surprised Ashni hadn't sneaked away. She had heard of lovers doing that after getting what they wanted. Apparently, the Queen wasn't like that or the Queen hadn't gotten enough of what she wanted. Nakia knew she hadn't gotten enough.

"You okay?" Ashni asked, pulling Nakia close to her. It was a little hard since Nakia was already lying on the Queen. Her head was on

Ashni's shoulder and she wouldn't mind staying there.

"Perfect," Nakia purred, running her leg up against the Queen's thigh. She had never felt so right in her entire life. It was like she was meant to be here.

The Queen shivered a little and moved her hand down to stroke Nakia's thigh. "I'm glad. There's a little lunch if you want to eat something." Ashni reached over her, moving the hand that caressed her thigh.

"No, not yet." Nakia moved Ashni's hand right back where it had been.

"All right." Ashni kissed her forehead.

Nakia sighed and snuggled into Ashni. For a while, the room was blanketed in a comfortable silence. Nakia could feel Ashni's heartbeat against her chest and it soothed her in so many ways. It was like nothing in the world could touch her while she was pressed against Ashni. Maybe this was wrong, but it felt perfect.

As Nakia became more aware, she realized she could feel more than Ashni's heartbeat, but also her naked skin. The sensation was beyond her to describe. Was this why people liked to cuddle? This could become a favorite thing if she allowed it. Would she be allowed to?

"Ashni..." Nakia had to test the name on her tongue. While it was easy to coo and scream while her mind was flooded with ecstasy, it took conscious and careful thought now. When she saw the Queen's face light up, she knew it was safe to proceed. "Was this...was this...what was this?"

While it was happening, Nakia hadn't thought about anything. She had needed to feel Ashni without the heady wine in the way. This was much better than flashes and phantom touches in dreams, but what was it? Was this just pleasure? Like when someone called in a slave to take care of some urges? Men did that all the time. She had been warned about it to make sure she never fell for some man's falsehoods. Her virtue was important and needed to be protected at all costs, but she didn't feel compromised here.

"I will follow your lead on this, kitten. I know this is not usual for you," Ashni said. Her fingers made light circles on Nakia's thigh.

"No, it's not. Far from it, really. But, if this is to continue, I will not be your toy," Nakia said. Royalty had their toys. She knew of many slaves who were such for her father. She also knew noblewomen who were such for her father. She wouldn't be reduced to being some bed warmer.

190

Ashni blinked. "My toy?" She had the nerve to look like she didn't know what Nakia meant, but they both knew that was a lie.

"I am not some toy. You will not find your way to my bed out of boredom or summon me for entertainment."

Ashni chortled. "You do realize I only summon you for entertainment."

Nakia glared at her. "I'm serious."

Ashni sighed. "I very much doubt you'd allow me to treat you as a toy. The second you thought I saw you as such, I know anything we have would come to an end. I like to think I've proven I'm not ready to let you go just yet."

"And there will be no others." Nakia knew that having multiple lovers was common in the Roshan Empire. She also recalled the tale of Ashni's parents and the people who tried to convince Ashni's father to take on other wives.

Ashni took a deep breath. "I don't think I need anyone else, kitten. I mean, if I have a hellcat in my corner, why would I need anyone else?"

Nakia brightened, unable to contain the joy she felt. When had Ashni began to mean so much to her? She couldn't pinpoint any time where she began to like Ashni. All the Queen did was tease and taunt her. Well, except for when she was allowing Nakia to eat with her, or teaching her games, or keeping her warm, or letting her say whatever was on her mind. Maybe Bashira was onto something.

"So..." Nakia wasn't sure what she wanted to ask. She wasn't sure what their relationship was called, if it was called anything. It obviously wasn't courting. Maybe the Roshan had a term for it.

"There is you and only you, hellcat. Isn't that enough?" Ashni shifted so that she was completely flat on her back. "You're a handful as it is. I wouldn't have time for anyone else."

Nakia narrowed her gaze on Ashni as she adjusted her body to make sure they were still in contact. "And what's that supposed to mean?"

Ashni beamed as her hands slid up and down Nakia's back. "It's a compliment. I promise."

Nakia narrowed her gaze. "No, it's not. Like I said, I'm not going to be your toy or your joke or whatever the hell you think I am. If you know anything about my culture, you know this meant something to me." Nakia hadn't meant to say that, but now it was out there. Physical intimacy couldn't be just pleasure for her. She wasn't raised that way.

Ashni's expression dropped. "Hellcat..." She wrapped her arms around Nakia's waist. "I told you, you're precious to me. Honestly, do you think I go around apologizing to everybody? Do you think I even care whenever someone calls me a monster? Do you think it matters to me when someone decides they don't want to see me anymore?"

Nakia had thought about all of that. It was good to hear Ashni saying it. Still, she didn't know what this was between her and the Queen. It wasn't some epic love story, not when they were two females. She was about to ask, but Ashni beat her to speaking.

"Now, do you want something to eat? I know you're hungry. You didn't eat breakfast and I wore you out," Ashni said with a smirk.

Snorting, Nakia gave the Queen a withering stare. "Oh, don't look so proud of yourself."

Ashni's expression grew into a wide grin. "Oh, but I am proud of myself. I'm also proud of you. You lasted longer than I assumed you would."

Nakia had a feeling that was a backhanded compliment, but couldn't bring herself to care. She was quite hungry and her stomach had the poor manners of letting the whole room know it. Ashni chuckled, but didn't say anything. Turning her head, Nakia could see the tray, but she didn't feel up to lifting her arms for anything. She didn't have to. Ashni grabbed a small slice of bread and put it to Nakia's mouth.

"All of that and you're feeding me?" Nakia smirked.

"Don't let it go to your head. You're not *that* special."

Nakia knew that was untrue. Maybe this was all right. She could take her time to understand these feelings she had for Ashni and understand whatever they had between them.

Chapter Fifteen

ASHNI HAD TO GET up the next morning as she had work to do. She wasn't surprised Nakia was still in a dead sleep. She had exhausted the princess since they had spent all day in bed. It was a pleasant way to spend the day and they would have to do it again sometime, especially since Ashni still hadn't gotten her fill. Maybe she would never be sated, but it would be fun to find out. Unfortunately, the kingdom wouldn't run itself and the two people who could run things for her were busy, so she had to do some governing.

She gave Nakia a soft kiss, earning a sleepy coo from her. Ashni smiled. She was ready to face the day. "When she wakes up, send her to me," Ashni told the nearest servant, who stood outside the room, ready to be of use.

It would be nice to spend the morning with Nakia again. For now, she went to her own rooms to clean up and put on clean clothes. Once she was done and refreshed, she made her way to the throne. Work and breakfast waited for her.

For the first time in a long time, she didn't mind working. She plucked an apple slice from the breakfast tray, but decided against it. These could not compare to the other apples and honey in her life. Instead, she grabbed a hard-boiled egg.

"Hmm...is it good to eat eggs when I'm probably going to put my tongue down someone's throat?" The idea of Nakia's mouth made her body tingle. She slapped herself in the head. "Why did I even get out of bed?" She thought about the things she could be doing to Nakia, showing her how amazing her body could feel.

All day yesterday, she had touched Nakia and was fine with that. She looked forward to when she could show Nakia how she liked to be touched, but for now, she wanted to do any and everything to Nakia. Her sounds alone were worth it, but her taste was the best reward. She licked her lips.

She glanced down at the documents before her and refocused. She needed to work. She needed to keep up with what was going on with her kingdom. If she couldn't govern a kingdom, how did she plan on governing her own empire once she took over the West? She could always leave the administrative work to Adira. If Saniyah was with her, Adira would do paperwork until she died with a smile on her face. Getting Saniyah there would be the trick.

"And none of this is getting my work done, so come on," Ashni told herself. She slapped her cheeks and took a deep breath before looking at the documents again. She ate another egg and got to work.

She got through quite a bit before Nakia came to the throne room. Ashni was a little disappointed Nakia wasn't walking funny. She thought she had taken care of the princess quite thoroughly. She wanted Nakia to remember her even when she was doing something as mundane as walking. Well, that was something to work toward the next time they were together.

Nakia made her way onto the dais. Ashni was about to pull Nakia onto her lap, but Nakia took the space she occupied when she was the royal cupbearer. Ashni almost snickered, but held it in. Maybe Nakia was still a little asleep or maybe Ashni had made Nakia come so many times she was a bit brain-dead. The latter was an entertaining thought. *Maybe I should mess with her a little and see how long it takes her to really wake up.*

Ashni picked up her wine cup and waved it at Nakia. Nakia took a step and stopped. Ashni laughed until those emerald eyes narrowed. *Uh-oh.*

"What the hell? Is that how this is going to be?" Nakia bellowed. "I'm good enough for you to warm my bed, but you still treat me like a slave here to pour your wine."

"Kitten—"

"Don't 'kitten' me!" A fire blazed in Nakia's eyes and she glared at Ashni as if she was the worst person to ever live. "I already told you, I'm not your toy and you can't play me." Nakia stormed off, feet slapping against the floor so hard that the noise echoed through the room, reminding Ashni of thunder.

Ashni considered chasing after her. It wouldn't take much to catch Nakia and explain what happened, but she let the princess go. There was always a possibility this wasn't about her little joke, but something deeper that Nakia needed to come to grips with. After all, her world was turned upside down yesterday when she realized she was attracted to women, something she hadn't known was possible until coming to Khenshu.

"Not that I get why someone would be attracted to a person just because of their sex or would rule someone out because of their sex," Ashni muttered, rubbing her chin. The West was weird.

Either way, she wasn't sure she was totally equipped to handle Nakia's issues with her growing sexuality. If it was truly bothering Nakia, she would probably get in touch with Bashira and Bashira would work her magic. Ashni already knew she wasn't great at helping Nakia when she was distressed. Bashira knew what she was doing and didn't mind helping. For the moment, Ashni needed to work on taking care of her kingdom rather than coddling Nakia.

"Eventually, I'll have to learn how to take care of this woman as well. Why the hell didn't Mommy teach us about that? Six sons and a daughter who follow anything pretty and she didn't think we needed to know how to take care of women? Or at least teach us how to read women?" Ashni scowled. *Damn useless mother.*

***

Nakia retreated to an empty garden and paced. She sent a servant to fetch Bashira. She would spend the day with someone who respected her. Screw the Queen. Well, no, she had already done that and that was the problem. Well, never again.

She was a Lady and she'd behave like a Lady, even if she was no longer a maiden. Hell, it might not even count since she had been with a woman. How could it count? Sex involved a man penetrating someone. She had seen enough pictures on pottery and mosaics and asked her governess enough questions about them to know that. Sex was not two women doing whatever the hell the Queen had done to her. No one at home would believe such a thing was possible. She was safe.

"I can go home and no one will ever know," she mumbled, wringing her hands as she walked.

Her stomach flipped with each step and her throat burned with her temper. This was worse than the first night the Queen took her. At least then there was the excuse of alcohol. This was the Queen using her and then making a fool of her as well. *How could I have been so stupid to believe her?*

"Heartless bitch," Nakia snarled. She wanted to punch something, but she didn't know how to throw a punch and it would undoubtedly hurt her hand if she did.

At the sound of a gasp, Nakia turned toward the entrance of the garden. Staring at her was a familiar face. She knew she knew him, but she couldn't recall who he was. She tensed in case he was a threat.

"I'm sorry. I didn't know this space was occupied," he said. From his short hair and braids holding his brown locks down at the top, she suspected he was a member of the military.

"It's fine." As far as Nakia could tell, the palace gardens were public places. It seemed like an insane and dangerous thing to do, but what should she expect from a barbarian like the Queen?

"Are you the foreign princess? The one the Queen forced to be her cupbearer?" he asked.

She arched an eyebrow, folding her arms across her chest. "What's it to you?"

"It's...you seem upset. I know how the Queen can be. She's very disrespectful and selfish when it serves her will. She's well known for her clever, deceitful tongue, playing with people and using them."

"What did she do to you?" This was going somewhere. Nakia decided to see where. Maybe it'd help her get back at the bitch. *I'll teach her to try to play me.*

"Disrespected me, same as you. She put a princess in the role of a servant and she reduced a mighty warrior to a babysitter." He scowled and made a fist.

Now, Nakia recalled who he was. This was Captain Majeed, the man the Queen blew off at the Festival of the Moon. What was his real problem with the Queen?

"She took you from your home as she took me from mine and stripped us both of anything that made us worthwhile," Majeed said.

His words hit home and curled in her stomach. The Queen had taken everything from her, including her dignity. She was nothing but a toy for this savage, who took so much joy in making her feel like nothing. At least her father pretended she was an important game piece, not just some sacrificial pawn. *Why does no one care? I am not worthless and I am not some toy or bargaining chip or anything like that.*

"She took you, too?" Nakia whispered. It wouldn't surprise her if the Queen often stole people and brought them to ruin.

"Conquered and killed my people, destroyed our culture, and then forced me into her army to follow her orders for the rest of my life. That is what she does."

The Queen planned the same for her home. Her home would be conquered and made part of the Roshan Empire. Their culture would be lost. People would be lost, murdered or sold into slavery. How could she—a princess of Phyllida—allow that to happen? And while it happened, she would be a plaything for the Queen, made to be a whore for the rest of her life or until the Queen tired of her. Who knew what would happen after that.

"You wish something from me," Nakia said.

"I only offer you a way home, a way to save your people from the same fate mine suffered. You have a chance to be a hero and save your city. You know she's called Lady Death for a reason, yes?"

Nakia had heard many nicknames for Ashni when she was home. She had also heard tales of the terror the Queen wrought. The worst she heard was something called a Bloody Orchard. The descriptions of it were frightening. The nobles with her father were horrified and fearful that the Queen would do worse to them.

"What would you have me do?" Nakia asked.

"Well, you are her cupbearer."

Nakia pursed her lips. "I am."

"Then, you know your job and why your job is so important."

"I am aware. Is that what you would have me do?" It would teach the Queen not to place her enemies in important positions.

"Think on it and then meet me back here at sunset."

"What should I be thinking on?"

He gave her a stern look. "You know."

She had an inkling. There were not many ways for her to get home or save her home, not with the Queen alive. He seemed to think she would agree to assassinating the Queen, which she should. The Queen planned to destroy life as she knew it, both in a personal and in the grand sense of the scheme.

"Be sure before you agree."

Nakia nodded and Majeed took his leave. Nakia didn't have much time to think about him as Bashira arrived shortly after. Bashira looked at her and decided they needed to spend the day shopping. Shopping had been quite fun, so she gave in without a fight. Bashira grinned all the way to the market.

***

Ashni wasn't sure why, but for some reason, Layla decided to land on her when she came to the throne room this time. Shoving Layla off, she glared at the obviously insane girl. Layla grinned back, her dark eyes dancing with mirth.

"You're in a mood. What happened?" Ashni asked. Her sister only acted like this when she had something too juicy to contain.

"Majeed met with your little hellcat," Layla replied said in a singsong voice. Well, that explained her mood. She might have caught Nakia in a compromising situation, thus justifying her hatred of the other princess. Never mind the fact that Majeed was trying to kill her sister, apparently.

Ashni curled her upper lip. "You're psychotic, you know that?"

"As are you, but I never hold it against you. In fact, I like to think it's one of the many things that keep us close." Layla continued to grin.

Sighing, Ashni couldn't dispute that. "Okay, so you think my kitten is going to betray me?" *I really don't need this right now, but I'd have it coming at this point, as far as the hellcat is concerned.*

Layla snorted and rolled her eyes. "I might hate her—and believe me I do—but, I know she's not going to betray you. I'm not stupid."

"No, only your spouse is."

Layla hissed. "Hey, I can make spouse digs now, too. You and your kitten, who you swear you don't have feelings for, but you're always so concerned about her and want her to be everywhere with you. You and your outsiders. A barbarian this time, too."

Ashni shrugged. "Hey, you were once a barbarian."

"No, I'm pretty sure that was always you. And, I think you prove it every time you get caught up with an outsider."

"Outsiders are interesting. I mean, imagine if I was around Amal for the rest of my life? Or even worse, Jay?" The very idea of being around her older brothers made Ashni want to bash her head against a wall.

"At least Jay wouldn't try to kill you."

Ashni nodded. "Which would probably make him a favorite brother, if I didn't want to punch him in the throat whenever he started talking. But, speaking of Amal, is he still around?"

"Of course not. He packed his bags and left a week after the Festival. You were too consumed with your kitten to notice."

"Yeah. I would have thrown a party to celebrate his departure. What did Majeed want with Nakia?"

"I think she is meant to be the sword. He didn't say as he whet her appetite. She seemed to seriously consider it. What did you do?" Layla narrowed her gaze at Ashni.

"Why is it always me?" Ashni leaned back and threw her arms up in the air.

Layla tittered. "Because you screw up all the time. I say that with a sister's love, but you're the person who sees a twelve-year-old fighting against your army and you go punch her in the face because you can't stand that your battle isn't going the way you want."

Ashni rolled her eyes. "I didn't punch you in the face. I slapped you in the head."

"I'm pretty sure you punched me in the face. Adira witnessed it, so we can ask her. Either way, I was twelve and I was kicking serious butt and you couldn't take it. Anyway, the point is, you're always at fault. You should remember that. Sort of like Adira is always at fault with Saniyah. That's just the way it works." Layla propped her feet on a work tray.

Ashni sniffed. "I am not the person always at fault. I'm the Queen around here."

Layla's mouth twisted to one side. "Your dad was probably always at fault, too."

Ashni grimaced at such blasphemy. "Never. Emperor Khalid Akshay, the Great Amir, son of the Great Eagle was always right."

Layla chuckled. "Except when Chandra said something totally opposite."

Ashni's nostrils flared. "Don't you have work to do? A mook to follow? Can we at least pretend you're trying to keep me alive?"

Layla beamed, but thankfully made herself scarce. Ashni sighed and ran her hand through her hair. Majeed wanted to tempt her hellcat—after Ashni had angered her, treated her like a joke. Ashni was hit with a sudden realization. Holy shit, Nakia was going to try to kill her. She groaned.

She threw her hands up. "It's always something."

***

Today, Bashira wanted to see jewels while Nakia people-watched. She felt hyper-aware of what happened last night and she wondered if everyone could tell. She noticed not only the servants tending to nobles, but also people walking with who she would have at one time thought were friends because they were the same sex. Not just women, but men as well. They held hands or cuddled close, not like friends.

"How is that normal?" Nakia blurted out.

199

"The pottery? You guys don't have glazing where you're from?" Bashira asked.

Nakia blinked and realized they stood in front of a potter and his wares. "Oh, sorry. No, I didn't mean that. I meant...well, is it normal around here for people of the same sex to be involved and to marry?"

Bashira shrugged. "As normal as anything else. My aunts have been married for years."

Nakia blinked. "Your aunts?"

"Yes, my father's sister is married to a woman." Bashira snapped her fingers. "You actually know them, Saniyah and Adira."

Nakia's eyes opened wide and she feared they might fall out of her head. "They are your aunts?" *How could Bashira be related to such barbarian women who flaunt their relationship out in the open and don't even pretend to be humble and demure?*

"Yes."

Nakia wasn't sure how she felt about that. Was Bashira like her aunts? Was she attracted to women? Was Bashira attracted to her? Could she trust Bashira?

"And you're okay with them?" Nakia managed to ask.

Bashira arched an eyebrow. "Okay with them being my aunts? I don't really have a say in the matter, eh?"

"Is that why you tried to push me to be with the Queen? Telling me she liked me and such nonsense?" Nakia demanded, glaring at her friend. Well, maybe her former friend or not even a friend at all. This may have been a setup.

"No. First of all, I only wanted to help you feel better and be your friend. But, the things I said about the Queen were quite true. I did tell you those things because it's clear you have feelings for each other and it was better for you to get them out into the open. I know this is all weird for you, but it doesn't have to be. I mean, look at you." Bashira motioned to Nakia.

Nakia wasn't sure what she meant as she looked down at herself. She was dressed in Roshan garments. She had put them on when she woke up because she thought the Queen would like to see her in the outfit. She hadn't bothered to change after the Queen showed her true colors. It was for blending in. At least that was what she told herself. But, she was also comfortable in the clothes. She was comfortable with the food and some of the customs. She was comfortable with...she shook her head.

"I know we seem odd to you as a whole. But, take it step by step.

Dissect it and pull it apart then put it together in ways you understand," Bashira said.

Nakia's throat was tight. She didn't understand any of this, not just the barbarians, but her own emotions, her own thoughts. "How?"

"I've learned from my aunt, Adira, and from Layla, who I hang out with on occasion, that cultures aren't better or worse. They're different. You adjust as best you can."

"Adira and Layla are from different cultures?"

Bashira tittered. "The Queen likes her outsiders."

Nakia's stomach fluttered and she had to swallow around a lump in her throat. "So...Layla isn't even her real sister?"

"They're as real as any others. They love each other and fight for each other and they're there for each other. Love isn't just about blood around here. In fact, blood is probably the least of all bonds for the Roshan."

Nakia's brow furrowed. "What do you mean?"

"There have been stories that the Queen wasn't even Amir Khalid's daughter. It's probably nonsense, but he had only sons and then, in the middle, this daughter. But, do you know who his favorite child was?"

"The Queen?" She couldn't fathom a father loving a daughter best of all, but these people were backwards. Sometimes, backwards seemed so much better than the things that made sense.

"He adored her. She's the one who was closest to him. She's his legacy and many people believe he saw that from when she was little. Even if she wasn't his blood, he put his legacy on her. Out of all the brothers the Queen has, who does she trust with her life, her kingdom, and her people? Layla above all others. They have a bond beyond blood."

Nakia took this in and compared it to her own learnings. Blood ties trumped all and no man accepted a child that might not be his, which was why women were supposed to be chaste until they were with their husbands. How could there be a bond that went beyond blood? But, she could see it with the Queen and Layla. She was certain they loved each other more than she loved her sisters, more than her sisters loved her.

"There are spiritual bonds and they know no gender for us. You meet someone and click in some way. Maybe as siblings, as with the Queen and Layla, maybe as lovers, as with my aunts, and maybe something else. Maybe it's the thing that first makes friendships and then if we allow it, it explodes into something else."

Nakia nodded. She felt like there was something here, something

201

she hadn't had the chance to experience. She hadn't been surrounded by many people in Phyllida to bond with them. Was that what made the Roshan so different? She could meet people who were more than servants, or hired by her father, and interact with them? She could bond with people?

"Are you okay?"

"Fine. Come on. I want to see some jewelry. I need bracelets." It was the least the Queen could do for her after treating her the way she had. Maybe the Queen had a bond with Layla, but there was nothing between them. And, yes, maybe same-sex couples were normal here, but the Queen obviously didn't consider them a couple. For all she knew, the Queen was on top of some other foreigner right now. It wasn't like she could be trusted to keep her word after this morning.

***

Nakia met with Majeed after she returned from shopping. It was late and she was surprised he waited this long. He obviously needed her more than she needed him, even if he claimed he could help get her back home.

"Ah, so you've come." He gave her a crooked smile.

"What do you want me to do?" Nakia asked, folding her arms across her chest.

"Are you in?"

"I wouldn't be here if I wasn't," she snapped. *Is he serious?* He had to think she was an idiot to not understand the danger they were in and yet here she was. "Now, are you going to tell me what you need from me or are you going to waste my time, like the damned Queen?" She glowered at him. She wasn't one to be played with and it was time for these damned barbarians to learn that.

Majeed sneered. "You are feisty. I have a little gift for you. I'll give it to you tomorrow and all I need you to do is put it in her wine."

She narrowed her gaze on him. "And then?"

"And then I promise you get to go home."

"How?" Her voice remained hard. She wouldn't let him sell her a pipe dream.

"Well, let's say I have friends in very high places." He smirked.

She wondered what he meant and then she remembered the Festival. Did he mean Amal? No, it didn't have to mean Amal. He was in the military. It could be one of the generals who wasn't loyal to Ashni or other captains who were unhappy. For all the talk of bonds, there didn't seem to be much loyalty among the Roshan. But, what should she expect of savages? Eating each other made more sense than them ruling the world.

"So, all you need me to do is put something into the Queen's wine and I'm free to go home? What of my home? Will it be invaded later?"

"I can guarantee it will not."

She wished she could believe him. She also wished she knew the line of succession to the Roshan throne. It was quite possible Layla would get the throne and Layla would definitely attack Phyllida. But, since Layla wasn't related to the Queen by blood, she might not inherit the throne. Maybe one of her brothers would be inherit the kingdom and they didn't seem as active as the Queen was.

"I'll be here in the afternoon. We shouldn't spend any more time together," she said.

Majeed smiled. "You're right. And you're making the right decision. You'll be a hero when you go home, celebrated and praised."

Nakia doubted it, but didn't say so. She was tired and wanted to retire to her rooms. A hot bath and dinner would be nice. Afterward, she'd crawl into bed. The plan went awry after she got ready for bed and went to her room. There was an unexpected guest in her bedroom at the end of the night.

"What are you doing here?" Nakia glared at the Queen, who had made herself comfortable in Nakia's bed. Nakia wanted to kill her just for the assumption. Did the Queen honestly think she could treat Nakia any old way and it would be acceptable? Did the Queen honestly think Nakia would share her bed with the Queen ever again after this morning? To Hell with her. Maybe even literally, tomorrow.

Chapter Sixteen

"KITTEN, ARE YOU SERIOUSLY still mad?" Ashni asked as she lay in Nakia's bed as if it were her own. She watched Nakia and could feel the anger coming off her. It made Ashni's body tingle. She wanted to pounce on her hellcat right now, but she was fairly certain if she made a move right now, Nakia would hit her with the nearest object.

"Still mad because you completely disrespected me this morning? Still mad because you treated me like your own personal whore, which I'm sure you have plenty of? Still mad because you proved to be a liar hardly eight hours after you convinced me to trust you?" Nakia barked. She paced in front of the bed.

Ashni winced. None of what Nakia said was exactly a lie, except for the personal whore thing. Yes, she had sex slaves, but she wouldn't use them since it bothered Nakia. She hadn't treated Nakia like her personal whore, and she hadn't lied. She never lied. She had no reason to do so.

Ashni needed to clear this matter up. "Kitten—"

"And stop calling me that! My name is Nakia, Princess Nakia Lysand of Phyllida. My father is a king." Nakia's face was bright red.

Ashni rushed off the bed and tried to gather Nakia in her arms. As expected, Nakia fought, struggling in vain. Ashni held her tight, but with caution, not wanting to hurt her. Never wanting to hurt her. They ended up sitting on the floor. Ashni settled her back against the bedframe and pressed Nakia to her chest.

"Princess Nakia Lysand of Phyllida, daughter of King Dorian Lysand, please, listen to me."

"No!" Nakia howled, trying to push away. She beat her fists against Ashni's chest and Ashni barely felt it on her body. Inside, each strike echoed through her, cutting through muscle, bone, and soul. A dull pain spread through her that had nothing to do with a physical ache and everything to do with a spiritual one. This little thing would be the death of her, one way or another.

"This morning was just a joke. I had to work, which is why I left the bed before you woke up. When you came out, I planned to let you sit with me, but you seemed dazed and you went to stand where you usually do, so I thought I would have a little fun and waved my cup at you. I wanted to see if you were so out of it that you'd actually fill it. I only meant it as a joke," Ashni said, pleading in Nakia's ear.

Nakia's frenzy had her breath coming in pants and she tried once more to break free. She grunted and groaned, pushing against Ashni. Ashni refused to release her. She let Nakia wear herself out a little more and cuddled her closer when she stopped to catch her breath.

Ashni pressed her forehead to Nakia's, wishing Nakia understood the gesture. *We are linked in mind and soul. We are bonded. We're united.* "I told you that you're precious to me. I don't say that to anyone, especially not someone I plan to disregard. It was only a cruel joke and I was stupid to do it." *Damn it, Layla better not be right. I can't always be at fault.*

"Do you always play around so viciously with those you claim to care about?" Nakia huffed, puffing out her crimson-stained cheeks. She glared at Ashni as best she could while pressed into her chest.

Ashni's face pulled into a bit of a grimace. "Uh...yeah, I do, actually. You see what I do with my sister."

"She's not even your real sister," Nakia hissed.

Ashni scowled. "She is closer to me and dearer to me than most of my brothers, so, yes, she is my real sister. I trust her with all things and when I play with her, it's brutal. You've seen. She can take it and dish it out and I adore her for it."

"Oh, so I'm supposed to take your horrid joke as some sort of declaration?" Nakia practically spat at her.

Ashni tensed. "I thought you could handle it, like you've been handling other things. But, maybe I'm wrong. Maybe you haven't been handling anything. Your bite and wit are because everything is scary to you and you don't know how to deal with it." For a moment, she felt disgusted by Nakia and would go to great lengths to wash Nakia from every cell and memory if this were true. How could she have misjudged someone so drastically?

Nakia's eyes ignited with that lovely fire as she tried to stare Ashni down. "Handle it? Handle it! How would you handle being used as bait by your father and dragged across the sea into some strange barbarian world where the Queen mocks you at every turn? How would you handle knowing you're only worth your weight in gold because your father can't muster enough of an army to handle a woman after he's spent your entire life telling you that the only thing you're good for is marrying into an alliance because you are a woman? How would you handle being treated as a slave by someone you think is a savage, even though you're a princess and have always acted the part of a Lady? You have everything and you want more and you look down on me. When have you ever known pain and suffering?"

Ashni chortled, glad to see the fire in her hellcat once more. *I knew I couldn't have misjudged someone so badly*. But, that hadn't stopped her from being nervous for a long moment. Nakia glowered at her. Ashni knew laughing right now was the wrong thing to do. She gazed at Nakia.

"I've known a great deal more of it than you have, I'd wager. I've only lived on this planet a few more years than you, but you know what? I've felt true agony. No, I don't know the pain where your father looks at you as if you're unworthy of his name, but I've been betrayed more times than I can count by those who should've been loyal. I know how precious people truly are. Maybe your father doesn't, but I do. Gender will never have anything to do with it. Culture will never have anything to do with it. And blood will never have anything to do with it. Are you here for me or not is all I care about. We all have our strengths and weaknesses. We all have moments of pain and doubt. We all have moments where it seems like the world will stop at nothing to crush us. But, what we do in those moments is what I care about. I watched my mother find my father's dead body, the only man she had ever loved, and she cradled him and she wept and she beat her breast over how unfair it was for the gods to call him back so young and then do you know what she did?"

"Mourned forever?"

"She fought off jackals trying to tear the empire she helped build right out of her hands. You think your father is the only man alive to think women are inferior? Cowards who wept over my father with her tried to stab her in the back immediately after, dared to rally against her to put her son on the throne, even when Jay wouldn't dare take anything from our mother without asking her. She could've crumbled. She could've tucked herself into a ball and ducked away. She could've bent and let Jay have what she helped create. But, she fought. She fought and she won. She pulled those she knew she could count on together and she destroyed those who tried to destroy her. And, now, she continues to sit as Empress of the Roshan Empire. A barbarian woman from the hills."

Nakia was silent for a long while. Ashni held her and waited. She enjoyed feeling Nakia breathe against her. *I want this for as long as I can have it. Grant me this.* She should feel selfish asking for more considering what she had in life, but she'd fight for Nakia and she always felt that if she fought for something, then she'd earn it in the end.

"What do you want from me?" Nakia whispered.

"I want you to keep that fire burning in you, hellcat. Show me you're as fierce today and tomorrow as you were when you first arrived. That Princess would've thrown wine in my face this morning." And Ashni would have laughed it off. Maybe even pulled Nakia into her lap and kissed her for such actions.

"That princess hadn't slept with you, nor had you told her she was precious."

Ashni had to concede that. Nakia had changed and change was often good. Maybe Ashni was the one who had made the wrong decision in the moment. Maybe she should have chased after Nakia and explained her actions before pulling her close, wrapping Nakia in her outer robe, and returned to the throne with the only person she wanted at the moment. Instead, she made a joke. *Okay, yes, I'm probably going to be at fault a lot.*

"In a fight or battle, I'm a genius," Ashni said. "At governing, there are things I can do and things I can't. I learn and adjust when I can't do things. At this…" She motioned between them. "I'm new."

Nakia let out a weak giggle and wiped her nose with the back of her hand. "Me, too."

"It was a poor time to make a joke." Ashni put a finger under Nakia's chin and gently tilted her head, so Nakia would look at her. "You are precious to me. So precious, I'm going to kiss you right now even though your face is totally red and your nose is running."

Nakia laughed and sniffled, apparently taking it as a joke. Ashni leaned down and gave her a brief, but tender kiss. The laughing stopped; the sniffling not so much. A soft smile settled on Ashni's face as she pulled away to see Nakia smiling as well.

"I just realized, I was the one who had the moment, not you, and I totally failed in the moment. I'll get better if you give me a chance. I'm a pretty fast learner," Ashni said. Or Nakia would learn to deal with her awful sense of humor and bad timing. One of the two.

Nakia sighed. "Why should I believe you?"

"Good question. First off, I don't lie. My word is my word. Always has been and always will be. Beyond my horrible mistake after the Festival, have I ever hurt you? I've been intrigued by you since the first day, kitten, and everyone can see it."

There was a crushing silence for more time than Ashni was comfortable with. This was the only time she felt like she fell out of the gods' favor. Her father was supposed to be looking out for her.

"That captain you blew off, he wants to kill you."

Ashni blinked. Okay, she hadn't been expecting that, but it was something positive. Nice to know her hellcat didn't want to assassinate her. *See, you haven't misjudged her at all.*

"How do you know this?"

"He approached me in the garden today. He wants me to put something in your drink."

Ashni nodded. This show of trust deserved the same. "I know."

Nakia blinked and then narrowed her gaze on Ashni. "You know? How do you know? Are you having me followed?"

"I'm having *him* followed." Okay, she was also having Nakia followed, but not for the same reasons. She needed to make sure Nakia was safe, be it in the palace or when she was outside. Whenever the Princess was on her own, there were a few invisible followers with her.

"You suspected him?"

"Yes, I suspected him. I didn't think he'd approach you with this foolishness. It's quite reckless to trust you with this plot. He doesn't know you." Majeed really was an idiot. It was a good thing she never felt comfortable giving him any real responsibility.

"He thinks I believe he'll send me home if I help him."

Ashni shook her head. "More like you'll take the blame and be executed when someone realizes my wine was poisoned."

"I figured that as well. He seems to think I'm gullible or an idiot."

"Well, fortunately for us, he's the gullible idiot and he doesn't know you at all. When he comes to give you the poison, will you take it?"

Nakia's brow furrowed. "You mean will I participate in an assassination attempt I just told you about?" She gave Ashni a deadpan look.

Ashni chuckled. "It'll help make this whole situation easier to deal with."

Tilting her head slightly, Nakia arched an eyebrow. "What would you have me do?"

"Well, before we go into that, are we all right?" Ashni put her hand on Nakia's cheek, glad to see the color back to normal. She gently stroked Nakia's cheek with her thumb. She pressed her forehead to Nakia's again.

"I think we both need to adjust."

"Agreed. Just know that if I do something stupid, it's more likely a joke than something malicious...for you anyway. Other people, I'm probably being malicious to."

Nakia sniggered and leaned in for a kiss. Ashni smiled against her lips. She liked this feeling. She wouldn't jeopardize it again. At least, she'd try her best not to jeopardize it again.

* * *

Nakia whined as she felt sleep slipping away. But, then she felt light kisses on her cheek and neck. Without opening her eyes, she turned into the kisses, which floated from her neck to her lips. She wrapped her arms around Ashni's neck and pulled her closer even as Ashni pulled away.

"I want you to know I'm getting up. I have work to get to and plots to foil," Ashni whispered.

"I should get up..." Nakia made no move to do so. She was so tired. Ashni kept her up all night after they made up and made plans.

"No, don't. You need your sleep. The sun's barely up. When you get up, join me."

Nakia nodded and there was one last kiss before she fell back to sleep. When she woke up, she found breakfast waiting for her instead of her having to wait for it to be served. She knew it was Ashni's doing. When she was finished eating, she dressed, putting on traditional Roshan clothing. She had a date with an assassin, after all, but then she also had a date with the Queen.

Majeed was in the garden when she arrived. She wondered who was watching him and where the person was hiding. This was serious, so it was probably Layla or Adira hiding. Nakia couldn't spot either, as she approached Majeed, but she didn't look too hard. She didn't want to seem suspicious or paranoid.

"Good day, sir. I see you're enjoying the gardens again," Nakia said, wanting it to make it seem like she was being normal and trying to cover up their rendezvous.

"It is peaceful," Majeed replied with a slight shrug. "I'm sure you agree."

"I do," she said. She stood close to him and whispered, "Pass me this thing quickly and quietly."

"There's usually no one here, unlike so many of the other gardens. The ones with the statues are especially infested with the servants' wild offspring," he said as he eased a tiny vial into her hand.

She gave him a polite smile. "I've seen some of those gardens, but never bothered to walk through them or really see them up close. They never seemed to be enough to draw me in." She hoped he understood her meaning. She couldn't believe the small bottle he passed her was enough to do anything. *This can't be enough poison to put down a mouse let alone someone like the Queen. Is he testing me?*

Majeed's eyes danced with devilish delight. "Oh, they are more than enough, but sometimes one just needs to be alone with one's thoughts. If only for a few seconds." He wiggled his eyebrows.

Nakia swallowed. This tiny potion would work in seconds? This was serious and Ashni trusted her to retrieve it. *Wow.* She took a deep breath.

"Is everything all right?"

"Oh, yes. Fine. I didn't expect that. I mean, that you've been to the other gardens." *I didn't expect this poison to be so powerful.*

"Oh, yes. Every place, like every person, has its function."

"I suppose. A few seconds seems to be all I need. Now, for a fun day of shopping," Nakia found it hard not run from the scene. She was surprised that neither Layla or Adira appeared to take the vial from her.

Instead, Ashni met her in one of the palace hallways as she made her way back to the throne room. Before she could ask about why no one took the vial from her, Ashni yanked her into a secret room. She yelped and Ashni laughed.

"You're cute when you're startled." Ashni's eyes sparkled as she kissed Nakia.

"You're demented."

Ashni put her hands on Nakia's hips and pressed against her. "I can't help it. You're sweet and I'm all about sweet things." She latched onto Nakia's neck, kissing and tonguing the area.

Nakia moaned, tempted to get lost in the feeling. "Wait, wait, wait. This isn't what we're supposed to be doing."

"I'm Queen. I can do warit I want, and I really want to do you right now."

Nakia glared at Ashni. "You just did me a few hours ago." Besides, she refused to be taken up against the wall in a room hidden from the wide, open hallway by only a thin wall.

"This is true. I also had apples for breakfast, but that won't stop me from having them for lunch. If it makes you feel better, I'll wait until tonight."

"Good, because you should focus on the fact that someone is trying to kill you and that I'm too much of a Lady to allow you such liberties in a public place."

Shrugging, Ashni chortled. "Attempts on my life happen at least once a year. I'm sure your father has to deal with it, too."

Nakia frowned. "That's not the point. Here." She pulled the vial from a pocket in her belt and handed it over.

"Thank you. You're even cute when you're helpful, kitten." Ashni beamed.

Nakia sighed and shook her head. "You're so annoying. I should have let him kill you."

"I'm sure you would have a way to blame him."

"Of course. After all, I wasn't sure I'd tell you until I was telling you, but I knew as soon as he tried to draw me in that he wanted me to take the fall. Speaking of that, do you really trust me enough to believe that's the real vial?"

Ashni smiled even more. "I wouldn't have sent you if I didn't."

"Was Layla or your monkey general watching me on the way over?"

"No, Layla has to stay with Majeed. Adira is handling other matters. No one followed you. I trust this is the right vial." Ashni shrugged as if it was no big deal.

Nakia smirked at Ashni. "Maybe you're the fool."

Ashni still smiled, her eyes sparkling. "Maybe I am." She leaned down and kissed Nakia. Nakia returned the kiss and whimpered when Ashni pulled away. "But, if I am to die, you have more reason than he does, so I'll accept it."

Nakia pursed her lips. "You're a smooth talker when you want to be, but we both know you wouldn't let me just kill you."

Ashni gave her a lopsided grin, looking quite diabolical. "Well, I wouldn't make it so easy."

Nakia had no doubt this was true. "Well, you work things out with your goons. I'm meeting with Bashira and we're going shopping."

Ashni groaned. "Can you try not to bankrupt me in the process? I have a campaign to conduct once the weather settles down and would like to be able to feed my troops."

An impish smile settled on Nakia's face. "Maybe this is my true scheme. It would save the West, after all. Save Phyllida."

"If you want to save Phyllida, kitten, all you have to do is ask me."

Nakia wanted to doubt that she had so much sway over Ashni, but she believed her. Ashni continued to open up to her, trust her, so she believed it possible. Ashni would give her the world. Without thinking, she wrapped her arms around Ashni and pulled her close.

"Don't mess up," Nakia whispered.

"I won't. Go enjoy your day." Ashni kissed her forehead. This simple show of affection flooded Nakia with so many emotions that all she could do was obey or she'd embarrass herself.

"I'll be back for dinner."

"I'll miss you until then."

Nakia chuckled a little. Ashni was certainly smooth. She hoped she hadn't made a mistake.

***

Majeed didn't seem to suspect anything about being invited to dinner at the last minute. Ashni did things like this with soldiers she liked every now and then. She had no reason to invite him until now. He probably thought he had impressed her in some way or that she finally recognized his value. *Idiot.*

She enjoyed watching Nakia pretend not to notice him when he sat down at the table. Nakia had been regulated to her position as the official cupbearer for entertainment purposes. He waved a greeting to the other guests, who included Layla, Naren, Adira, and Saniyah. The dinner would be construed as a strategic meeting for their trip back West in a couple of months since her top people were there. Majeed might think he was being picked to go on campaign with them. He might even think he had a promotion coming to him, considering high status of those around him.

"Wait, wait, wait. How is this dinner without any dip?" Naren asked, surveying the food with great interest.

"By the Great Eagle, I wish you showed this much interest when we're on campaign," Adira said.

"Dips are vital to dinner," Saniyah said with a smile, obviously teasing Adira. Ashni shot Nakia a look, hoping she understood that couples joked around with each other. If Nakia understood, then Ashni wouldn't get in as much trouble over it the next time she teased Nakia.

"Really? I always thought dumplings were vital to, well, any meal." Ashni used a skewer to collect a dumpling and pop it in her mouth. She glanced at Majeed, who fidgeted on his cushion.

"Oh, please, we all know if you could eat pastries at every meal and not lose all of your teeth, you would," Adira said.

Ashni couldn't argue that one. She ate another dumpling and, for a moment, imagined feeding one to Nakia. *Save that fantasy for later.* It wouldn't be a fantasy for long once they got this dinner/trap out of the way. She eyed Majeed and watched him squirm a little more. He scanned the table.

"Captain, is the food not to your liking?" Ashni asked, moving from the dumplings to something to satisfy her sweet tooth. Some shredded beets worked for the moment.

He blinked. "Huh?" He glanced up at her.

"I was wondering if the food wasn't too your liking. You haven't touched anything." Ashni looked over the meal. It wasn't huge by any stretch of the imagination. In fact, it was the dinner she would have if these, those closest to her, were eating with her rather than having to foil a very poor attempt on her life.

"The chicken is always amazing," Layla said. She made a show of popping a piece of shredded chicken into her mouth. She licked her lips as she chewed.

"Maybe the food isn't good enough for him," Adira said, frowning at him. She didn't have to pretend to like him.

"No, no, no." Majeed shook his head. "It's not that. I imagined we'd talk about the upcoming invasion and that was why I was invited. It's almost time for me to leave the desert, yes? I can be of much better use to you in the West." Majeed beamed.

Ashni couldn't understand why he thought that. There was nothing outstanding in his record to show he could handle serious warfare. Even the men who trained him suggested he'd do best as a sentry in a calm territory. Almost everyone who met him claimed he was skittish, but he didn't accept that. He hadn't done anything at his station beyond complain and almost get killed by some playful teens once, which seemed to prove everyone right.

Ashni took some bread and broke it in half instead of answering. She bit into the bread before gathering some of the shredded roasted chicken, careful of the gravy with the chicken. She ate that with the rest of her bread. Chewing slowly, she watched him and saw that he was sweating enough for a bead to slide down his cheek.

"Is that right? General, is he right in assuming he will be better use to me in the West?" Ashni asked.

"I could always use someone to test Saniyah's new catapults on," Adira replied as Saniyah fed her a piece of bread.

Ashni nodded and Majeed's face fell. "I have plenty of combat experience."

Ashni almost laughed aloud. Naren snickered, but covered it up by shoving food in his mouth. Layla laughed outright, which made Ashni laugh. Majeed had the nerve to glare at them.

"You mean the combat experience where three teens throwing rocks at a tortoise almost killed you?" Adira asked with an arched eyebrow.

Majeed narrowed his gaze on Adira. "They were attacking me and it was an ambush."

Everyone except Majeed chuckled. There had been witnesses, all who said it was an accident. Majeed had been trying to get the teens to leave the area without paying attention to what they were doing. A rock hit him on the side of the head and knocked him out. He tried to have the kids arrested and executed, not thinking about how there were investigations when people were to be executed. He would have done well to leave the matter alone, but now the whole army knew the true story thanks to the investigation.

"I'm bored," Ashni said. She grabbed her wine cup and motioned for Nakia.

Nakia poured the wine and Majeed leaned forward as Ashni was about to drink from her goblet. For a second, Ashni swore there was delight in his eyes as she put the cup to her lips. She downed her wine in one gulp. Majeed was practically on the table by the time she lowered the cup. He watched her intently. She ate another dumpling as sweat gathered on his forehead.

"That is some delicious wine. I'll have more," Ashni said and held up her goblet again. She sipped this time as Majeed's expression fell and his face paled. "Captain, you look as though you're expecting something."

His breath hitched. "Something? What would I be expecting?"

"For my sister to fall down dead, maybe." Layla drew her sword and aimed for his throat. He gasped and another bead of sweat ran down his face.

"Ex...excuse me?" he stammered, gulping as the tip of the finest cursed steel touched his neck. He probably could feel the damned sword breathing the fires of Hell on him. If Layla's hand slipped, he'd feel the burn all the way to the ends of his hair before his head fell off his shoulders.

"You dare to think you can poison the Queen?" Adira asked, leaving the 'idiot' unsaid, but clear in her tone.

He gasped again and put his hand to his chest. "I would never! If anything, she's the one who would attempt to kill you." Majeed pointed at Nakia. "This filthy outsider is the one serving the Queen wine." He had the nerve to growl at Nakia.

"You should tell whoever spies for you that just because someone is unhappy with me one day doesn't mean they will stay unhappy with me." Ashni held up the vial and feigned examining it for a moment. "And she wouldn't have known what this is to purchase it in the first place."

"I would never!" Majeed broke into a serious sweat as he stood up. Layla still pointed her sword at him.

"I'm sure you wouldn't. Just like you would never bad mouth foreigners in the presence of three of them." Ashni sucked her teeth. *This guy really is a moron.*

Majeed turned and ran right into Naren as he tried to escape. Naren wasted no time putting Majeed in a hold, subduing him with ease. Shaking her head, Ashni cackled.

"Sometimes I forget you can even fight," Ashni said to Naren.

Naren made a face at her and strengthened his hold on Majeed as the idiot tried to wiggle away. Majeed grunted and shouted, but Naren ignored him. "Can we get back to dinner now?"

"Guards." Ashni waved for the men, who took Majeed from Naren.

They dragged him away screaming. "You can't do this to me. You can't prove I did anything. Don't do this!" Thankfully, his pleas and voice faded into the distance.

Naren wasted no time sitting back down to eat. Sighing, Layla sheathed her sword. Ashni beckoned for Nakia, who sat down next to her, on her pillow. She put her hand around Nakia's waist.

"Adira, you'll handle Majeed after dinner," Ashni said.

Adira glanced at the end of the hall. "After breakfast. Let him sweat it out. I want him to admit he didn't buy that vial."

Nakia blinked and her forehead wrinkled. "Wait, he didn't buy it? Then why did he have it?"

"The seller of this particular poison will only sell it to a select number of people. A lowly captain wouldn't be among that number. Unfortunately, if he doesn't tell us who gave it to him, we can't accuse the person we suspect," Ashni explained.

"I better put some good men on him or he might not last through the night," Adira said.

Ashni waved it off. "I've done it. The guards know which cell to place him in and they have orders to will watch him. Let's enjoy the meal." After all, how often would she be surrounded by her favorite people?

S.L. Kassidy

Chapter Seventeen

MAJEED NEVER GAVE UP who purchased the poison. A couple of weeks after his arrest, he was found murdered in his cell, which didn't surprise Ashni. She knew who was behind both the assassination attempt and his death, but she wouldn't breathe the accusation without proof beyond her word and Adira's findings. If she didn't have true evidence, she would end up embarrassing herself. Adira decided to keep digging, but they both knew nothing would come of it. Ashni now focused on Nakia.

Nakia's bed became her bed, mainly because she couldn't convince Nakia to share her bed. It wasn't like she'd take away Nakia's rooms and Nakia liked having a space of her own. Ashni respected that. Besides, it didn't matter whose bed they were in once they settled in.

"Let me hear you, kitten," Ashni whispered into Nakia's ear.

Ashni was behind Nakia, one hand massaging a plump breast and the other enjoying itself between Nakia's legs. Nakia purred as Ashni caressed her, two fingers inside, feeling quite at home. Nakia's hips moved with her. She was not shy in the slightest anymore.

"You feel so good, kitten," Ashni said before kissing Nakia's neck. She considered marking Nakia, right there where everyone could see, but there was no point. She'd already left marks all over Nakia's chest and by now everyone knew who pleased Nakia at night.

Nakia whined and arched into Ashni. The pressure of Nakia's wonderful ass against her made Ashni moan. This was one of the most amazing things she had ever experienced and she would be with Nakia all day if she could. All too soon, she felt Nakia flutter around her fingers and go slack with only her hand holding the Princess up.

Before Ashni could say anything, Nakia turned and kissed her. Ashni liked this and could get used to this. She needed to make sure Nakia liked it as well, checking in with her every now and then. It was a lot to take in, after all, even if they had been at it for weeks now.

"You are so delicious," Ashni said, nuzzling Nakia's neck.

"You're all sweet talk," Nakia replied, weakly wrapping her arms around Ashni and pulling her close.

"Goes well with you being all sweet. You all right?" Ashni stroked Nakia's side, enjoying soft skin and feeling Nakia relax from her touch.

"How could I not be?" Nakia yawned. "Stop checking on me."

"I just want to make sure..." Ashni glanced down to see Nakia was asleep. It was not out of the norm, especially when Ashni had her way with Nakia for a few hours.

As far as physical intimacy went, Nakia seemed quite accepting of it now. There were times when she initiated kisses and she was eager for Ashni's touch. She hadn't worked up the nerve to touch Ashni beyond curious caresses to her arms or running her hands through Ashni's wild mane. Ashni wanted to go with the flow, but she also wanted to make sure Nakia wasn't doing it to do it. Despite her words, there were times when Nakia would reach out, as if needing to touch Ashni, and then pull back, like she wasn't sure of herself or if she was allowed to touch Ashni. Ashni wanted her to know it was all right, but Nakia always pulled back.

"This has gone beyond pleasure for me. Has it for you?" Ashni whispered, her eyes stuck on Nakia.

Sighing, Ashni shook the thought away. She enjoyed being able to touch and take Nakia. It didn't matter if Nakia was still unsure about touching her. They'd get there eventually. Ashni fell asleep, needing at least a few hours. The next morning, Ashni woke first and went to work.

***

Yawning, Nakia awoke shortly after Ashni left. A servant informed her that the Queen had been gone for almost an hour. She inhaled Ashni's scent on the pillow and it caused her to sigh in contentment.

She bathed and dressed, putting on the garb of the Roshan Empire. It was comfortable and felt better against her skin than her tunics did. The servants agreed the new clothing suited her, which made her smile. She shouldn't care about slaves and servants' opinions, but sometimes she had them pick outfits for her to wear, and they never failed to get Ashni's attention.

She wandered to the throne room and wasted no time cuddling next to Ashni. She greeted Ashni with a kiss to the cheek. The Queen didn't object, smiling as soon as Nakia's lips touched her.

Ashni adjusted her body, so that Nakia sat between her legs. She wrapped her outer robe around Nakia, which was normal for them now. Nakia settled against her warm body. She felt secure and safe against Ashni. She remembered how Ashni stopped Amal with a look when he thought he could strike Nakia. She wondered what would happen if someone genuinely came at her while she was with the Queen.

"Do you want to sit with me while I see people?" Ashni asked.

"Do I have to sit here quietly like a good girl?" Nakia countered with a teasing smile.

Ashni chuckled. "I never like you quiet."

Nakia snickered slightly, trying to cover up the blush that burned her face by ducking her head. It would be easy to assume this was all about sex for Ashni if the Queen didn't let her cuddle up to her like this, on the throne, and in front of any and all who happened by. So, she relished the Queen's body heat while she ate breakfast, which was cold.

"Do you want me to send for a hot meal?" Ashni asked.

"No, no. I'll eat the fruit and bread. The hard-boiled eggs aren't bad cold either." There was plenty for her to eat, even if the main things were cold.

Ashni dared to arch an eyebrow. "You're going to kiss me with egg breath?"

Nakia sneered. "Well, not with that attitude."

Ashni made a face at her and Nakia was beginning to see that the Queen could be quite a child when given the chance. Instead of engaging, she focused on eating, needing to build her energy again. While she busied herself with food and tea, which was thankfully warm, Ashni's first appointment arrived. Nakia listened with half an ear until something caught her attention.

"Wait, why would you need a budget increase if you have already cut workers?" Nakia asked, poking her head up from the tray.

"I was going to ask that," Ashni said in a slightly singsong voice.

Nakia wanted to smile, but held off. It was good Ashni didn't reprimand her for speaking out of turn. For the moment, she glared at this man, who was trying to put something over on them.

The man gulped. He stammered and ran his hand through his hair. Apparently, he thought he could come in and make demands and no one would question him. *Idiot.*

While they waited for an answer, Ashni's hand found its way under Nakia's shirt and caressed her abdomen. Nakia held in a purr and went back to her meal. By the time she again checked into what was happening, someone new was there. Nakia listened and found she had more questions to ask. The official had the nerve to look at Ashni, like Ashni was supposed to stop the interrogation.

"What? She's got a solid line of inquiries there. Any answers?" Ashni asked with an arched eyebrow.

"You're just going to let this barbarian question me?" The official stomped her foot. Maybe the whole Roshan Empire was immature.

"I think I just did. I also wouldn't refer to her as a barbarian again, unless you dislike your position that much," Ashni said.

The official yelped and looked back at Nakia. An impish grin curled onto Nakia's face. *That'll teach you to call me a barbarian, barbarian.* Not that she meant the 'barbarian' remark. Nakia was coming to accept that a different culture didn't automatically make people savages. As she opened up to the people around her, she began to even appreciate their culture. The official apologized.

"Please, forgive me, my Lady." The official bowed.

Nakia smiled, pleased with the show of respect, even if Ashni was the one who forced it out of this insolent woman. Once she was done with her questions and breakfast, Nakia left to go do things with Bashira and not have to worry about being called a barbarian to her face.

***

Ashni rubbed her eyes as she scanned the reports in front of her. A light tapping sound caught her attention. *It's about time.*

"Your kitten and my niece are going to bankrupt me and the Empire, I imagine," Adira announced as she strolled into the throne room.

"Well, we'll have to make sure to storm into the West and raid every treasure box there is to be had," Ashni said. That was the plan anyway.

Adira sneered. "Is your kitten going to allow that? I mean, I know Saniyah would have my head if I raided any other treasure boxes."

Wrinkling her nose, Ashni shook her head. "You're so vulgar."

Adira sucked her teeth. "Oh, please. I knew you before the hellcat showed up, so don't try to pull that with me. Are we doing this budget or what?"

"Yes, let's get to it. I want to be done by the time Nakia gets back."

Adira's eyebrow went up. "Who are you and what have you done with Ashni?"

"Because I don't want to spend the day budgeting? Who does? My father died to escape a budget meeting." Ashni threw up her hands. "Died with a smile on his face, might I add. He might've been on to something."

Adira snorted. "Oh, yes, and you totally hate budgeting and making sure everything is right for the next invasion. You're never involved in those."

"Your sarcasm is noted and hated. Sit down." Ashni pointed to the table she had set up for Adira's arrival.

Adira smirked at her. Ashni wanted to punch Adira in the mouth, but she was more than an arm's length away. Adira sat down and gave her a knowing look. Ashni had to throw something at her and opted for a small pillow tucked at her back. She very nearly bashed Adira in the face with it, but the General dodged at just the right moment. She was good at that for a woman with one eye.

"Wait, wait, wait, where's the Princess?" Adira picked up a document and looked around, checking the ceiling.

"She's on her way. She had things to pick up first," Ashni replied.

A soft chuckle escaped Adira. "She isn't bitching about you using her as an errand girl? Color me surprised."

"She is bitching, of course, but she's the only one I can trust with this errand. I need the special ops numbers and anyone else might betray us for the right amount of gold eagles."

"Hell, I might betray you for the right amount of gold eagles."

Ashni blew out a breath and waved her off. "Oh, please. I could offer you your own country and you'd still ride with me if only to harass me for the rest of our lives. Sometimes, I think you're here just to nag me. No glory, no money, just nagging."

"It's not my fault you're an idiot and need a babysitter."

"No, I don't. You're a worrywart and you need someone to worry about and for some freaky reason you chose me. You've got a niece you can worry about, you know?"

"No, Bashira can take care of herself. You, on the other hand, need constant supervision."

"Says the woman whose niece is currently bankrupting her and the nation."

Adira couldn't argue that one and they got to work. Layla arrived not too long after. There was a lot of work to do to prepare for the upcoming warring season. They had taken the West by surprise, but now, with the information from the surprise attack, they planned to stay this time. They needed a base of operations and to know where they would go from their established foothold. They worked until Nakia returned. Ashni dismissed them soon after.

"Don't even say anything." Ashni pointed at Adira, who opened her mouth, but then closed it at the order.

"Can I say something?" Layla had a cruel, twisted grin on her face and if she had the time, Ashni would slap it off, but she wanted to be with Nakia.

"Do you want me to say something back?" Ashni countered.

Layla shrugged. "I think what I have to say will be better than anything you have. After all, you've been saying things for years while everything I can say is new."

"You can both leave me alone and get the hell out of here. We've all got things to do," Ashni said, pointing to the door.

"Don't you mean people to do?" Adira chuckled and wiggled her eyebrows.

Ashni groaned and shook her head, but rushed the pair out of the throne room. She made her way to Nakia's rooms and found Nakia about to sit down for dinner. Ashni eased down next to her and kissed her lips. Nakia returned the kiss and cuddled against her. They both sighed.

"Good day shopping?" Ashni asked, surveying the meal Nakia had before her. A few of the foods were imports. This was generally what happened when she took her meals in Nakia's rooms. She made note of Nakia's favorite Roshan foods and now she could note what sort of Western foods Nakia liked to eat.

"What makes you think I was shopping? I know you have spies following me."

"They only report to me if something dangerous happens. You have your privacy. I promise." She wanted to make sure no one touched Nakia, but she'd never go so far as to have her people report on what Nakia was doing, even if it was something dangerous. She made sure her people knew they'd better rescue Nakia, even if it was from herself, if something happened. But, only if something happened. "I know you were shopping because Adira mentioned it when she arrived."

Nakia brightened and kissed the end of Ashni's nose. "I never expected you to be so sweet."

Ashni wasn't sure if that was an insult or not and let it be. Instead, she busied herself with a new favorite past time—feeding Nakia. Sometimes, Nakia fed her. When they finished eating, they decided to play chess. Ashni was pleased with Nakia's progress. She was certain she could get Nakia into shape and by the time of the next Festival of the Moon, she could leave Nakia to slaughter Amal in the game. Of course, she would still have to be there as he was a sore loser on a good day and he would probably try to kill Nakia once she won on her own.

There was something peaceful about spending time with Nakia. Ashni couldn't put her finger on it, nor did she care to. She enjoyed it and looked forward to it each day.

***

Bashira had made sure she saw much of the capital, but the marketplace had become Nakia's favorite place in Khenshu. The theaters were interesting. Many people liked telling stories about Amir Khalid and Empress Chandra, as well as stories of Ashni's conquests, especially with her father. Nakia even caught a tale about Ashni's childhood and how she proved herself a warrior by killing a fully grown male lion in the cirque. That was how she became a member of the Order of the Lion. According to the story, Ashni wore the beast's teeth around her neck. Nakia had noticed such a necklace. One day, she'd have to remember to ask Ashni to tell her the whole story.

The theaters taught her the history, but the marketplace taught her the culture—to a degree anyway. She could see what people sold and brought, see what they wore, what they ate, how they interacted with each other, and dozens of other small things. She wondered what the marketplace was like in Phyllida. Was it like this? Were all marketplaces the same? She doubted it. Places were too different for every marketplace to be the same.

"I was thinking of taking you to meet my dance troop," Bashira said as they eyed some beautiful, soft fabrics. The bright colors never failed to attract them. The soft, light material was always a delight to Nakia.

"And why should I want to do that? You're the rebel among us," Nakia replied with a teasing smile.

Bashira gasped and gawked at her. "*I'm* the rebel? Boy, you are either in some heavy denial or don't have an ounce of self-awareness." She scoffed. "I'm the rebel. Anyway, I think you'd do well with us."

"What makes you think that?"

"Come on, there's nothing worse in the Empire than a coward. One of the reasons my aunt hasn't said anything about me dancing is because she's impressed by my bravery. Besides, you'll learn dances to

225

entice the Queen."

Nakia glowered at her. She didn't need any help enticing the Queen, for the moment anyway. Ashni had had a variety of lovers before she showed up. All of whom had to be more practiced in the sexual arts than she was. Maybe learning to dance would help.

"Would she...would she mind me knowing how to dance?" Nakia asked. Dancing was lower than acting, after all. Slave girls danced.

Bashira eyes twinkled with mischief and mirth. "As long as no one's around, I'm sure she'll only delight in it."

Nakia felt this was true and learning to dance was now tempting. Before she could make a decision, someone seized her. She turned around and glared at quite possibly the largest man she had ever seen, which said a lot around a city like Khenshu.

"Hey, what do you think you're doing?" Nakia yanked her arm away.

"Come with us." His voice was gruff and he motioned to a dozen men behind him. They were dressed in familiar tunics with long hair and beards. Beyond them was an enclosed palanquin. Her stomach dropped when she saw the insignia on the side.

Nakia was about to object, but was cut off when a man in dark blue pants appeared in front of her. She rubbed her eyes as he gently pushed her aside. She took a step back and saw another man in front of Bashira.

"Stand back, Princess. I've got these idiots." The man drew a sword from his back and pointed the blade at the man in the tunic, who pulled his own sword from his side.

Nakia's mouth fell open and her voice caught in her throat, preventing her from objecting. The men clashed swords. The sound of the metal scraping together sent people in the market running for cover. There were shouts and clamoring as items fell from stands and chaos moved around them.

Nakia tried to press forward, wanting to stop this nonsense, but the man in front of Bashira grabbed her and pulled her away. Suddenly, two female warriors came out of nowhere and fought with the other men in tunics. Nakia supposed Ashni would be getting a report eventually.

"Who do you think you are?" one of Ashni's spies asked, knocking her opponent's sword away.

"We are emissaries for King Dorian." The man flashed his badge. It was time for Nakia to go home.

***

Ashni rubbed her palms together as ambassadors from Phyllida made their way into her throne room. They showed up unannounced, which was enough to upset her, but she knew they had a deal. Adira was there, standing by the throne and frowning.

"Such manners," Adira said.

"We come with your gold," the main ambassador said. Chests were brought in after him.

Ashni tilted her head, regarding the boxes with a scowl. She narrowed her gaze upon him. He eyed her with defiance, as if he was above her, despite the fact that she was looking down on him. Her decision was made.

Ashni flicked her wrist at him, bangles ringing. "Take it away. I don't want it." There were gasps all around and Adira looked at her as if she had lost her mind. Maybe she had.

"Wha...what?" the ambassador stammered. His face was tight and his forehead dotted with sweat. It was possible he now understood the dangerous position he was in.

"I have what I want and I don't need your gold." That wasn't entirely true. The tribute was to help finance her invasion of the West, but she could get the money elsewhere. Most of her troops were loyal enough to ride with her for the prestige more than the money. The money was nice and they knew they'd be paid eventually.

"You have what you want?"

"Is there an echo? I have what I want. Now, away with you," Ashni ordered. She turned away, done with him.

"You'll forgive me, but the exchange has already been made."

Ashni's head snapped back in his direction and her gaze narrowed solely on him. "Excuse me?"

"I had my men fetch the Princess. The gold is yours and the Princess is ours. Good day." The bastard had the nerve to turn his back on her and walk away.

The world shattered around Ashni and she let loose an ungodly noise. Thunder roared outside and Ashni launched herself from the throne, fully intent on destroying the man. Lightning crackled from her entire being and covered her form. She extended her hand, ready to turn the ambassador to ash—consequences be damned. Before she could, Adira stood in her way, looking her squarely in the eye.

"General, stand down!" Ashni eyed her. Lightning popped from

Ashni, gathering in her hands, wanting to reach the official from Phyllida.

Adira wouldn't be moved. She leaned in close, so no one would hear her words. "Be calm. Do you wish to go back on your word? Gain that reputation?"

Ashni snarled. "I wish to keep my kitten," she said through gritted teeth, her voice low as well.

"There are other ways. You made a deal and you must honor it. Besides, we need this gold."

It was true, but she didn't care. "I can get gold elsewhere."

"You would ask your mother to finance this march?"

Ashni's jaw tensed. "Never."

"Then, be calm and accept the gold. We both I know we'll think of something else." Adira stared at her, trying to reach into her soul. "We'll think of something."

Ashni growled again and thunder blared outside. There had to be another way. There had to be some way for her to keep Nakia.

"Go get her," Ashni ordered.

Adira waved her hand. "You heard the Queen."

People moved off in every direction, but it proved to be in vain. Moments later, the smell of smoke filled the room. Ashni turned to see black smoking disappearing, revealing her spies with Bashira.

"They took her!" Bashira threw herself on Adira.

"Her?" Adira echoed, clutching her weeping niece.

"They took Nakia. They battled in the market. She went peacefully in order to stop the destruction, but they stole her." Bashira bawled.

Ashni gnashed her teeth as she stared down the main spy. "What happened?"

"She told us to stand down. They were her father's men. She went with them on her father's orders."

"On her father's orders?"

"There were papers. She assured us it was his writing, his seal, and they were his orders. Were we to defy her, Highness?" he asked.

Sighing, Ashni shook her head. She had given them their orders. Protect Nakia, but also obey Nakia. "She is me."

He bowed his head. "Understood."

Ashni turned her attention back to Adira, who held her hysterical niece even tighter. "Take care of her and then think of something. And someone get Princess in here." Layla might be able to think of some way around this.

***

The trip to Phyllida was bumpy and lonely. No one engaged with her. Seconds into the journey she regretted leaving on her father's orders, but she knew Ashni would keep her word. Ashni always kept her word. Of course, Nakia would be returned to her father once the gold was delivered. Knowing that didn't stop her from feeling sick and her heart from hurting.

When she arrived at the royal palace in Phyllida, she wasn't announced and there was no celebration. She was taken to her old rooms and her father came as soon as she was alone. He eyed her as if he expected her to transform into some monster right before his eyes, like he knew what she had done while with the Roshan. She didn't betray herself.

"Good to see those barbarians did not harm you."

"I'm sure."

King Dorian didn't care if she was harmed or not. He was just happy her presence had held off the invasion. He offered her something of a smile, but it didn't reach his eyes. "You did us well, daughter. Holding up in that Hell. It could not have been easy, but you gave us time to prepare."

Her brow furrowed. "Prepare for what?" They didn't have the men to fight Ashni before and she doubted they managed to gain so many troops in the months she was gone.

"To strike against those barbarians." He threw his fist in the air. "We'll show those savages that they cannot march into our territory and devour us."

She blinked. He really thought they could take on the Roshan Empire? "How do you propose to do that?"

"I've called forth allies."

She wondered why that concerned her, but she didn't have to wonder long. She was promised to one ally. She'd be his bride in exchange for his troops, forever the sacrificial pawn in her father's game. For the first time, she hoped her father lost.

Fini — for now

Warrior Class — Taming the Wind

Ashni tries to negotiate with King Dorian to get Nakia back. When it is clear Dorian won't deal with Ashni, she decides she will simply take everything she wants. She plans to get Nakia back from her new husband and conquer the city of Phlylida from right under him. But, will she be able to achieve her dream with her brother Amal trying to steal her land from her while she's out on campaign? Will Nakia be able to chase after her own dreams with her new husband and her father standing in her way? Regardless, no one is about to go down without a fight.

About S. L Kassidy

What is there to know about me? Not much. I was bred, born, and raised in New York and I have no desire to live anywhere else. One day, I would like to travel to a few places, but for now I am content where I am.

I started out writing poetry in junior high and continued to do so for ten years. I wrote short stories, usually fantasy and romance stories, for my own entertainment throughout high school and college. Back then, I wrote strictly for me and those stories remain locked in the back of my closet in little notebooks, written in my almost unreadable, tiny handwriting. In between writing those stories and poetry, I managed to get a college degree in history.

After graduating college, I had a semester off before graduate school and I didn't really have anything to do with my time. So, I took a chance and wrote a fanfic and dared to upload it to the Internet. I was surprised that other people enjoyed my work and I've been posting ever since. I had quite a bit of fun with fan fiction and eventually decided to try my hand in original fiction. I suppose it was sort of like coming back around to what I had been doing in high school and college, except this time the stories were for whoever wanted to read them. I uploaded my first original story a few years ago and haven't looked back. I plan to continue writing as long as I continue getting ideas for stories and it continues to be fun.

Contact Information
E-mail: slkassidy@gmail.com
Facebook: SL Kassidy

Other Books by S. L. Kassidy

Please Baby
ISBN: 9781311485137

Jayce Newton's life is going downhill after she rescues her little niece from an awful situation. She plans to hold onto her niece and gain custody of her, but there are some factors against her. Her girlfriend doesn't want the baby around. Her mother wants to take the baby from her, and her brother has disappeared. Things only seem to get worse when Gus Tucker comes into her life.

Gus Tucker's life isn't going much better. She recently divorced her wife and moved into a new home. She's looking forward to a new start and spending time with her sister. Before she can do that, though, she ends up causing trouble for Jayce Newton, getting her fired from her job and kicked out of her home. She tries to make it up to Jayce by taking her in during her time of need. Now, it's just a struggle to see if they're able to coexist in the same house with a baby between them.

Desert Palm Press

Scarred Series

Scarred for Life
ISBN: 9781310171352

Dane Wolfe is a loner. Forsaken by her family and betrayed by people close to her, she has lost all faith in people and spends her days wandering the streets with no direction or meaning. She drifts through life, existing and nothing more. Nicole Cardell is a successful attorney. She has too much faith in people and is being taken advantage of by her boyfriend, Tyler, Dane's cousin. She's tired of his selfish ways and tosses him out. The bad relationship leaves her questioning her judgment. Circumstances bring Dane and Nicole together and a friendship brings them closer. They're able to heal each other and bring balance to each other's lives. Their peace is shattered when family causes trouble and tears them apart. Will they find their path back to each other and to the love that was slowly growing?

New Cuts, Old Wounds
ISBN: 9781310217289

In this sequel to *Scarred for Life*, Nicole Cardell and Dane Wolfe have been together for a year. They are doing their best to move forward with their relationship and open up to each other. It's time to meet family members. Dane's nervous about meeting Nicole's family, but she's even more nervous about Nicole meeting her family. Nicole is eager for both. Nicole thinks Dane should bond with her family while Dane thinks she needs to get as far away from them as possible. The Wolfe family seems to agree with Dane, but keep inviting her to things and Nicole keeps accepting the invites. Will family make or break Dane and Nicole?

Bandages
ISBN: 9781942976103

Nicole and Dane return in the third installment of the *Scarred* series. Life is good. The musician gave the lawyer a ring, a not-engagement ring, a promise; this is forever. But, they both still had some growing and healing to work through.

Healing is strange. There are those days when the bandage falls off on its own and you think you're good to go. Days when laughter comes easy and you forget the past. And there are days when the past doesn't want to be forgotten; you still need a stitch or a cast to hold yourself together. There are even relapses when the poisonous past needs release.

Share their journey through eighteen short stories of play, passion, and a deepening partnership. You'll enjoy the journey as much as where it leads.

First Degree Burns
ISBN (epub): 9781942976257

Dane and Nicole are back in this sequel to Bandages. Nicole arranges a camping trip for Dane to meet her father's side of her family. Nicole is trying to move their relationship forward, but things do not go the way that she planned. Dane has a lot more excitement on her first camping trip than either of them thought. Hopefully, it doesn't ruin what they have already.

Learning to Walk Again
ISBN (epub): 9781942976851

In the final installment of the Scarred series, Nicole and Danny are going through life changes with their families, friends, and new people in their lives. Nicole is about to finish school and feels the pressure to decide if she's ready to seek out a new career in the unknown or to keep her stable position. Danny gets a job and doesn't expect the stress that comes with it. Their relationship strains under the evolution. How much can they take before they shatter and break? Can their family and friends help them pull it together or will seemingly good things be the ones to destroy them?

Desert Palm Press

Note to Readers:

Thank you for reading a book from Desert Palm Press. We have made every effort to edit this book. However, typos do slip in. If you find an error in the text, please email lee@desertpalmpress.com so the issue can be corrected.

We appreciate you as a reader and want to ensure you enjoy the reading process. We would like you to consider posting a review on your preferred media sites such as Amazon, Smashwords, Bella Books, Goodreads, Tumblr, Twitter, Facebook, and/or your blog or website.

For more information on upcoming releases, author interviews, contest, giveaways and more, please sign up for our newsletter and visit us as at Desert Palm Press: www.desertpalmpress.com and "Like" us on Facebook: Desert Palm Press.

Bright Blessings